SPARKS AND SHADOW

RISING ELEMENTS BOOK 1

CEARA NOBLES

RIVERSIDE PRESS, LLC

Contents

CHAPTER ONE

Seattle was full of monsters.

I'm not talking about the petty criminals, drug dealers, and other miscellaneous jerks that flooded the streets every day. No, I'm talking about real-life, stuff-of-nightmares monsters—but these weren't confined to the midnight recesses of the mind.

They stood in line at Honey Hole, waiting for a sandwich like it was the most natural thing in the world.

It was one o'clock in the afternoon, just past the lunch rush, and most couriers in the area had gathered at Honey Hole for Al's gourmet sandwiches. A line of pedal bikes leaned haphazardly against the building's cement wall and my co-workers sprawled on the sidewalk, gossiping about the day's deliveries between bites.

I sat on my bike, leaning forward against the handlebars, and watched a tall, horrific monster covered in scales have a friendly chat with the woman in line behind him.

Part of me—the part that never learned—wanted to run inside and yank the woman away from him, but there was a big problem with that.

I was the only one who could see them.

Tapping my foot, I forced myself to look away from the big window and down at my phone. The smell of freshly baked bread tantalized my nose. My stomach growled, but I ignored it. Since everyone else was eating, it was the perfect time for me to get a few good gigs with no competition.

"Hey, Everly." Peter leaned forward, crossing his arms over the handlebars of his ridiculously expensive Diamondback. His overly gelled blond hair gleamed in the afternoon sunlight. "Get any good gigs today? I got one that paid a hundred bucks to deliver a letter across town."

I smiled sweetly through clenched teeth. "That sounds like a gig I would've had if someone hadn't kicked my tire and made me crash."

Into a hot dog stand. In the middle of the morning rush. With fifteen witnesses.

I hated Peter's guts. He'd stolen dozens of good gigs from me with underhanded moves like that.

Peter threw back his head and laughed. He glanced around as if we had a captive audience, but everyone was busy with their lunch. "That's unfortunate," he said. "I guess you just weren't fast enough."

My eyes narrowed. I took a step forward to show him exactly how fast I was, but the 'ding' of an app notification stopped me. A similar tune echoed from the pockets of all the surrounding couriers. I flipped open the old phone and unlocked it. There, in snappy red letters, an announcement blazed up at me.

NEW GIG, GO-CARTERS!

I tapped the notification with my thumb and a map appeared on the screen with a route from my location to a red X. Just underneath the X, a small yellow box read, "$250.00."

Peter let out a long whistle and shifted on his bike, placing his right foot on the pedal. His dull brown eyes met mine, and the challenge there sent a shot of adrenaline through my veins. "Don't bother with this one, E. I'm especially motivated this afternoon."

I slid my phone into the pocket of my jeans and gave him a cool smile. "We'll see about that."

Peter laughed and pushed away from the concrete wall of the sandwich shop. I heard the metallic click as he switched gears and took off down the street. Several couriers called out encouragement as I set off after him. Our rivalry was a source of endless amusement for our co-workers.

My old cruiser didn't have gears and it wasn't as fast as Peter's fancy mountain bike, but it was my baby. I'd found it in a dumpster a few months before. The rusty frame was slightly bent, but I'd spent a week's savings to buy two new tires and now it ran like a dream.

It didn't take me long to catch up to Peter. Despite his superior bike, he spent more time eating fast food than peddling. His lunch had clearly slowed him down, and I gave him a two-finger wave as I cruised past him a couple blocks down the road. He snarled something that sounded like the feminist in me should take offense.

The street began a slow downhill descent toward the port and I stood, shoving hard on the pedals to gain some speed. Car horns sounded as I whipped around a corner, narrowly missing a parked van. I ignored them, cutting up onto the curb and weaving in and out of tourists walking along the boardwalk.

I got held up near Pike Place. The boardwalk clogged with bodies and nobody listened to my shouted, "Move!" so I glided back onto the street. Even traffic was at a standstill; the cars were packed too closely together for me to squeeze through.

A sharp whistle drew my attention to the left. Peter flipped me off as he sped by under the freeway.

I cursed and cut across traffic to follow him. His laughter floated back to me.

I leaned forward, panting as I pumped my legs to pick up speed. The wind tossed my dark hair across my face and I jerked my head to keep it out of my eyes.

After we passed Pike Place, the traffic grew sparse. The surrounding shadows lengthened as the sun disappeared behind massive warehouse walls. The buildings grew closer together, the alleys winding and narrow. Grimy faces peered out of the darkness and around corners at the sound of our approach. Frayed blue tarps stretched between buildings and lamp posts, and bundles of clothing and blankets shifted underneath. Small groups of people scattered as we pedaled past, skittering into the darkness like cockroaches.

Ahead of me, Peter's feet slowed. His head swiveled in every direction.

I grinned into the cool afternoon air. He obviously hadn't looked closely at the map before he accepted the gig.

The address listed was at the center of Vagrant Seattle.

"What's the matter, Peter?" I asked, drawing my bike next to his. "Scared of a few homeless people?"

I didn't tell him that there was much more to be afraid of in this area. Most of the inhuman threats didn't come out around here until after dark though.

Peter shot me a nasty look. That was the only warning I got before he veered sharply and lowered his shoulder, ramming it into me.

My bike made a beeline for the curb. I jerked the handlebars to keep myself on the road, but the bike's frame wobbled dangerously. I was going too fast.

Someone screamed.

A little girl stood in my path. Her mother was running from across the street, but she wouldn't make it.

I couldn't stop.

Cursing, I jerked to the right and jumped the curb, narrowly missing the toddler.

"Out of the way!" I shouted at the group of people standing on the sidewalk. "Move!"

They scattered.

A blur of black fur skated across my vision. Before I could process what it was, I was flying over my handlebars.

Time slowed. I saw Peter's smug expression as he picked up speed and rode away.

I landed hard on my back and laid there in shock for a few heartbeats—my heart was still beating, thankfully—before I moved.

Nobody came to check on me. I had seen a few familiar faces in the crowd, but by the time I struggled to a sitting position, the street was empty.

I wasn't surprised. In Vagrant Seattle, as I fondly called the area where the homeless population gathered, it was every man for himself. It was hard to focus on helping someone else when you could barely fend for yourself.

Hot breath on the back of my neck had me shooting to my feet. I whirled around, ready to fight, but it was a dog. He sat next to my overturned bike, tail wagging and tongue lolling to one side of his open mouth. Intelligent brown eyes regarded me without a hint of reproach for almost killing him.

"Sorry, boy," I muttered. I gave him a good scratch on the top of his head. "You don't look like you belong out here. You should go back to where you came from. The people around here would eat you as soon as look at you."

He cocked his head to the side.

"And I'm talking to a dog," I continued, hauling my bike upright. "Maybe I hit my head on the way down."

Glancing at my phone, I smiled. There wasn't much distance left to the gig location, and Peter didn't know these alleyways like I did.

I jumped onto my bike and took off. The handlebars were bent, so I had to keep them angled at forty-five degrees to ride in a straight line. Swerving into an alley, I cursed Peter's name as I swerved between makeshift shelters and yelled at bystanders to move.

He was going to pay for humiliating me twice in one day, starting with the two hundred and fifty dollars this gig would pay when I stole it from him.

I cut around the back side of the waterfront warehouses, riding along the narrow edge next to the water. Peter would go all the way around the pier to the gig's address on the other side, but I knew the area like the back of my hand. I had spent a year living in these alleys after I ran away from the foster home at fourteen.

A few people acknowledged me as I passed. Nobody waved, but some familiar faces nodded in my direction. Body odor and the smell of garbage burning in metal trash cans permeated the air, mingling with the smell of sea salt. It smelled like home.

Even I could recognize how messed up that was.

A large cargo ship greeted me at the pier, a narrow wooden walkway connecting it to the shore. I hopped my bike onto the ramp. The frame wobbled as I crossed the expanse with water far below. Luckily, the ship was deserted as I rode through and down the ramp on the other side, landing safely on the opposite side of the pier.

I couldn't help but grin as I pedaled faster, picking up speed to weave through the last alleyway separating me from my destination.

I burst into the shadowed street, grinning like a fool, and slammed on my brakes. My back tire screeched against the pavement. The sound reverberated against the tall metal and concrete walls surrounding me. The force of my sudden stop about flipped me over the handlebars again, but I threw my weight back and managed to gain control of the bike.

The hair on the back of my neck stood on end.

This place was very, very wrong.

There were monsters everywhere.

When my dad was still around, he and my mom had always laughed about my "imaginary friends." After Dad left, though, everything changed. Mom couldn't stand the embarrassment of having a daughter that was likely crazy, and then she stopped caring about that and started caring more about her next hit.

By the time I was on my own at age thirteen, I had no idea how to handle my weird ability. Like everything else in my life, I didn't have a choice. I had to figure it out or die trying.

Now, four years later, I knew a thing or two about the monsters that stalked Seattle's streets. Most were active at night like something out of your worst nightmare; they creeped, crawled, and slithered through dark alleyways, preying on passersby regardless of age, ethnicity, or gender. Most looked like humans with the exception of oddly colored eyes or skin, but a select few still caused me to wake in a cold sweat some nights. Monsters with horns and beady eyes and sharp teeth who could devour a human in two seconds flat.

I didn't know why they were in Seattle or where they came from, and I didn't care. My priority was always survival, so over the years, I'd learned what I needed to know to avoid them. I knew their patterns, when and where and sometimes even how they hunted.

There shouldn't be any monsters on this side of the pier. They stuck to populated areas where the pickings were good, and even the homeless didn't come here. It was a ghost town of abandoned warehouses and metal shipping containers that hadn't moved in years.

But this warehouse was downright bustling—just not with people. Monsters hurried in and out of the building, some carrying briefcases, like it was just another day at the office.

I stood in the middle of the narrow street with my jaw almost touching the pavement. I was so stunned that I didn't immediately register the sound of Peter's approach. By the time I did, it was almost too late to react.

Dropping my bike, I sprinted across the street. A few monsters glanced my way, but I kept my eyes forward.

First rule of surviving Monstrous Seattle—don't let them know you can see them.

As far as I knew, I was the only one who could. Sure, some monsters interacted with humans, but they wore some sort of illusion. Sometimes, if I squinted and tilted my head to the side, I could see the disguise too. It flickered, shimmering in front of their true form like a mirage, and gave me a splitting migraine if I focused on it for too long.

I reached the door of the warehouse as Peter whipped around the corner. He swerved, narrowly avoiding my abandoned bike, and swore viciously when he saw me. Normally I would've given him the middle-finger salute with a cheeky grin, but my stomach was too busy trying to claw its way out of my throat.

Leave, I urged him silently. Get out of here before it's too late.

The warehouse door swung open. The hinges screeched like they hadn't been used in at least a hundred years. I turned away from Peter to face the monster standing in the doorway. It was at least eight feet tall, probably male, with blue skin and jagged tusks that extended from his canines and past his chin. My eyes automatically rose to his face, well above mine.

I realized too late that his illusory face was much lower. The face of a handsome red-haired man shimmered in the middle of the monster's massive chest.

I'd just broken rule number one.

My heart jack-knifed in my chest. I allowed my eyes to travel casually past the monster's real face and up to the ceiling of the warehouse, as if I was admiring how tall it was.

Yeah, real convincing, Everly.

After a moment of pretend-reflection, I looked at the monster's chest and smiled brightly. "I'm here from Go-Cart. You had a package to deliver?"

The monster's shimmering face regarded me for a long moment. In my experience, this type of monster wasn't the brightest bulb in the box. If I was lucky, he wouldn't catch on to the fact that I had just met his eyes. His real eyes.

After a moment that stretched into eternity, the monster nodded and retreated into the warehouse.

I leaned slightly to the right, hoping to get a discreet glance at the interior. What could be so important that a whole horde of monsters would hang out in this area? It was too dark for me to see anything, and before I could look further, the monster returned. He held a manila envelope in his meaty hands. One palm was easily the size of my head.

I swallowed hard and accepted the envelope, careful to keep my smile in place. "Thanks!"

I showed him my phone and he unlocked his, tapping my ID into his app. Another address popped up on my screen, along with a flashing green dollar sign.

GIG RECEIVED.

I'd never been more disturbed to see those words.

Without a word, the monster closed the warehouse door with another shriek of protest from the rusty hinges.

"How did you get here so fast?"

I turned to see Peter scowling at me. I ignored him, hurrying to where I'd left my bike.

Before I could reach it, his hand closed around my arm.

I planted my feet and yanked it out of his grasp, whirling to face him. "Touch me again and I promise you'll regret it."

Peter's expression turned mocking. He crossed his arms over his chest. "What, are you scared of a few homeless people?"

I forced a deep breath. This idiot had no idea what he'd walked into. Monsters surrounded us, many of them staring at us with hungry eyes. They were at the top of the food chain and we were the main course. "If you know what's good for you," I said to Peter in a low voice, "you'll get out of here. Right now."

Peter must've caught the tone in my voice. His eyes narrowed and he glanced around, but he didn't move.

Fine. He could get eaten for all I cared.

I pulled my bike upright and hopped on, securing the envelope in my backpack. I would deliver the cursed thing and then be done with this freaky place forever.

Without another word to Peter, I rode away.

CHAPTER TWO

I delivered the stupid letter to a human in a business building at the heart of Seattle without incident. Part of me wanted to ask the dude if he had any idea who he was doing business with, but that was liable to get me thrown in the loony bin, so I left it alone.

It was dinnertime when I rode my bike through town toward home. The handlebars were wobbly, and my arms were sore from riding with them turned at a forty-five degree angle. I'd have to spend some time tomorrow straightening them back out, or work would be a nightmare. I cursed Peter's name for the millionth time that day. It was his fault that I'd wrecked my bike and his fault that I'd stumbled onto some kind of monster den. He was lucky we weren't both dead already, and that I hadn't kicked him in the shins for being an idiot.

A muffled scream drew my attention to the left, and I nearly crashed my bike again. A hulking, hairy monster was dragging a man down an alleyway across the street. The man tried to scream again, but the monster had an enormous arm wrapped around his throat, cutting off his ability to release any sound.

Wait—I knew that guy.

I slammed on my brakes, skidding to a stop in the middle of the bike lane.

It was Arthur, a crazy old guy I'd known for a few months now. Why wasn't he at home? It was past six.

My eyes met his, and he reached out a shaking hand, silently begging me for help. I clenched my bike's rubber handles, my gaze darting between him and the monster dragging him away. I had never seen what the monsters did with the humans they preyed upon, but my imagination had drummed up all sorts of possibilities, none of them pretty. If I didn't stop this, I would sentence Arthur to death. But what if the monster realized I could see it? What if it dragged me away too?

My mother's face flashed in my mind.

Screw it—I couldn't watch this happen. I tossed my bike to the ground and started across the street, squaring my shoulders. I may not have superhuman powers like these monsters did, but I could throw a mean right hook—

HONK!

I jerked around. The screech of tires on concrete filled my ears, and I threw out my hands as if I could stop the car skidding toward me with sheer force of will.

By some miracle, the car's bumper stopped less than an inch from me. The driver rolled down his window and yelled, "What are you doing? Get out of the road!"

"Sorry," I yelled back, and raced across the street before another car could decide to end my life today. My heart slammed against my ribcage as I entered the alleyway.

There was no sign of Arthur.

I scanned the concrete, the brick walls, the dumpster. There was no other exit. No doors they could have disappeared through, no convenient sewer entrances. Where had the monster taken him?

Arthur's terrified expression, the way he had reached out to me...

I was too late.

I trudged back out of the alleyway and across the street. My bike lay in a crumpled heap next to the curb, and I glared at the crooked handlebars.

How many people had those monsters preyed upon? How long until they tried to prey upon me next?

I kicked my bike, snarling a curse when it did nothing except possibly break a toe. Then I hauled it upright, climbed on, and started pedaling home.

By the time I reached Hammond House, it was well past seven. The tidy red building sat on a corner in a slightly less sketchy neighborhood on the east side of town.

I swung one leg over, riding the last few yards on one pedal, and rammed my front tire into the bike rack. Locking the bike was pointless—everyone around here knew not to steal from me, or they'd regret it—but I wound the chain around the rim anyway, securing it in place with a simple padlock. If nothing else, it made me feel better.

Because the hour was so late, the line that usually extended from the front door, down the street, and around the corner was gone. It was strange to waltz right up the steps and inside the building. A wall of stuffy air assaulted me as I entered the lobby.

Hammond House didn't believe in air conditioning.

"You're home late tonight." Helen gave me a friendly smile from behind the front desk and nodded to the clipboard sitting atop it. She was one of two people in this place that I actually liked. While I signed in, she added, "Mary Beth was looking for you."

For a second, my stomach dropped to my toes, but people didn't deliver bad news with smiles like the one Helen was wearing.

"She looked fine," Helen added, seeing my face. "I think she ate already, so she's probably getting ready for bed."

"Thanks." I slipped past her and into the main hall. A few stragglers ate dinner at the long tables along the wall, their voices joining the low din of conversation. My stomach growled at the smell of marinara sauce in the air, but I hurried past the picked-over buffet table and into my bedroom.

I say "my bedroom," but really it was everyone's bedroom—a huge, high-school-gym-sized room stuffed with long rows of twin beds. Hammond House didn't believe in privacy either, and that was fine by me. No one could sneak up on me that way.

I walked past bed after bed, making my way to the back corner. A few people called my name, followed by greetings or taunts, and I responded with a smile or a rude gesture appropriately, ignoring the churning in my gut. Arthur was likely dead, and here I was acting like nothing had happened. But what else was I supposed to do? This was the reality of life on Seattle's streets. People disappeared all the time, and there was nothing I could do about it. Even if it kept me up at night.

My bed location wasn't ideal. There was one door to the gym, and my cot was the farthest from it. If there was ever an emergency, I'd be dead meat.

Not that administration cared if I liked where I slept. When I'd mentioned it to Nancy, the night manager, she'd told me that if I didn't like it, she'd give my bed to the next person on the waiting list. That had moved her to the top of my enemy list for a week until Peter's usual shenanigans knocked her off the top spot.

I found Mary Beth sitting on her bed, right next to mine. About two feet separated our mattresses, just enough room to sidestep and slip off my boots before bed each night.

Mary Beth's expression lit up as I approached. By that, I mean her eyes widened a little and her mouth turned up at the corners. Her face usually remained set in stone, so common standards of expression didn't apply to her.

"There you are," she said in her soft voice. "I was worried when you didn't show up before they unlocked the doors." Her eyes swept over me, lingering on the new scrapes on my arms and cheek. Part of me wondered if she saw what was underneath all that, too. "What happened?"

I shrugged, forcing a bland expression. "Arch nemesis stuff. Nothing new."

Mary Beth didn't laugh. She never did. "Peter knocked you off your bike again?"

"Yep."

She pushed badly shaking hands through her wispy blond hair, shoving it away from her face. The ever-present circles under her eyes seemed darker today, and it looked like she'd lost weight again. If the wind blew too hard, she'd fall over.

Mary Beth was quiet and many people probably thought she had the personality of a pet rock, but I owed her a life debt. I didn't know why she was out on the streets, but I knew she'd been married once. He wasn't a nice guy, some things happened, and Mary Beth ended up in a homeless camp. Everyone in Vagrant Seattle had a story, and most didn't want to share it. She never asked me for details about my past, and I never asked for hers. It was the way our tenuous friendship worked.

"Everly, I hate to ask, but..." She hesitated, biting her lip, and her gaze went to her lap.

I already had my right boot off. With a quick glance around, I shoved my hand into it and pulled out a wad of bills. "How much do you need?"

"Just enough to get by. I'm weaning off." Mary Beth swiped her hand across her nose, which was already red and chapped from her last purchase. Her hands shook so badly that she dropped the fifty dollars I gave her. She was quick to snatch it from the ground where it fell, stuffing it in her shirt.

I didn't argue with her. Instead, I gave her an encouraging smile and climbed into bed. It was still early to go to sleep, but my appetite had disappeared, and Hammond House didn't believe in entertainment.

Mary Beth rustled around next to me for a while, probably finding a good hiding place for her drug money, before she finally fell asleep.

I lay awake for a long time after that, listening to her breathing. The lights turned off at nine o'clock and slowly, the dull buzz of voices tapered off as everyone around me fell asleep too. The gym was dark, but a beam of moonlight shone through the windows near the ceiling. It cast a blue spotlight on the floor below, illuminating a few beds in the middle of the room.

My thoughts turned to the events of the day. Arthur's face would forever haunt me, but I had to push that aside. There was nothing I could do about it now.

Or could I?

That warehouse I'd seen today had been full of monsters, more monsters than I'd ever seen in one place. It was like a base of operations. What if... what if that's where they took the people they kidnapped? What if Arthur was there right now, still alive?

An idea took root in my brain and I couldn't get it out. The longer I stared at the ceiling, the more firm it became.

You know that saying about curiosity and the cat?

My whole life, I've been the cat.

CHAPTER THREE

Mornings started early at Hammond House.

The lights turned on at 6:30 a.m. From that point, we had ninety minutes to shower and eat breakfast before they kicked everyone out for the day. I dragged myself out of bed, bleary-eyed—had I even slept?—and stumbled into a cold shower. There were far too many people for warm water, but I didn't mind. The icy water sent the blood pumping through my veins.

Once I'd dressed in the same clothes I'd worn the day before, I coaxed Mary Beth awake and gave her a cup of coffee that smelled like road tar. She smiled vaguely in my direction, gulped it down, and wandered off toward the front door, muttering something about errands she needed to run.

I bit back my worry and called a cheery goodbye after her. What else could I do? I had no doubt what her "errand" was. His name was Zayne, and he was the man in charge of the drug trade in Vagrant Seattle. I'd met him a couple times doing different deliveries around the city. Gigs in the homeless district paid well, and the competition was light because most couriers were terrified to ride through there. Even Peter stayed away.

People said Zayne once had a man killed for looking at him wrong. Having met him, I believed the rumor.

Mary Beth had been one of Zayne's loyal customers ever since she'd arrived in Seattle. She'd been addicted to pain pills, and an acquaintance had introduced her to Zayne. He, of course, had sent her down a path lined with much more than pain pills. Now she was in too deep, like many of the people who lived in Vagrant Seattle. The only hope I had of getting her out was to leave the city and check her into a well-guarded, off-the-beaten-path rehab center.

While I worried about Mary Beth, I wandered into the dining hall for breakfast. Hammond House provided a long table full of crusty muffins and the bread you could buy for a discount at the grocery store. The stuff was like gold for the residents of Hammond House. They stuffed their pockets every morning, hoping to hoard enough to get them through until dinner.

I was a little late this morning and barely snagged a piece of wheat toast with a bite taken out of it. My stomach rumbled its discontent, reminding me I hadn't eaten dinner the night before either. I might have to dig into my meager spending budget and buy myself something on my way to do the stupid thing I'd been thinking about all night.

"Everly!"

I looked up to see Carol, Hammond House's no-nonsense social worker, striding toward me. It was too late to run, so I pasted a smile on my face and nodded a greeting.

She was a pretty woman in her mid-thirties who always wore a blouse and a pencil skirt, no matter the season. Her heels click-clacked on the tile floor as she approached, a binder clutched to her chest. "I've been looking for you," she said.

"Here I am. I'd love to talk, but I have to—"

"Have you had any luck finding a job yet?"

Wow. She got right to the point, as usual. I stuffed the toast in my mouth and chewed, giving myself a few precious moments to think.

Carol's polite smile didn't slip as she waited for me to answer.

"I'm making money," I said, my mouth still full. "I'm doing the courier thing."

"You know our policy. You need to have a consistent, permanent position. If you're not making an effort to enter society…"

"My bed disappears. I know." I stuffed my hands in my pockets.

Her expression gentled. "You can't stay here forever. You're young. You've got such a bright future ahead of you. It's time that you move on and do something great with that brain of yours."

Mary Beth's face flashed in my mind. I couldn't move on anywhere until she was taken care of. She needed me.

I pasted a smile on my face. "I know. I'm trying. I had a job interview yesterday, actually."

She brightened. "Where?"

"McDonald's."

Her eyes narrowed and she opened her binder, peering at a document inside. "Didn't you have an interview there last week?"

By the time she looked up to confront me, I was gone.

I hurried down the stairs and yanked my bike from the rack before Carol had the presence of mind to chase after me.

The morning was chilly and overcast, a typical spring day in Seattle, and the trip across town was uneventful. I gave up on the idea of a decent breakfast when I saw the line extending out the door of my favorite bakery. It was eight a.m. and the rush hour crowds clogged the streets and sidewalks.

I passed a few monsters along the way, but I was on my guard after what happened yesterday. One monster reminded me of the one I'd seen at the warehouse, but his disguise was a small child, a boy with messy brown hair and a mischievous smile. I shivered, sliding my eyes over the boy's face—roughly at the height of the monster's waist—and on to the next person in the crowd.

By the time I reached the unofficial morning meeting point for the Seattle couriers, it was nine o'clock. Peter was nowhere to be seen, but several other couriers I knew lounged against the railing on the edge of the pier, munching on bagels. Fresh coffee steam swirled from cups sitting on the railing next to their elbows. My stomach growled again.

My plan for the day was this: take a few gigs in the morning, rack up as much cash as I could before lunch, and then act on the Stupid Idea that had ingrained itself in my brain the night before.

The Stupid Idea was likely to get me killed.

After I took the time to mostly repair my handlebars with a few well-placed kicks and yanks, I set out for the day. I delivered flowers for an apologetic husband and a forgotten camera to an anguished tourist. I even delivered a catered lunch to a staff of twenty—now that was a sight to see, me balancing eight huge bags of steaming food on my handlebars. I didn't have a fancy basket and trailer like some of the other couriers did, but I made up for it in speed and efficiency.

By lunchtime, I made two hundred dollars. After seven dollars for my sandwich from Honey Hole, I had a decent chunk to put into my savings for Mary Beth's rehab program. Good thing, too, because I doubted I'd be making any money that afternoon.

To my surprise, Peter didn't steal any jobs from me. He must have decided to work in another part of town. Maybe my reaction the day before had scared him enough that he'd leave me alone for a few days. A girl could dream.

After lunch, I rode back to the warehouse. I took the long way this time, looping all the way around the water to the other side of the pier so I could approach the building from the opposite direction. I kept my eye out for monsters, but I didn't see any lurking in the alleyways. The few people around ignored me, as usual, but didn't seem surprised to see me there. Then again, a lot of them stared at me with eyes that were glazed over, seeing me without really seeing me.

Zayne's handiwork, no doubt. Sometimes he handed out drugs like candy to the folks who couldn't afford it. I still didn't understand why. I assumed he wanted to get them addicted so they'd be desperate enough to find some money, often by resorting to crime, to buy more.

The people here were just like Mary Beth, in too deep with no way out. I tried not to think about it, though my heart still tugged whenever I spent time in Vagrant Seattle. I'd save them all if I could, but I was just one person, and many of them didn't want to be saved. Sometimes I wondered if Mary Beth even wanted to be saved, but I owed her a debt. I refused to resign her to the same fate my mother had suffered, another nameless drug death in the city. I couldn't save my mother, but I would never give up on my friend.

By the time I reached the warehouse, it was just past two o'clock. I stashed my bike behind a dumpster and continued the rest of the way on foot. I had no idea what I would do once I figured out if Arthur was in there and why the monsters were gathering like this. It couldn't bode well for the people of Seattle.

And if Arthur was in there, I had to do something. But what? Call the police? The FBI? The CIA? I had no idea. All I knew was I couldn't stand by and do nothing. Not again.

I circled the warehouse, keeping an eye out for anything suspicious. All I found were a few broken windows and a big loading dock door. Thankfully, it looked like it hadn't been opened in years. I didn't hear any loud noises coming from the interior, and there weren't any monsters guarding the back door.

Maybe there wasn't anything here. Had the delivery from yesterday been a fluke? A one-time thing? Had they already killed Arthur and disposed of his body somewhere?

My gut didn't think so.

I crouched behind a dumpster across the street from the main entrance. The front door was closed and the foggy windows were dark.

Okay, maybe it was nothing, but it couldn't hurt to stay for a while. Maybe the sketchy stuff didn't happen until later in the day. Everyone knew bad guys worked at night.

An hour passed. Then two.

I kept myself busy by mentally counting the money I had saved. It was dismally small compared to what I needed. Maybe Carol was right. Maybe I needed to find a stable job, somewhere I could sit at a desk all day and get bi-weekly checks I could count on.

The thought made me sick.

I needed activity, a change of scenery. Maybe I could deliver pizza? That was considered a stable job, but it wouldn't pay enough to accumulate the amount I needed in a decent time.

Over the past few weeks, Mary Beth had grown more absent. Some nights she didn't even acknowledge my presence. An internal countdown had started somewhere in my mind, and Mary Beth didn't have much time left. She was hopelessly addicted to whatever Zayne was selling her. If I didn't get her out soon, it would be too late.

With every day that passed, Mary Beth reminded me more of my mom. In the weeks before the end, her eyes had been completely vacant. Luckily, I'd been old enough to feed and take care of myself, because I could've danced the Irish jig on the kitchen table and she wouldn't have noticed.

I shivered and shook myself out of the nasty memory. That was the past. I wasn't that scared little girl anymore, and I wasn't helpless. There was something I could do for Mary Beth, and I was determined to do it.

Movement in the street jarred me from my thoughts. The clicking of bike gears moved closer and closer, and finally Peter rode into view.

What on earth was he doing here?

He cast a furtive glance around, then looked down at the phone in his hand as he rolled to a stop in front of the warehouse. The basket on the front of his handlebars was empty, so he wasn't making a delivery, and I hadn't gotten a notification for a gig pickup in this area.

Peter hopped off his bike and lowered his kickstand just as the warehouse door opened. Two burly men stepped out into the late afternoon air. Well, they looked like burly men. Past their glimmering disguises, one was covered in red scales with yellow eyes and long claws. The other was covered in dark hair—fur?—and two horns curled from its head.

Just like the monster that had dragged Arthur away yesterday. Was it the same one?

The two monsters approached Peter, and they exchanged a few murmured words. One of them grabbed his bike, hefting it in meaty arms like it was a child's toy. The other stepped close to Peter's side, and they escorted him toward the building.

My muscles tensed. Should I run out? Should I try to stop them?

Indecision froze me for a second too long. By the time I darted out from behind the dumpster, the door to the warehouse was closed and Peter was inside.

Okay. Okay okay okay. What could I do now?

I stood in the alleyway, hands clenched into fists.

Option one: leave Peter to die. He was my arch nemesis, and that's what you're supposed to do, right? Trying to save him would put my own life in danger, and survival was always my priority. But Arthur could be in there too, and I didn't hate Arthur. Even if I did hate Peter, I didn't want him to suffer gruesomely before he died.

Option two: be an idiot and try to save him and maybe Arthur too. I couldn't dwell on that one too long. It was just a stupid idea, and that was all.

I gritted my teeth, my eyes never leaving the warehouse door. Finally, I surged forward, turned right, and ran around the building.

Peter was a jerk, but he didn't deserve to die. And I couldn't sit around and let Arthur be devoured by those monsters.

The broken window on the back side of the warehouse was just taller than I could reach. On my third jump, I caught my fingertips on the ledge. I hauled myself up, baring my teeth, and got my chin over the edge. The window looked in on a small room filled with wooden crates.

Empty. Good.

Shards of glass stuck out at all angles from the sides of the window. After a few agonizing seconds, I got one elbow up, then my torso. Holy crap, I should've worked on my upper body strength more. Give me anything that involves leg muscle and I'm your girl, but pull-ups were never my thing.

The window was just wider than my body. I shimmied my front half through, grimacing as glass shards scratched my exposed skin.

Peter better worship the ground I walk on after this.

It took far too long, but I managed to get through the window. A wooden crate rested only a few feet below the windowsill, so I dropped onto it. Giving myself a cursory glance, I scowled at my ripped T-shirt.

Great. Just great. Now I'd have to dig into my meager savings for supplies to sew it back together. Or buy a new T-shirt.

I slid off the crate and crept toward the door. The doorknob protested when I turned it, but thankfully the hinges were silent when I cracked it open.

The middle of the warehouse was wide open, with skylights providing light to the building. Thick metal chains hung from steel beams in the ceiling, as if they had been hooked to large machinery at some point. A metal folding table and a couple chairs sat discarded in the corner, the only furniture in the expansive room.

Monsters were everywhere. Dozens of them lounged on the floor or leaned against the walls, conversing in low voices. Horrifying monsters straight from my nightmares stood next to some that looked mostly human.

In the center of the gigantic room, Peter stood with the two monsters from before. His bike was nowhere to be seen, and I didn't see Arthur either. The group stood next to what appeared to be a tall brick wall. It looked out of place, as if someone had built it by hand in the middle of the warehouse, but the red brick was scuffed and aged.

Peter stood with his arms crossed over his chest. He shifted from foot to foot as the monsters conversed, and I could see his gaze flitting around the room. His shoulders were stiff under his white polo.

I craned my neck, but I couldn't see who the monsters were talking to. It was probably the guy in charge of this whole operation.

What did they want with Peter? Whatever it was, it couldn't be good.

My fingers clenched the side of the door until my knuckles turned white. Every logical thought in my brain was screaming at me to close the door and throw myself back out that window before anyone saw me.

But even if Arthur wasn't here, I couldn't leave Peter. I had no idea what the monsters wanted from him, but it could only end in death.

Squaring my shoulders, I silenced the voice in my head that was screaming, "You idiot!" and yanked the door all the way open.

The hinges made a horrible screeching sound. I forced myself not to panic as thirty pairs of eyes swung my way. Before I could change my mind, a man appeared at my side. His eyes glowed red and his face was far too angular to be human.

This was the biggest mistake of my life. Worse than the time I had let go of my mom's hand in Pike Place and followed a monster through the crowd. Worse than the time I had mouthed off to an ex-convict in my first homeless camp and he made my life a living hell.

I let a small smile steal across my lips and strode into the center of the warehouse as if I owned the place. "What do we have here? My invitation must've gotten lost in the mail. I wouldn't miss a party like this."

The warehouse was so quiet that I heard the distant drip, drip, drip of water somewhere. Dozens of eyes stared hungrily at me as I approached the center of the room.

I was in big trouble.

CHAPTER FOUR

"Everly?" Peter asked, astonishment clear in his expression. "What are you doing here?"

I kept my pace leisurely as I walked toward him. If I made any sudden movements, the red-eyed guy trailing behind me would probably kill me before I could take another breath. My thoughts raced a million miles a minute. I wished I had a plan, but as usual, I was flying by the seat of my pants.

"Do you know this girl, young man?"

The two monsters next to Peter stepped aside to reveal a figure in a dark cloak, a hood covering his face. The fabric extended to the floor, pooling around black-booted feet.

This had to be the boss.

I met Peter's gaze and shook my head slightly, warning him with my eyes to keep his mouth shut.

"We work together," he said. "She delivered your package yesterday."

Okay, why was I saving this idiot? Did he have a death wish?

The cloaked figure stepped forward, reaching two black-gloved hands up to pull back the hood.

The boss was a woman.

Well, 'woman' was a relative term. She was a monster, but she was beautiful. Her skin was light grayish-purple and dark purple stripes streaked across her face like a tiger. She looked kind of like a pixie, with petite features, but her black eyebrows were drawn into a frown. She examined me, her eyes sweeping from the top of my head to my booted feet. Then she took a step forward, her gaze narrowing on my face.

A five-alarm chorus sounded in my head. I forced myself to hold my ground and keep my chin high.

"So you're the one who delivered our package yesterday," she said. "You did good work. You impressed our client with your speed."

Peter made a sound of annoyance behind the woman's back.

"What's your name?"

"None of your business."

"My name is Bria," she continued, nonplussed. "I'm the one who hired you. I must tell you, though, it was foolish to come back here. Brave, but foolish." She looked at Peter. "What's her name?"

"Everly," he said grudgingly.

"Shut up, Peter," I snapped.

Bria smiled coldly. "Everly. A pleasure to meet you." She raised her voice, addressing the group of monsters that had gathered around us. "This girl intrudes on our territory. Normally, this is grounds for death."

A cacophony of cheers erupted around us.

I kept my expression stoic as my heart tried to claw its way out of my throat.

"However," Bria continued softly, "I am impressed by your bravery. You don't strike me as a normal human."

Did she know I could see them—the real them? I couldn't possibly have given that away.

We had to get out of here, and fast.

I met Peter's eyes. They were wide and frightened. He'd finally realized something was going on here, something much more than he had signed up for. We had to escape now, or we'd never leave this warehouse alive.

"Tell me," Bria said, drawing my attention back to her. "What would you do if I gave you ultimate power?"

Ultimate power? That was random, and definitely not what I'd expected to hear before they mauled me to death.

Growls and yells of disapproval sounded from the crowd. Obviously, they would've been much happier if she'd turned me over so they could eat me or suck me dry or whatever they did to unsuspecting humans. The red-eyed man stepped forward to stand at Bria's side, adding his voice to hers as they addressed the crowd. The hoard was restless. A few of them shoved at each other and a fight broke out. The red-eyed demon rushed forward, yelling at them, but his voice echoed off the cavernous walls and I couldn't understand what he was saying.

Bria turned back to me. Her expression was unruffled despite the chaos around her.

"Ultimate power?" I asked slowly, gaze darting around the room. "I'd use it to get you out of the way. But since I don't have that..."

I leaped forward and sucker-punched her before she could react. She went down in a heap, thanks to my great right hook.

I sprinted for the door, grabbing a fistful of Peter's T-shirt as I went by. He didn't resist as I dragged him along with me, his eyes still wide on the crowd. What did the scene look like to him? A bunch of bloodthirsty humans fighting each other for the chance to kill me?

If he only knew.

We were halfway across the warehouse before someone screeched an alarm. I heard Bria's voice barking orders—I guess I didn't hit her hard enough—and three monsters broke away from the throng to give chase. I shoved Peter in front of me. "Run!"

He obeyed.

We reached the door to the warehouse and Peter flung it open, nearly slamming it into me. I would've punched him too if I wasn't so busy running for my life.

Then Peter was outside, running into the darkening city. My heart soared, but we weren't out of the woods yet. If we used the ship as a shortcut, we could—

Pain seared through me. I screamed and went down. My chin whacked against the hard pavement and I tasted blood. One monster, a tall one with yellow eyes, had his claws embedded in my right calf. Red liquid oozed around his black talons.

Ahead of me, Peter glanced over his shoulder. His eyes met mine.

I don't know what I expected from him. The monsters would rip him to shreds if he returned for me. I doubted he could throw a punch, let alone fight off a bunch of monsters. Especially when he didn't know they were monsters.

I still yelled a curse after him when he kept running.

He didn't look back.

The monster held me down with his claws until two more caught up to us. They hauled me to my feet and back into the warehouse. The crowd had calmed slightly, but many of them shifted and paced with barely quelled hunger. A hush fell over the room as we reached the center and Bria approached me.

It didn't look like my punch had affected her at all. Her skin was still perfectly intact, no swelling or bloody nose or split lip.

She didn't even look angry. Instead, she appeared thoughtful as she examined me.

"My master will be most pleased. He would love to mentor someone like you." She reached out and brushed my hair out of my face. I shook my head violently to dislodge her, but she fisted her hand in my hair, holding me in place while she stared at me. Those expressionless eyes seriously freaked me out.

"Let go of me," I snarled, tossing my head again. My scalp burned, but I'd rather pull out my own hair than let her touch me.

"You have no idea who you face," she hissed. "It would be wise for you to remain still."

She raised her other hand a few inches from my face. A ball of flame winked to existence in her palm, glowing brightly in the darkening room. The sudden heat threatened to singe my skin.

I tried to jerk away, but her other hand still gripped my hair.

This was not happening. She was not holding a ball of fire in her bare hand.

I'd observed a lot of monsters over the years, but I'd never seen anything like this.

Abruptly, Bria let me go and stepped back. She turned her unnerving gaze from me and addressed the red-eyed monster. "Erza, take her to the master."

Erza nodded and stepped forward. He took one arm and another monster took the other. I pulled against them as they dragged me away. "Where are you taking me?" I demanded. "Let me go, you idiots!"

"I'd remain silent if I were you," Bria said from behind me. "The master appreciates bravery, but he will slay you without hesitation for your insolence."

Erza pulled me toward the brick wall in the center of the room. Instead of going around it like I expected, he quickened his pace, dragging me right toward it.

Was he going to tie me to it? Wait for Bria's master to come and kill me?

I renewed my struggles. My foot connected with Erza's shin and I bit the other monster's bicep. Neither of them so much as twitched. "Let me go!"

They didn't.

I dragged my heels on the ground, but I couldn't slow them down. By the time we reached the brick wall, we were running. I squeezed my eyes shut, preparing myself for the impact.

It didn't come.

Instead, I felt a strange sucking sensation, like the air around me grew a hundred times thicker. It was like running in jello. My body grew stiff. I would've remained there forever if Erza hadn't forced me forward. My lungs couldn't draw oxygen from the air around me.

This was it. This was how I met my end. Suffocation in a giant room of jello.

After an agonizing moment, we plopped out on the other side with a slurping sound. I fell face-first to the floor.

Except it wasn't a floor. It was tightly packed dirt and rock.

I glanced up, squinting through the darkness, but all I could see was rock on all sides. Rock walls, rock ceiling, rock...

We weren't in Seattle anymore.

CHAPTER FIVE

I had to be dreaming. People didn't just slurp—that's the only word I could think of to describe it—from one place to another in the blink of an eye. And as far as I knew, there were no caves in Seattle, especially in Vagrant Seattle.

Bria and her goons were gone, the warehouse was gone, and I was in a strange cave with Erza lying on the ground next to me.

He hopped to his feet and dusted himself off as if this was the most normal thing in the world, then reached down to grab my arm again.

I slapped his hand away, scrambling to my feet. "Where am I going to go?"

His red eyes narrowed and he looked like he wanted to do more than reach for me again, but he didn't.

I turned around to look behind me. There was nothing but a rough cave wall to indicate where we'd come from.

What in the actual—? Okay, monsters were one thing, but I was not emotionally or mentally capable of handling this right now. It wasn't possible to slurp from one place to another through some magical portal. Portals weren't real.

Then again, monsters weren't real either.

My brain was two seconds from exploding.

Wait. Hadn't there been two monsters with me?

"Where'd the other guy go?" I demanded, looking over my shoulder at Erza.

Erza eyed the rock wall. "The gate is temperamental."

Great. Not only were portals apparently real, but they were temperamental.

I turned to look at the cave wall again. If I walked into it, would it spit me out back in the warehouse? Or would I get stuck in the jello forever or slurp somewhere else entirely like the other monster had? Did I really have another choice?

Before I could try it, Erza grabbed my arm—harder than before—and dragged me toward a light on the other side of the cave.

"Where are you taking me?"

"Silence, human." His claws dug into my skin.

I clenched my teeth and stumbled along behind him. I kept my eyes focused on the ground, blinking against the bright light until my boots sank into soft, mossy earth. When I looked up, my stomach dropped to my toes.

The gigantic trees surrounding us had to be a figment of my imagination. Seattle had trees, but they were nothing like this. These were impossibly tall, stretching higher than I could see in a tangle of thick branches. A dark green canopy of leaves blocked the sky, shrouding the area in deep shadows.

What was I doing? I didn't have time to admire the scenery.

I jerked my attention back to Erza, who had stopped abruptly.

"Erza," a smooth voice said from somewhere ahead of us. "It has been ages."

Erza let go of my arm and stepped in front of me, raising a hand. Fire erupted from his fingertips, engulfing his hand in heat and light.

Oh, great. He could do it too. With every second that passed, I further regretted trying to save Peter's life.

"Ah, no time for a friendly conversation? I'm offended."

I should've shoved Erza from behind and immediately ran away, but instead I peeked around his shoulder. Through the flickering light of his fireball, I could see the outline of a man. His face was shadowed, but he stood relaxed, as if Erza wasn't seconds away from lighting him on fire.

"You shouldn't be here," Erza said.

"But I am. And I see you've brought a friend." The man stepped forward, and I glimpsed dark hair. Honey-colored eyes met mine for a fraction of a second before he turned his attention back to Erza. "You know humans aren't allowed in Thios. The queen would not be pleased."

"Bria wants her taken to the master." Erza shifted, blocking my view of the stranger.

"Does the young lady have a say in the matter?"

I almost snorted. Did the young lady look like she had a say in the matter?

"Will you interfere?" Erza's voice took on a dangerous edge. "You know the power I wield."

"Power?" The man's voice held a smile. "I would truly like to see that."

Erza threw the ball of flame like a baseball. It flew toward the other man at the speed of a Major League pitcher, but faster than I could blink, the man was gone. Muttering something that sounded like a curse, Erza conjured a flaming orb in each hand.

Across the clearing, a black wolf emerged from the darkness. It took a step toward Erza, teeth bared, golden eyes glowing in the retreating light.

Okay, nope. Fire I could handle, but men turning into wolves went way past the line.

I turned my back on them and sprinted into the cave. I wouldn't wait around for some wolf-man to save me, but I would use his distraction to make my escape.

My eyes struggled to adjust to the cave's darkness. I pulled my phone out of my pocket and turned on the flashlight. It was a pinprick in the oppressive blackness, but it was better than nothing. I tracked the light across the uneven cave wall, searching for some sign of the portal we'd come through. If I could find it, I could slip back into it before Erza and that other dude realized I was gone. With any luck, I could slurp back to Seattle, somehow fight off Bria and her pack of angry monsters, and be home in time to eat frozen lasagna with Mary Beth and the other residents of Hammond House.

Frozen lasagna had never sounded so good.

There. That portion of the cave wall looked portal-ish.

I ran at it without a second thought.

There was no slurp. Instead, I bounced off the wall like a pinball and landed on my back.

Okay, maybe that wasn't the best approach. Or just the wrong wall.

I got to my feet with a curse and stepped up to the wall again. This time, I placed both hands on it. The stone was rough and cool against my fingers. I walked the length of the cave, waiting for my hands to sink into the wall somewhere.

They didn't.

I wanted to scream in frustration. Where was this stupid portal thing? Did I have to do something special to open it?

Movement sounded at the cave's entrance. I flipped around and put my back against the wall. If I had to beat the crap out of Erza and force him to open the portal...

The black wolf padded into the darkness. He sat just inside the entrance and looked at me with golden eyes, his head cocked slightly to the side.

I didn't know whether to be relieved or more concerned.

I was leaning toward the latter.

"Open it," I demanded, pointing at the wall next to me.

The wolf bowed his head. When he looked up, it was the man's face staring back at me. He unfolded from a crouch, fully clothed, and brushed invisible dust from his jacket.

That was a neat trick. I tried not to show him how creeped out I was.

I pointed at the wall again, with emphasis. "Open it, wolf boy."

The man folded muscular arms across his chest. "I can't."

I looked at him like he was crazy. "What do you mean, you can't? I just slurped through there a minute ago."

A cool breeze fluttered through the cave, lifting my hair and tossing it across my face. I used one hand to shove it out of the way, and when I looked at the cave entrance again, there was a second man standing there.

Okay, I was already sick of this magic mumbo-jumbo.

"Who the heck are you?" I demanded.

It wasn't Erza. It wasn't the wolf man. This guy was NBA tall. I couldn't see his face because the light was behind him, but he stood with his hands clasped behind his back.

"This complicates matters," the man said in a lilting accent.

Wolf man inclined his head silently.

They both stared at me like I was the weird one here.

I couldn't decide whether to attack them or plead for help. These guys were obviously monsters like the ones from Seattle, but they didn't seem bloodthirsty like the others.

"Where am I?" I demanded. "Who are you?"

"I apologize," the tall man said. "We have been terribly rude. My name is Aki. This is Shadow. You are in the land of Faery. Thios, specifically."

"Faery...?" Surely I had cracked my head open on the warehouse floor. Maybe I was in a coma and this was all some weird hallucination. Fairies weren't real and portals weren't real and I was two seconds from passing out.

Okay, no. If this was a hallucination, I would roll with it. Maybe if I played along, I would wake up in a hospital room soon. "I was brought here—wherever here is—against my will. Will you please open this portal thing so I can be out of your hair and go back home?"

Aki regarded me for a moment. "I'm afraid I cannot."

I struggled to keep my voice level. "What do you mean, you cannot?"

"The portal only opens during the equinox." Aki nodded to the wall behind me.

"I just went through it."

"From your world, it is continuously open. Here in Faery, that is not the case."

I narrowed my eyes. My hallucination wasn't being very cooperative—big surprise.

Wolf boy—Shadow—sniffed the air and whispered something to Aki.

"You're injured," Aki said.

"I…" I glanced down. In all the chaos, I'd forgotten about the gash in my calf. Now that I was aware of it, it throbbed with a vengeance. Was it possible to feel pain in a dream? Because it hurt. "Yeah. I guess I am."

"Come," Aki said. "You must have that treated before infection sets in."

I didn't move. "I'm not going anywhere, thanks. I'll wait here for the portal to reopen."

"The equinox is in three weeks, and this forest poses many threats to those who aren't familiar with it. Come." Aki turned and walked out of the cave, clearly expecting me to follow.

I didn't.

Shadow remained where he was, watching me. "More like Erza will be here soon," he said, his deep voice echoing in the cave. "You don't want them to find you. Trust me."

Trust wasn't something I gave easily, especially to dark-haired men who could turn into dogs when they wanted to, but I didn't want to run into more monsters like Erza. Even I could recognize that an encounter like that wouldn't end well for me. Could all of them summon fire like Bria and Erza could? I swallowed hard. "Where is Erza?"

"He was no match for me." Shadow gave a self-satisfied smile. It looked more like a wolf baring its teeth.

A shiver skated down my spine. "He's dead?"

"Seraphine will take care of him now." Shadow waited for me to pass him, then followed me out of the cave.

"Seraphine?"

"Mother Earth."

Of course. How did I not know that Seraphine was Mother Earth? Even my hallucination was crazy.

But I had felt that slurp myself, hadn't I? And the pain in my calf felt very real.

This couldn't be real. Could it?

As we stepped out of the cave, I blinked until my eyes adjusted to the light in the clearing. Aki stood a few feet away, waiting patiently for us. Now that we were out of the cave, I got a good look at him for the first time. He really was tall, especially to my five-foot-nothing, and he wore an ancient-looking dress suit complete with vest and silver tie. Even though the style was old, the suit itself looked brand new. It was at least three hundred years out of fashion, but maybe this place was three hundred years behind Seattle? His hands were covered by pristine white gloves, and a mask covered the right side of his face. It was white, made from what looked like bone, with intricate carvings around the edges.

Aki looked at Shadow. "Tell the others what happened here. We'll need to set up a patrol of the area. Others will come looking for Erza; perhaps we can use one of them for information."

Shadow nodded. Without a glance in my direction, he bent into a crouch. In the space of a blink, a black wolf darted into the underbrush, disappearing without a sound.

I stared after him—I'd never get used to that—and turned my attention back to Aki. "Where are we going?"

"Home. Come." Aki began walking. Again, he didn't look to see if I would follow.

This time, I hurried to keep up.

I prided myself on my ability to sense and avoid danger, and flashing red warning lights were going off in my head. The problem was, they were coming from both directions; in front of me and behind me.

If I stayed here, I would run into Erza's people, and that wouldn't end well for me. If I went with Aki, I might be safe, but I would be away from the portal and my only chance to go home. I'd probably regret it, but I had to trust Aki for now. He was my best chance at getting home, and he seemed less inclined to kill me or turn me over to some scary "master."

I'd been avoiding these monsters my entire life, and now I had somehow been transported to wherever they came from.

Part of me was curious about this place—the part I could never fully extinguish—and the other part of me screamed that I needed to get home.

My curiosity would have to win for now. Hopefully it wouldn't get me killed before I found a way back to Seattle.

Chapter Six

Monster Land was... not what I expected.

The further we walked, the bigger the trees became. Soon it took a full two minutes to walk past a single moss-covered trunk. I squinted up, and up, and up—I could barely see the canopy of green hidden behind fluffy white clouds. The damp, humid air crowded my lungs as I walked.

Aki remained a few yards ahead of me; he seemed to trust that I wouldn't run from him or attack him from behind. Not that I had a choice—my limp became more pronounced with every step and I had to grit my teeth against the throbbing pain. I wouldn't be running anywhere soon, and if he had magical powers like Erza or wolf-man, I wouldn't stand a chance attacking him.

Soon—but not soon enough—the trees thinned and the soft, mossy earth gave way to cobblestone. We passed monsters bustling around tree roots large enough that they needed a ladder to climb over. Unlike the ones I'd seen in Seattle, they all wore clothing that covered them from neck to toes. The females wore long dresses and the males sported flowing robes. I could only differentiate them by their faces—crazy colored skin, some with long fangs or pointed ears —and their sizes. They kneeled at the base of the tree trunks, picking bright berries from the bushes there and dropping them into rough woven baskets. Most of them didn't bother looking at us as we passed, but occasionally I received a double take and an audible gasp as they laid eyes on me, followed by murmured comments I couldn't quite hear.

I kept my chin high despite the dread crawling up my throat. A few monsters in Vagrant Seattle was one thing; now I was in a forest full of them, and there was no escape. They seemed less threatening —less inclined to eat me as soon as looking at me—than the monsters back home, but that didn't ease the nerves that formed a knot in my belly.

The cobblestone path led us into a clearing broken by a wide, slow-moving river. A low stone bridge arched across the water, crowded with creatures. To my right, the river meandered around a corner and disappeared into the forest, and to my left, it curved toward a group of trees lit with lamps on one side and rolling fields of what looked like farmland on the other. The path headed that direction too; the town, perhaps?

We were forced to stop several times as we crossed the bridge to allow creatures rolling large wooden carts to lumber by. Flickering lanterns lined the path, bathing the area in golden light. The low din of conversation filled the air, and more double takes and whispered exclamations of, "human?" made me step closer to Aki's back. Not hiding... just concealing myself from any threat.

On the other side of the bridge, the trees changed. They were still massive, but their bases were no longer covered by underbrush. Instead, they were cleared and neatly swept, some even featuring large pots filled with flowers next to... doors. Tall, arched wooden doors with round metal knobs in the middle. Circular windows cut into the tree trunks glowed with soft yellow light and shadowy figures moved behind the frosted windowpanes.

The monsters lived in literal tree houses. It was such a far cry from the nightmarish images I'd created in my head over the years.

I'd imagined they would live in dark, spooky caves like the one I'd come through with Erza, not behind these brightly colored doors and flower pots.

Soft creaking drew my attention upward. Above our heads, rope bridges swung between the trunks, connecting the small houses to their upstairs neighbors. I watched in fascination as a short, round woman with a bright pink face and purple hair walked across the bridge directly above us, her feet sure and steady on the wooden planks. She carried a basket under one arm and towed a similarly pink-faced child behind her with the other.

By the time Aki stopped walking, the road around us was empty and night had fallen completely. I stopped behind him, forcing myself to stay standing when I wanted nothing more than to fall over at his feet. We stood in front of a dark wooden door carved with intricate designs. I didn't see a knob. "Are we here?" I asked.

Aki looked down at me for the first time since we left the cave. "Does your wound ail you?"

"Uh, yeah, it ails me." I shifted, taking the weight off my injured leg.

"I did not realize humans were so frail."

"I'm not frail. I've had a day from hell. There's a difference."

"So you say." Aki reached out, touching a gloved palm to the intricately carved wood. With a soft click, the door swung open.

"What the—" I began, but I stopped short when the glowing light from inside was interrupted by a body that hurtled out of the doorway. It collided with Aki's chest.

It took me a moment to realize it was a woman, and her arms were wrapped around Aki's waist. She was tall—the top of her head reached Aki's chin—and she squeezed him fiercely.

Aki stayed still, hands at his side. I couldn't see his expression, but his shoulders were stiff.

When the woman pulled away, relief and irritation warred on her features. Long, snow-white hair fell halfway down her back and her dark blue eyes glowed in the warm yellow light coming from inside the house. Her skin was sky blue, light compared to her eyes, and the points of her long ears stuck out of her hair, and...

She wore a faded gray Metallica T-shirt and black leggings, complete with black Converse shoes.

I blinked. They had Metallica in Monster Land?

"Mina," Aki said. "We have company."

Mina dropped her arms and took a step back, looking at me. Her eyes widened, and then a huge grin split her face and she squealed, "A human! Shadow didn't tell me you met a human."

"Erza brought her through the gate."

Mina gave a little hop, her excitement bubbling over. Then her gaze snagged on my leg. "Oh my, you're injured! You poor thing. Shadow never relays the most important information. We should ban him from delivering messages. Come, let's look at it."

Before I could protest, she elbowed Aki out of the way and grabbed my hand, pulling me inside.

The interior of the house was one huge room, as big as the gym where we slept at Hammond House. A fire burned in a stone hearth to my left—that seemed risky inside a giant tree—and a plush couch sat in front of it. To my right, there was a kitchen and a worn table and chairs. Bookshelves lined the walls, filled to the brim, and a set of spiral stairs led to an upper level.

The smell of damp wood and coffee made me want to curl up on that couch and sleep for days.

Mina led me over to the table and plopped me down on a rickety wooden chair, then moved to the kitchen area. It was a strange combination of smooth white countertops, aged cabinets, and an ancient cast iron wood stove. She opened a cabinet beneath the large farm sink and pulled out a woven basket.

As she set the basket on the table next to me, Aki skirted the room and leaned against a bookshelf nearby, arms crossed over his chest. He watched us without a word.

Mina pulled a second chair over and leaned forward, smiling gently at me. "Let's get this taken care of."

I searched her gaze, my nostrils flaring. Her eyes were guileless. I didn't trust that one bit, but what choice did I have? I had no intentions of dying in Monster Land. So I gave Mina a tight nod.

She beamed and guided me to rest my foot on the chair, then lifted the fabric of my pants.

I hissed a breath between my teeth as it peeled away from the cuts on my calf.

Mina looked up at me, her white eyebrows lowering. "Did you walk all the way here from the gate on this leg?"

Unsure how to respond to this monster's kindness, I just nodded again.

Mina scowled at Aki. "You let her walk on this? She's a human, Aki."

"She didn't complain."

I bristled. As if I would admit any weakness to Aki or any monsters here. And what did Mina mean by human? I may not be able to summon fire in the palm of my hand, but I wasn't fragile, and I wouldn't let a scratch be the end of me.

Mina shook her head and grabbed a small jar from the basket on the table. Popping off the lid, she reached two fingers inside and withdrew a blob of green gel. "It's a salve," she explained as she rubbed it into the wound. "Made from local herbs provided by the Great Mother, Seraphine. You won't find it in the human realm. It's extremely effective."

A burning sensation started at the wound and spread upward. Before I could panic and jump away from her, a deep cooling followed with a wave of sweet relief. My tense muscles turned to jelly. Okay, that was freaky and amazing. If I had something like this in Seattle, I'd never have to visit a pharmacy again. The next time Peter made me crash on my bike, I'd be back on the streets in no time.

Mina wrapped strips of clean white cloth around the wound and tied them firmly. "There," she said. "That should do it."

"Thank you." My voice was gruff. I let my pants fall back into place. Now that my wound was taken care of, all I wanted to do was crawl in a hole and sleep for years, but I was in Monster Land so I doubted that would happen soon. Aki and I had business to take care of.

I looked up at him. "Tell me what I need to know to get home."

Aki clasped his hands behind his back. "As I said previously, the gate only opens—"

"During the equinox or whatever. Yeah, I got that." I nodded in thanks to Mina as she grabbed the basket and returned to the kitchen. "So I just show up on that day and walk through? I don't have to dance naked around a fire or something?"

Aki blinked. "I haven't the faintest idea what you're talking about. There is no... naked fire dancing involved."

Mina burst out laughing. When Aki shot her a look, she covered her mouth with one hand, but her shoulders shook with the effort to remain quiet.

Aki returned his gaze to me. "Tell me, human. What were you doing with Erza? Why did he bring you through the gate?"

"I'd love to ask him the same question. Too bad you killed him."

He crossed the room and stood at the end of the table, towering over me. "It couldn't be helped."

"I have to disagree with you there. Most people are more useful alive." I stood, ignoring the zing of pain in my calf, and lifted my chin to meet his eyes. The top of my head didn't even reach his shoulders, but it made me feel better. "Look, I don't know why he dragged me through that brick wall or how I ended up here. All I know is that I need to get home. Are you going to help me or not?"

Aki paced to the bookshelf and back. "Where was Erza taking you?"

"I don't know. To his master? He gave me a henchman vibe."

Aki turned to stone. Not a muscle moved. "Did he say where?"

I looked from Aki to Mina, whose eyes were wide as saucers. I was clearly treading in dangerous water and I had no idea how to navigate the current. "No," I said slowly. "I didn't get the chance to ask. I was too busy getting slurped into a world I had no idea existed."

The front door slammed open.

I jumped in the opposite direction and flipped around to face the intruder.

A broad-shouldered monster leaned against the door jamb. His dark brown hair was long enough to hang in his eyes and a thick beard covered his chin. He looked remarkably human, except for his size. Human men didn't have shoulders that wide without steroids or a lifetime spent at the gym. A dark leather belt slung low on his hips and a matching band stretched across his chest from left shoulder to right hip. Both had several loops and buckles, probably to attach a variety of weapons, but they were empty.

He swaggered into the room and dropped into the chair across from where I stood. A frosted glass bottle thunked onto the table in front of him, almost empty.

"Gideon," Aki said, as if this was a perfectly normal occurrence.

"Heard you had a guest," the man said, shooting me a grin complete with razor-sharp fangs. His hazel eyes didn't reflect his smile. "So Shadow was telling the truth. You're a human."

"He was. And I believe he should have asked you to guard the gate's entrance." Aki's tone held an unspoken warning.

Gideon waved a hand. "Shadow'll take care of it. He's a good dog."

My lips twitched. Did Shadow think he was a good dog?

"How about some coffee?" Mina asked, eyeing the bottle on the table.

"I don't want coffee."

"You need something in your system besides whiskey."

"I like whiskey."

Mina shot him a look and turned to the stove, her long white braid trailing behind her. She placed a teapot on the burner and smiled at me. "You must be hungry. I made scones this morning. I'll get you one. Do you like honey butter? Of course you do. Who doesn't? How do you like your coffee?"

"I don't." When she gaped at me, clearly appalled, I added, "Coffee. I don't like coffee. But a scone would be...nice."

"You'll like my coffee. Everyone does. Well, except for Aki." She made a face at Aki as he perched in a chair next to Gideon. "I just haven't found his flavor combination yet. I'm still working on it."

I sank into the chair I'd vacated earlier, eyeing the two monsters across from me. The world had gone crazy. I was sitting in a tree about to eat scones and drink coffee in some weird place that wasn't Seattle. How did they even get coffee in Monster Land?

Any second now, I would wake up and realize this was all a horribly vivid nightmare. Any second now.

Of course I wasn't that lucky.

Gideon tipped his bottle over his mouth. Nothing came out. He shook it a couple times and scowled.

Aki ignored him and steepled his hands, elbows resting on the table. "Tell me everything you saw today."

I searched his face—well, the bit of his face that I could see. The mask made it hard to read his expression, but my spidey senses told me that my answer was more important to him than he let on.

This was it. My ticket home.

I squared my shoulders. "I'll tell you whatever you want to know, but first I want a guarantee that you'll get me home."

Tense silence. Aki regarded me thoughtfully.

"Sco-ones," Mina sang, turning around with a platter in one hand and a tea kettle in the other. If she was aware of the tension in the room, she didn't care. Or maybe she was trying to dissipate it. She set the platter on the table and poured dark brown liquid in a few mugs, sliding them in front of us. "Brazilian blend coffee with one caramel square and a splash of almond milk."

I stared at the coffee cup. The flesh-eating monsters I'd grown up fearing drank coffee and lived in tree houses. They ate scones and read books and also turned into wolves and summoned fire in their hands. My brain wasn't wired to handle this much crazy in a single day. But the most delicious smell wafted up from the pastries, and my stomach was about to eat itself if I didn't do something about it.

"Honey butter. It's my favorite," Mina said with a big smile. She poured another cup of coffee, dropped in a piece of caramel candy, and handed it to Aki. He ignored it. "Human recipes are so fascinating, and so delicious. I have a whole collection of human cookbooks."

Gideon took a sip and whistled in approval. "It's delicious, darlin'. Not as good as whiskey, but it'll do."

"It won't be easy to return you home," Aki said slowly, his eyes on me. "Bria has held the gate successfully for years now. They will heavily guard it during the equinox, especially when she realizes Erza is missing."

Gideon slammed his coffee cup down on the table, and I jumped. Steaming liquid sloshed over the side, but he didn't seem to notice. "Listen, chicky. You're the first lead we've had on Asmodeus in too long. Whatever you saw today could be the info we need to finally take a step forward in this bloody war."

Asmodeus. A war. Monster Land was looking less and less safe by the minute. I had to get out of here, and fast.

I clenched my jaw. "I'm not in the business of giving away information for free. I'll tell you what I know, but in exchange, I want a guarantee that you'll get me out of this creepy forest and back home."

Mina busied herself at the counter, her back to us, but I could tell she was listening intently to our exchange.

"Very well," Aki said. "Provided that your information is sound, I will return you to the human world at the equinox."

"Very well," I mimicked in a British accent. I wanted to wilt in relief, but I kept my back straight. "What do you want to know?"

CHAPTER SEVEN

After I'd told him everything I knew, Aki sent me to bed.

Aki and Gideon had asked a million questions about my warehouse nightmare, demanding that I remember useless details. They'd been particularly interested in Bria, the creepy girl who seemed to be the leader of the monsters I'd seen at the warehouse. Apparently she was important. I hadn't paid much attention as Aki and Gideon discussed Asmodeus—whoever that was—and their plan to overtake the portal on the day of the equinox.

Mina showed me to a beautiful bedroom on the second floor, but I didn't spare a glance at the interior. I perched on the end of the bed as Mina bade me goodnight and closed the door. I waited thirty seconds, then jumped up and tested the doorknob. It wasn't locked.

I may have played the obedient child and followed Mina up here, but I had no intention of staying.

Adults always had the important conversations after the children went to bed.

If I would be stuck here for the next three weeks, I needed leverage. Anything to help me stay alive surrounded by monsters until I could get back to Seattle. I didn't trust Aki or his little crew; they had no reason to hold up their end of the bargain, especially now that I had given them the information they wanted. If they planned to eat me for breakfast, I would prefer a heads up.

I eased the bedroom door open, half expecting a creaky hinge to give me away like the warehouse in Seattle. Thankfully, it glided open without a sound. Careful to keep my footsteps light, I snuck down the hallway and to the banister surrounding the spiral staircase leading to the bottom floor. I didn't dare peek over to see them, so I settled for laying on my belly next to the opening.

Sure enough, they were in the middle of a debate.

"She can't stay here." Gideon's voice was indignant, and he wasn't trying to be quiet. "She'll draw too much attention to us. If word gets back to the queen that there's a human here, the Reyan Guard will overrun Thios."

"She's just a human," Mina said, voice so soft I could barely hear her. "She didn't ask to come here. I'm sure Senan would agree that we should shelter her. If he spreads the word, everyone will listen. The queen never needs to know."

"You're a fool if you think she can stay without consequences." A loud thunk sounded like Gideon had slammed down his coffee cup again. "She will threaten everything we've been building. Tensions are high with the Reyans already. Her presence here will add fuel to the fire."

"We can explain—"

"She's a human. She won't understand."

"Keep your voices down." It was Aki, calm despite Mina and Gideon's argument. "She stays. I will discuss the matter with Senan tomorrow; we can put safeguards in place. I understand your concern, Gideon, but I made an agreement and I intend to keep it. You know that Asmodeus's monopoly on the gate has impacted Thios more than anywhere else. Without access to the human world, supplies are dwindling and trade with Reya is suffering. Elyra isn't willing to help, and we haven't had a lead on Asmodeus's location in years. If we can capture Bria, we may finally gain the information we need to find him and end this once and for all. That is our goal, and it is more important than anything else."

Gideon muttered something. It was too low for me to hear, but Mina's outraged noise told me it wasn't flattering.

A long silence fell.

I shimmied away from the banister and climbed to my feet. It seemed the conversation was over, and I didn't want to be caught eavesdropping on my first night here.

At least they weren't planning to eat me for breakfast. Gideon clearly wasn't happy by my presence here, but Aki seemed intent on keeping his word. For now. That was enough reassurance for me to return to the bedroom and lock the door behind me before I fell into bed fully clothed.

The mattress didn't creak when I moved, and it was wide enough that I could roll over without falling off. The sheets were soft against my skin and smelled like flowers instead of body odor. I inhaled deeply and closed my eyes. I could almost pretend I was back home in Seattle, that I had somehow inherited a huge amount of money and Mary Beth and I were living in a penthouse apartment in the city, warm and full and worry-free. That the past twenty-four hours —actually, the past five years—had been a horrible nightmare. That I had met Mary Beth at the mall instead of behind a dumpster in the dead of winter. That we'd become friends slowly instead of overnight when she'd saved me from freezing to death. That my mom was still alive and my dad had never left and I had never become this cold person I barely recognized when I looked in the mirror. That I was like everyone else, and I had never seen monsters at all.

When I opened my eyes again, it was morning.

I blinked against the sunlight streaming through a large window. The quilt I'd used last night was tangled at the foot of the bed. At least that was familiar; my blanket at Hammond House often ended up the same way, the result of nightmares all night long.

My head pounded like Peter had run it over with his stupid bike and circled back around to do it again.

I looked around the room, really seeing it for the first time. Besides the bed, there was a plush armchair with a stack of folded clothes on top and a clawfoot tub full of steaming water. I eased off the bed and padded over to it, inhaling the scent of lavender. I couldn't remember the last time I'd taken a bath, and if I was anywhere besides Monster Land, I would want nothing more than to sink into that warm water and let it ease my sore muscles.

Instead, I walked past it and examined the large window. It led to a swinging wooden walkway like the ones I'd seen the night before. The walkway stretched across what looked like a garden and connected to another tree house. It looked like the perfect place to people-watch—uh, monster-watch?—and I could just imagine sitting on the wooden slats, swinging my feet over the expanse below.

Okay, I had to admit this tree house was pretty cool. If only I could transplant it to Seattle and leave the monsters here.

I made sure the window was locked and then shucked off my clothes and climbed into the bathtub. To my amazement, my gash from yesterday was completely healed; only a few pink streaks remained, as if weeks of healing had happened overnight. It weirded me out, but at least my leg didn't hurt anymore.

The water was the perfect temperature. With my history, it was the closest I would ever come to heaven.

I washed the dirt out of my hair using the different bottles of flowery shampoos and soaps. Was this bath tub magical? I couldn't find a faucet, and I had locked the door last night. How would someone have gotten in to fill it without me hearing them? And how had the water stayed this hot until I woke up and discovered it?

From what little I'd seen in Monster Land, I wouldn't be surprised if the water had appeared there in the blink of an eye.

As my aching muscles relaxed, my thoughts drifted back to Mary Beth. Today was the first day I'd woken without her beside me in years. Who had woken her up this morning? Who had made her coffee? Who had given her the money she needed to make it through the day?

Who would keep her from falling in deeper with Zayne?

And here I was, soaking in a bath like I had a right to relax. Guilt settled like a fifty-pound weight in my chest.

I couldn't do anything to help her right now; all I could do was focus on getting home. If I kept worrying about her, I would drive myself crazy. I had to keep my attention on what I could control.

When the water had turned a murky brown and I'd scrubbed every inch of me I could reach, I finally climbed out of the tub. I toweled off and pulled on a pair of leggings and a large Grateful Dead T-shirt. Mina's, probably. Where on literal earth had she gotten these, and why didn't she dress like the other monsters I'd seen on my way here yesterday?

Finally, the growling in my stomach coaxed me downstairs. It smelled like my favorite bakery back home, the one I hardly visited because the line was always out the door.

Mina looked up when I reached the bottom step. She was dressed in a Blink-182 T-shirt this morning, her white hair falling in a braid down her back. Her face lit up when she saw me. "You're awake."

My eyes slid past her and landed on Aki, who sat at the table. His chair was turned so he faced the stairs, the fingers of his right hand curled around a coffee mug. He was dressed the same as the night before, in an old-fashioned suit complete with vest and jacket, but his tie was navy blue today. The mask covering the right side of his face matched the pristine color of his gloves.

Mina bounced over to me and grabbed my hand, towing me to sit across from Aki. He didn't shift, but his eyes followed me. "I made fresh bread and jam. There's coffee, too. It's French roast. Aki doesn't like this one either." She set the steaming drink in front of me and followed it with a plate of buttered bread and a small bowl of dark purple jam.

My mouth watered. I ignored the urge to shove it all in my mouth before someone could take it from me. "Thank you."

Mina beamed and returned to the stove, stirring something in a pot.

I turned my attention to Aki. If their conversation the night before was any indication, he planned to hold up his end of the bargain, but I had to be sure. "Listen, I don't like handouts. If I'm going to be here for the next three weeks, I can work to pay for the roof over my head."

"That won't be necessary."

"I may not have magical powers like you guys, but I can be useful."

"We do not have magical powers." Aki pinned me with a stare. "We have made a pact with Seraphine and an element of her choosing. That bond is a great responsibility, one that isn't taken lightly by those who choose to take part."

"Seraphine," I echoed. I'd heard that name a few times now. "Is she your God?"

"She is the mother of all things in Thios, and in all of Faery. The Fae are here because she allowed it. Without her assistance, we couldn't survive in this forest."

Fae. Fairies. So that's what the monsters called themselves. I tried to picture one of the monsters from Seattle sneaking into a child's room to exchange their lost teeth for money. That was the stuff of nightmares.

"Okay," I said, ignoring that train of thought. "I think holding fire in your hands is pretty magical, but whatever. My point stands. If I'm going to be here, I'd prefer to help."

Aki's gaze was so cool it could've frozen the coffee in my mug.

I was so beyond the male posturing. It didn't work on the streets back home and it wouldn't work here, magical powers and towering height or not. I lifted my chin and stared back at him.

"Mina will take care of you while you're here," Aki said finally. "I'm sure you can make yourself useful to her. For your own safety, it would be wise to remain inconspicuous. Thios is dangerous. Humans aren't meant to dwell here for any length of time, and there are many who wouldn't be happy with your presence here. Listen to her instructions if you want to stay alive long enough to return home."

I ignored the chill that skated down my spine. Nothing like a vague warning of danger to freak me out first thing in the morning. I opened my mouth to ask for clarification, but he had already turned his attention to Mina.

"There's a meeting at the Great Tree later this afternoon, and I will meet with Senan to discuss the..." He glanced at me. "New developments. Gideon and Shadow will be there to keep an eye on things."

Mina turned from the stove with a bright smile. "Of course. Everly, you can join me while I run a few errands before the meeting. I'll give you a tour and you can tell me all about what's happening in the human world. It's been ages since we've been there. I can't wait to hear about all the new developments the humans are making!"

I should have said no. I didn't need to learn anything further about this strange place, and I wasn't interested in talking about human world events with Mina. But I had never been good at sitting still, and I could hardly spend the next three weeks holed up in this tree house with nothing but coffee and bread and a whole lot of time on my hands.

Plus, my curiosity was piqued. Wasn't there a saying about knowing thy enemy? I needed to learn more about Thios so I could avoid danger and get out of here without losing my sanity or my life.

"I guess it would be good to get the lay of the land," I said finally.

Mina beamed. "Yay! I have so many questions, and I'm sure you do too."

I gave her a half smile and took a bite of bread so I wouldn't have to answer. Aki remained quiet, his attention back on the book spread in front of him on the table. He said nothing else while I waited for Mina to finish cooking so we could go.

It was just a few weeks. The new, reformed Everly could bide her time and make herself useful until it was time to go home.

Yeah, right.

CHAPTER EIGHT

It was afternoon when Mina and I emerged onto the street in front of Aki's home.

It was bustling. Creatures pushed carts and hauled huge woven baskets full of berries, branches, and plants that looked like herbs. The air was warm and thick with humidity. Despite that, the females wore long, flowing dresses and capes with hoods and the males wore similarly modest clothing. It was just like when I'd come into town with Aki. There wasn't an arm or an ankle in sight. Did the Fae not believe in short sleeves? I didn't remember noticing the monsters in Seattle covered from head to toe. But then again, it was often cool at home, so that wouldn't be out of the ordinary.

The crowd moved one way, opposite of the direction Aki and I had come from the night before. Mina led the way and we joined the throng, merging into the procession. Nobody looked twice at Mina, even though she was the only female I saw who wasn't wearing a dress, but I received quite a few sideways glances. The trees here were huge, but apparently the town was small. Between my unfamiliar face and the fact that I wasn't dressed like everyone else, it was clear I was an outsider. That, at least, reminded me of home.

"This is the main path to the Great Tree," Mina explained. She walked beside me, a bounce in her step, her silvery white braid swinging back and forth behind her. She didn't seem to notice the sidelong glances directed my way. Or perhaps she simply ignored them.

"These all look like great trees to me," I said, gesturing at the skyscraper-size behemoths on either side of the cobblestone road.

"The Great Tree is at the center of Thios," she replied. "You'll know it when you see it. It sits at the bottom of the Falls. Every large gathering, celebration, and funeral happens there. It's the center of Thiosian culture. As a matter of fact, the summer festival will take place here the day before the equinox. You'll be able to see it in all its glory."

"You worship a tree?" That tracked, especially with Seraphine being the equivalent of Mother Earth. Three weeks sounded ages away, and I wasn't particularly interested in partying with a bunch of fairies.

Mina giggled. "I wouldn't say worship, but it's very important to us. All roads in Thios lead to the Great Tree. This just happens to be the main one."

We ducked around a large cart laden with what looked like potatoes, but they were far larger than they should have been. The Fae pushing it—a bulky, lumbering creature with horns curving from each temple—waved us along with a barely concealed scowl at me.

The street grew more crowded, and we passed small tents on either side. Each tent had a brightly colored awning and a Fae standing out front, shouting prices and pointing at their wares. Some in the crowd stopped to browse; others got into heated arguments with the shopkeepers, haggling over prices. That much wasn't any different from Seattle. Delicious, savory smells I didn't recognize filled the air, and I glimpsed smoke rising from one tent further down the line. My stomach growled.

"Hungry?" Mina asked with a wink. "You didn't eat much this morning. We can stop and get something. Everyone will head to the Great Tree soon, so we'll have to wait until after the meeting to do our shopping."

She led the way through the crowd and we stepped into the line winding from the blue awning with the smoke and delicious smells. My mouth watered. The Fae walking past held long skewers with steaming chunks of meat and strange vegetables on them.

"What is it?" I asked.

"Feoil. It's a Thiosian specialty." Mina inhaled deeply through her nose. "Chunks of muc thigh and assorted vegetables grown nearby. It's nothing compared to the foods you eat in the human realm, but it's delicious."

If the smell was any indication, she was right. I didn't have high standards when it came to food—Hammond House was as far from gourmet as you could get. I rubbed my hands up my arms and shifted onto my toes, trying to see over the heads in front of us. It was impossible when all the Fae were vastly different sizes.

When we reached the front of the line, Mina ordered our food. The shopkeeper, a portly male Fae with skin the color of wet earth handed over our skewers, pinning us with a suspicious look. I hesitantly took a bite as I followed Mina down the path. It was delicious, smoky and full of herbs I'd never tasted before. I could get used to eating food like this for the next three weeks.

"Look, there's the Great Tree," Mina said, pointing ahead of us.

I looked up, and up, and up. "Wow."

Mina wasn't kidding when she said the Great Tree was big. It was enormous, double the size of the other huge trees I'd seen here so far, and stretched up so high I couldn't see the top behind the clouds. At the bottom, a moss-covered cobblestone pavilion stretched wide.

Fae mingled in small groups, filling the massive space, and the din of conversation buzzed in the air. Behind the Great Tree, an even greater waterfall fell from the sky, crashing into a river below. Despite the volume of water falling from the sky, the river meandered into the distance.

"Is that the same river I crossed over last night with Aki?" I asked, pointing.

"It provides water for Thios and most of the forest. Senan says it eventually leads to the ocean, but none have followed it that far to know if that's true. Or if they did, they never returned."

"Wow," I murmured.

"Reya is at the top of the Falls," Mina said, and I followed her gaze to the sky. I couldn't see the top behind the clouds. "Queen Elyra and the Reyans live there. When the Fae settled here millennia ago, the king and the five Reyan houses built their manors and the palace at the top of the Falls while the Thiosians settled below."

I frowned. "That seems weird. Why didn't everybody just settle in Reya?"

"Reya sits on top of a mountain, and there's not much up there besides beautiful views. The king liked the location, but all the farmland and trade material is down here in Thios. Thiosians settled here to provide for the Reyan houses and the palace. Luckily, Seraphine provided the elemental bond that allowed us to survive here." Mina smiled. "But that's ancient history. Now it's just the way it is."

I glanced up at the sky again. No wonder tensions were high. There was a miles-high class divide between Thios and the Reyans. "How do you get up to the palace to trade with the Reyans?"

"Most don't. Not without a special invitation." Mina nodded toward the far end of the square. Next to the base of the Great Tree, I could see the top of what looked like a hot-air balloon. But no, not a hot-air balloon. It was elongated, with fins extending from each side and from the tail.

"Is that... an airship?" I asked in astonishment.

"Yes. That's the only way to reach the palace and the Reyan houses. Reyans sometimes use the ship to visit Thios, but it's mostly used for the Fae who work in the palace to commute back and forth. Aki is the only one I know personally who has ever ridden it."

"Amazing," I breathed. It looked like something out of a movie. I wanted to see the bottom. Did it look like the old airships I'd seen pictures of in school?

More importantly, how had an air ship ended up in Faery? Their technology seemed like a strange combination of new and old.

"It is," Mina agreed. "Maybe someday, there will be open travel and trade between Thios and Reya."

I followed her as she made her way through the crowd gathered in the pavilion. Several sets of eyes followed us, but I ignored them. "Why doesn't the queen allow anyone to visit Reya?"

"We used to, but the queen doesn't think much of us downworlders anymore." Mina's voice was matter-of-fact, but her shoulders were stiff. "A long time ago, two of the Reyan houses followed a Fae named Asmodeus and rebelled against the king in a coup called the Schism. A lot of Thiosians joined him and died fighting for his cause in the war. The king was injured, so Queen Elyra took the throne and stopped allowing visitors topside."

"But if the Thiosians joined Asmodeus to rebel against the king, why isn't he helping you?"

"Asmodeus isn't our ally." Mina led me around a group of Fae congregating in the cobblestone street. "The Thiosians thought he was back then, and a lot of them lost their lives before they realized the truth. When we lost the war, he fled and no one has seen him since. Now the queen is punishing all of Thios for that mistake."

Wow. No wonder Mina would rather be part of the human world. We had plenty of our own wars and discrimination, but Thios wasn't a peaceful place either.

I cleared my throat. "You said Aki has visited Reya. Did he work for one of the Reyan houses?"

"Aki grew up there."

"What?" My toe hit an uneven cobblestone and I nearly tripped. "He's a Reyan? But doesn't that mean—"

Mina glanced over her shoulder. "He was a Reyan."

"Why did he leave?" Despite myself, I wanted to know more. Apparently Aki had been born an aristocrat. It certainly explained his imperious attitude and obnoxiously formal clothing choices, but why would he leave a life of luxury to putter around down here with the commoners? Did he not share the queen's dislike for the Thiosians?

"That's not my story to tell." Mina looked around. "Speaking of, Aki should be around here somewhere. He is probably done meeting Senan by now. Ah, there he is."

I followed her pointed finger toward the base of the Great Tree. Aki's tall, masked face towered over the crowd. His back was straight, his chin high as he surveyed the gathering. It was too far away for me to tell who he was standing with.

The market huts on either side of us thinned and disappeared as we entered the pavilion in front of the Great Tree. Most of the crowd moved like a relentless tide toward the center, but a small group had congregated at the entrance, stemming the flow of foot traffic. They pushed together against the armored Fae guards, chanting something I couldn't quite hear.

"What's going on?" I murmured, pressing close to Mina so she could hear me over the noise.

Her eyes followed my gaze. "Protesters. You have them in Seattle, don't you?"

"What are they protesting?"

Mina's brow wrinkled. "Today? The weapon ban. Tomorrow, it will likely be something different. Many are unhappy with the laws Queen Elyra has put into place since the war."

Come to think of it, I hadn't seen any weapons since I'd arrived here. "Weapons aren't allowed?"

"Seraphine asks for balance," Mina said. "Weapons bring violence, and violence disrupts nature's balance. At least that's what the queen says. Only the Reyan Guard may carry weapons."

"Wait." I grabbed her arm. "We're supposed to storm the portal in three weeks. How are we going to fight Bria without weapons? They most definitely have weapons in Seattle."

Mina didn't answer, just pulled me forward to follow her. The shouting grew impossibly loud as we drew close to the pavilion entrance. The four Fae—Reyan guards, I guessed—stood steadfast, blocking the protesters' way. They held long spears in an X across the path, metal helmets covering their faces. As we passed, I couldn't help but stare. Unlike the protesters in Seattle, these ones didn't carry signs. Instead, they waved their fists in the air as if that would sway the guards. They weren't dressed like the rest of the Thiosians either; they wore sleeveless tunics, and a few of them had black tattoos winding down one or both arms.

Mina and I squeezed through the Fae bottleneck at the entrance, way too close to the protesters for my comfort. I started to shoulder Mina toward the other side of the crowd when I caught the eye of one of the sleeveless Fae in the group. His slime green gaze narrowed on me, then flicked to Mina, and he nudged one of his comrades. Soon enough, everyone in the small group was glaring at us.

"The Reyan's pet," one Fae yelled. He was tall, and swirling black ink covered his right arm. The others moved closer to him, and I picked him out immediately as their leader. His skin was a sallow yellow, a disgusting contrast to his pitch black eyes, and the sneering tone of his voice reminded me of Peter.

Every muscle in my body tensed.

Mina's step faltered, and then she grabbed my arm and pulled me forward. "Keep moving," she said low. "They're just looking for trouble."

Oh, they'd find trouble if that tall jerk didn't soften his tone and his expression.

But he wasn't sneering at me. His eyes were on Mina. "Useless brownie. Even Seraphine doesn't think you're worthy. Tell your Reyan to do something useful with his time and make the queen answer for her crimes!"

When Mina didn't stop, he reared back a hand and pushed it at us like some kind of demented karate move.

A gust of wind hit Mina in the back. She went sprawling, her long braid coming undone with the force of the gale. She released my arm and I barely avoided going down with her.

What the—?

The crowd around us scattered, shoving through the entrance to the Great Tree in their haste to get away. None of them gave us a backward glance.

A chorus of laughter had me whirling around to glare at the group of protesters. "What is your problem?"

The leader's attention turned to me. His eyes widened a fraction, and then he broke into a serpentine grin. "You don't belong here, human."

If someone called me that one more time...

Calm. I had to stay calm. Aki had told me to keep a low profile. I could hardly expect to last three weeks if I got into a fight on my first day here.

I glanced at Mina, who had gotten to her feet. The knees of her leggings were torn and dark blue blood dotted her scraped skin.

Actually, no. I couldn't care less about staying under the radar. It didn't matter if I was in Seattle or Monster Land or on Mars; I hated bullies, and I wouldn't let this Peter lookalike hurt my new... monster friend? Whatever.

I marched right up to the group of protesters and poked a finger in the leader's chest. "Listen here, buddy. I don't care who you are; you can't go around using your magic on people. Karma's a—"

The yellow Fae held up a hand.

My lungs deflated. The air stole from my body as if I'd stepped out of a space ship with no suit.

He cackled—honest to God, cackled—and his friends followed suit.

I scrambled backward, clawing at my throat, but there was nothing to grab on to. There was no oxygen in the air, nothing for me to suck into my burning chest. I was going to die. Day one in Monster Land, and I was going to suffocate to death in a pavilion full of monsters.

"Everly!" Mina rushed forward, putting herself between me and the protesters. "Stop it!"

My scrabbling fingers bumped against a small rock behind me and I grabbed it tight. Gaping like a fish out of water, I leaned around Mina and chucked it at the leader.

Hours spent throwing pebbles at distant seagulls while I waited for the next gig to come in had served me well. The rock smacked Fae Peter right in the forehead. He reared back, his yellow hand going to his face, and the invisible vacuum around me disappeared. I sucked in sweet air and scrambled to my feet. Mina grabbed my arm again, presumably to shove me behind her, while I tried to do the same to her. Neither of us got anywhere.

Fae Peter took a step forward, his black eyes narrowing to slits.

My eyes scanned the ground for another rock to use as a weapon, though I doubted the same trick would work twice.

"Friends," a booming voice said from my left.

The protesters turned to look toward the entrance to the Great Tree.

Gideon stood there. His cheeks were ruddy, and his teeth flashed in a grin through his dark beard. Where had he come from? He wasn't there a moment ago. Shadow stood calmly behind him as if they were about to have a friendly conversation over drinks.

For a moment I thought Gideon's large stature might intimidate Fae Peter, but then he sneered, "And what is Thios's greatest drunkard going to do to stop us?"

"Even a drunkard can realize this is not the time or place," Gideon said in a bored tone. "We empathize with your concerns. If you'd like to meet with Senan, he would be happy to hear your complaints, but as you know, he does not have control over the queen's laws. Your protests would be better served with her."

"I don't see Aki here; did he send you to do his dirty work, as usual? What a shame." His voice flashed me back to countless arguments with Human Peter, and I wanted to punch him in his smug face.

Gideon's eyes flashed dangerously despite his easy expression. "Aki would not be pleased that you bothered Mina and our new friend here. I would send for him, but he won't waste his time with you. I guess I'll have to do it."

Then he lifted one foot—he wasn't wearing any shoes, I realized —and slammed it on the ground.

The earth shook. I stumbled, but Mina's grip on my arm steadied me. Fae Peter wasn't so lucky. The cobblestones bucked him off his feet like an angry bull, cracking and groaning in protest. He and the other protesters went down in a tangle of arms and legs and angry shouts.

Before I could process what I'd just seen, the guards had them surrounded, spears pointed at their throats. One of them looked up at Gideon. "I shouldn't need to tell you that magick use is prohibited outside your occupation."

Gideon grinned. "You're welcome."

The guards exchanged a glance, as if deciding whether they should arrest Gideon too, but they seemed to think better of it. Without another word, they hauled Fae Peter and his goons away, jabbing their spears between the protesters' shoulder blades.

I stared at Gideon, my jaw hanging wide open. He exchanged an unreadable look with Mina. Then he met my eyes and winked before he sauntered away with his hands in the pockets of his brown leather duster, whistling a merry tune.

Shadow, who hadn't moved from his relaxed position behind Gideon during the exchange, stepped forward to meet us. "You have a knack for getting yourself into trouble, don't you?"

"Not always." A lie. From the ghost of a smile on Shadow's face, he knew it too. I glanced at Mina's skinned knees and back to her face. "Are you okay?"

Mina nodded. "Are you? I can't believe you threw a rock at him. Are you crazy? You're—"

"If you call me human one more time..."

"I was going to say you're a bad-ass." She grinned.

I sputtered out a laugh with the precious oxygen in my lungs, ignoring the warm glow at her praise, and followed her and Shadow through the entrance and into the pavilion in front of the Great Tree.

Dozens of Fae eyes stared at me as we joined the crowd waiting for the meeting to start.

So much for going incognito.

Chapter Nine

After the excitement with the protesters at the gate, the meeting at the Great Tree was uneventful—boring, really. I stood with Mina and Shadow among the large group gathered in front of a raised dais where Aki and a few other Fae stood. A woman stepped forward, raising her arms in a large circle, and the sound of rushing water from the Falls dimmed to nearly nothing. While I stared around, trying to figure out how she did that, a Fae man stepped to the front of the dais. He looked old. Even from this distance, I could see the wrinkles on his face. His white hair and beard were a stark contrast to his withered charcoal skin, and he wore long brown robes that reached the ground. Even from here, I could see his huge pointed ears, and he moved as if his old bones would crumble at any moment. The dude looked like he'd been around since the dinosaurs roamed the earth.

Wait... did Monster Land have dinosaurs?

"That's Senan," Mina murmured to me. "He's our leader."

"Does he work for the queen, then?"

"Technically, yes." Mina smiled. "The queen appointed him, but his allegiance lies with Thios."

"Then why doesn't the queen appoint someone else?"

"Senan is good at what he does," Shadow supplied from my other side. "He plays a delicate game of appeasing the queen while also looking out for our best interests. She doesn't dare remove him for fear that it would cause an outright rebellion."

I looked back at the old Fae. The more I learned about Fae politics, the more complicated they became.

"My people," Senan said, his voice booming over the now silent crowd. It was amazing that such a powerful voice could come from such a frail old man. "We are gathered here today to hear your concerns. Please, step forward..."

I let his voice turn to a dim buzz in my mind as my eyes wandered around the pavilion. I didn't care much about the Fae who said his crops weren't receiving enough water, or the female complaining about her neighbor's property. Instead, I observed the Fae around me. They came in all shapes and sizes, some looking remarkably human and some like they had stepped out of a fairy tale. How could a place like this exist with no one knowing about it? Aki had told me about the portals to the human world, and that Asmodeus currently controlled them. From what Mina had said, Asmodeus was the enemy. Did that mean all the monsters I'd seen in Seattle—the ones who preyed on humans—were his lackeys? They were all "bad guys?"

Somehow, this beautiful place existed free of weapons and full of magic. Clearly it had its problems too, but aside from the protesters, the Fae creatures I'd encountered here seemed... well, normal. They complained about their neighbors and water shortages. They bartered in the market and farmed for their food and talked and laughed like any human would.

I looked up, and up, craning my neck until I could see the Great Tree's canopy above. The clouds had cleared, revealing the massive branches and leaves blocking the sky. Sunlight filtered through, casting dancing shadows on the surrounding crowd. I let my gaze wander around again, and it snagged on movement beyond the pavilion. A faint white glow illuminated a creature in the Great Tree's shadow.

It was the most beautiful animal I'd ever seen.

It was a stag, but it was the size of a moose and covered in silvery-white fur. Huge antlers protruded from its head, but they didn't end in sharp points like normal antlers I'd seen. Each one split into four branches, curving into a C-shape and ending in a small glowing orb. The creature's legs were long and thin, with corded muscle ending in glowing hooves. It stood silently in the shadows, and I could've sworn it was looking right at me. Its eyes were pitch black, a stark contrast to the glowing white light emanating from its antlers.

A chill swept up my spine, and I nudged Shadow with my elbow. He was on the side closest to the creature.

He pulled his gaze away from the dais and looked down at me, his dark eyes inquiring. He didn't seem annoyed by my interruption; maybe he was just as bored by this meeting as I was.

"What's that?" I asked, pointing at the creature.

Shadow followed the direction of my finger. "What?"

"The—" I looked. The creature was gone. "Didn't you see that? It was like a reindeer, but it glowed."

Shadow raised an eyebrow, looking at me like I had a screw loose. "Beware of what you see in this forest. It can play tricks on the mind, especially for a human."

The forest could make me hallucinate now? Was that what Aki had been referring to when he said humans weren't meant to dwell here? Maybe, but I knew my own mind. That creature couldn't have been an illusion. Right? I scanned the forest around us, looking for another telltale white glow, but all I saw was green gloom and dancing shadows.

Maybe I did have a screw loose. Monster Land was weird enough to drive any human crazy.

When the meeting finally ended—which felt like hours—we said goodbye to Shadow and I followed Mina back through the pavilion toward the marketplace. I didn't ask her about the glowing creature I'd seen; now I was questioning if it had been real. My mind was still spinning from the things I'd seen in the past couple days. Maybe Shadow was right and the forest was causing me to hallucinate. Or maybe it was the strange meat I'd eaten on my way to the meeting.

We puttered around the market, visiting stall after stall to gather the items on Mina's list. The Thiosians seemed in good spirits now that the meeting was over; the air was alive with conversation and laughter. I mostly people-watched—monster-watched? Fae-watched?—while I followed Mina around. I spotted a few Fae wearing masks like Aki's and sporting finer clothes than I'd seen so far and assumed they were Reyans.

"Are the masks a Reyan thing?" I asked Mina while we waited for a blue-skinned Fae to fill a basket with vegetables.

She followed my gaze to two Reyans at the stall next door. They wore fine dresses—long sleeved, of course—and their masks reminded me of something from a masquerade ball, all filigreed and jeweled. "Yes. The mask's color indicates which Reyan house they belong to. See how theirs are blue? They're from the House of Water."

"Are all five houses named after the elements?"

Mina nodded. "Blue for Water, red for Fire, silver for Air, green for Earth, and black for Spirit. Only the houses of Water, Earth, and Fire are left, though."

"Then what does Aki's white mask mean?"

Mina didn't meet my gaze. "He's not affiliated with a house anymore."

I had so many questions, but the shopkeeper chose that moment to hand over the basket of vegetables, and Mina bustled away with a cheery smile before I could ask them.

It was early evening by the time we finished Mina's errands and reached Aki's house. Nobody else had returned yet.

"Aki is meeting with Senan, I'm sure. They'll both be here later," Mina said. "Senan will want to meet you. Gideon and Shadow should be here soon too, so I'll get dinner started."

I stood awkwardly by the table as Mina started banging pots and pans around in the kitchen. I thought about offering to help, but I had no idea how to cook. It had been years since I'd had a kitchen of my own, and even then, I'd mostly eaten stale pizza and peanut butter sandwiches.

I watched Mina chop strange vegetables, then slide them into a pot on the stove. The stove was metal, with ornate designs. Fire burned steadily from the burner. Glancing around the kitchen, I was struck again by how modern-ish it was. It had all the fixings of a gourmet kitchen, but the appliances were slightly off. A toaster sat on the counter, but it didn't look like any toaster I'd seen in stores. It was metal, with gears and pulleys, and I didn't see a cord to plug it in anywhere.

"Where did you get all this stuff?" I asked, moving to stand behind the counter so I was out of Mina's way. "I didn't see a Walmart on our way through town."

Mina glanced back at me. "What's a Walmart?"

I tried not to smile. "It's like... a shop. A really big shop, where you can buy pretty much anything you can think of."

"You humans think of everything." Mina tossed some herbs into the pot and gave it another stir. "We don't have that in Thios, though I wish we did."

"Then where'd you get all these fancy gadgets?"

"I created them." Mina beamed with pride.

I gaped at her and gestured at the toaster. "You made this?"

"I don't have a Gift like the others, so I create my own conveniences." Mina picked up the toaster and set it on the counter in front of me. Her blue eyes sparkled. "It's been ages since any of us have been to the human world, but I read a lot of your books. I love learning about all the new inventions your kind is creating. Senan and I take inspiration from that to improve life here in Thios for those who don't have Gifts."

"Why don't you use magic like Aki and the others?"

"It's called elemental magick." Mina's face fell. "Not everyone can use it. Seraphine only Gifts it to those she deems worthy. I performed the Rite, but I didn't pass her trial so I couldn't bond with an element."

I searched her face, feeling a pang of sympathy that I didn't appreciate. She was a monster like the rest of the fairies here, but... she'd been nice to me. She was also clearly an oddball. She couldn't use magic like the others and she seemed more interested in dressing in human clothes instead of what everyone else wore. Come to think of it, I had gotten a lot of strange looks today, but so had Mina. And those protesters had targeted her, not me. Was she an outcast here? I knew what that felt like, and it made my heart ache.

That was not a feeling I was comfortable with.

Clearing my throat, I picked up the toaster and examined it. It didn't have a power cord. "How does this work?"

Mina visibly shook off the gloom and pointed to a shiny disk near the back of the toaster. "I built a power source to heat a cell and toast the bread. I set it in the window and it stores sunlight to use as a power source."

I had to admit, I was impressed. She had created her own solar battery. "Wow. So you're like a fairy version of Elon Musk."

She cocked her head. "I don't know who that is."

"He... invents things."

"Things have certainly changed since the last time I visited, but yes, I consider myself a bit of an inventor. Do you know about Einstein?"

I laughed. "Yeah, he's an important dude too."

"His work inspired me." Mina put the toaster back in its place on the counter. "Before Asmodeus took control of the gates, Fae often visited your world. During the equinox, many would visit and bring back books and baubles. That's where I learned most of what I know about humans."

"Is that where you got all your T-shirts from too? Wait." I frowned. "If Fae visited my world all the time, how does no one know about you?"

Mina adjusted the temperature on the stove and stirred the liquid in the pot, then turned to face me. "When Seraphine first opened the gates, she used her magick to ensure that Fae could blend in when they visited the human world. To your kind, we look human."

That explained the disguises the Fae used, but...

"I could see them," I said. "Your true forms. Bria has lots of goons running around Seattle, and I've always been able to see them. There must be other people who can, too."

"That's impossible." Mina regarded me for a long moment. "Perhaps we should ask Aki about that. Are you sure you don't have Fae blood in you somewhere?"

I snorted. "No. My parents are both very much human." I didn't like the curious expression on her face, so I wandered over to the bookshelves on the far wall. Sure enough, brightly colored textbooks, cookbooks, and novels stuck out between leather-bound tomes with strange writing I'd never seen before. A lot of the human books had frayed bindings and title designs I had never seen before. "How long has it been since you've been to the human world?"

Mina thought about it. "The Great Schism happened hundreds of years ago—that's when Asmodeus went into hiding—but he took control of the gates maybe twenty years ago now. That's why Aki wants to capture Bria. He thinks Asmodeus is planning something, but nobody knows where he's hiding. Hopefully Bria can help us find him."

The front door slammed open. I jumped and whirled around as Gideon staggered inside. Did the dude ever knock?

His brown duster flapped behind him as he dropped into a chair at the kitchen table. He propped his boots on the chair next to his and laced his fingers behind his head. "Well, that meeting was boring. But hey, chicky, thanks for the entertainment earlier. At least I got some exercise today."

Mina came around the counter and pushed his feet off the chair with one hand, dropping a loaf of bread on the table with the other. "Thanks for your help."

Gideon eyed her, but he didn't put his feet back up. "You should be more careful, Mina. They wouldn't have bothered you if you didn't make yourself a target."

"I like my clothing, thank you." Mina smiled down at her T-shirt. It was still covered in dirt from our scuffle with the protesters earlier, but she somehow made it look good. "They were looking for an excuse to cause problems. We were in the wrong place at the wrong time."

Gideon tore off a hunk of the bread and shoved it in his mouth. "If you say so. I'm starving from all that fuss earlier. When is dinner?"

"Soon." Mina went back to the stove.

I cautiously slid into a chair across from Gideon. He shoved another hunk of bread into his mouth and gave me a semi-unfriendly grin. "What kind of magic do you have?"

"Ah, Seraphine's Gift," Gideon drawled. "My greatest strength and my greatest weakness. My element is earth."

"That earthquake today. That was you."

Gideon's grin widened. The table vibrated, rattling the coffee cup in front of me. I grabbed it before it fell off the edge.

"You'd never guess it by looking at him, but he's a skilled magick user," Mina said from the stove.

"I don't know whether to be flattered or offended, Mina dearest."

Mina gave him a droll look. "He's one of the few who can control his element with something other than his hands."

Gideon raised a leg, showing me his bare feet. "What can I say? It's all talent."

I looked between them. Their banter was cute and all, but my mind had snagged on something Gideon had said. "What did you mean by your greatest weakness?"

"Seraphine's Gift has a cost. It really shouldn't be called a gift at all." Gideon got to his feet. "Each element draws on something within us. Earth draws on body mass, water draws on the body's water, and on and on... You get the idea. Whenever I use my magick, I feel like I could eat a whole feoil. And that's the least of my problems." He shrugged off his jacket and threw it on the couch. Then he turned away from me and pulled up the back of his shirt. Inky black tattoos started between his shoulder blades and crept across his back in intricate designs.

"The protesters had tattoos like those," I muttered. "What are they?"

"This is my Mark." Gideon dropped his shirt and sat down again. "It links me to the elemental magick, and it grows in direct response to my bond with my element. If that link is severed, I'm dead."

"What do you mean, severed?"

"If the line is broken on my Mark, the magick will kill me. Even something as small as a paper cut could be the end." Gideon winked.

I forced myself not to roll my eyes. If he winked at me one more time...

But then the reality dawned on me. Those tattoos were a giant Achilles' heel, and they only got bigger.

I shivered. "Is that why nobody wears short sleeves around here?"

Gideon nodded, tapping a finger to his temple. "Now you're thinkin'. We can't let our enemies see how our tattoos have grown, nor where our weak points are. Hide your Mark, save your life."

I swallowed hard. This magick stuff didn't sound so fun after all. It would be nice to control fire in the palm of my hand, but I wasn't keen on having a weakness anyone could see and take advantage of.

"Anyway." Gideon leaned back in his chair and produced a bottle from his duster. "You don't have to worry. Elemental magick isn't meant for humans. Knowing about the Mark will help you if you're ever caught in a fight with a Fae, though." He paused, his brows lowering. "Don't know why I'm helping you. It must be the alcohol."

Mina plucked the bottle from Gideon's fingers. When he opened his mouth to protest, she pushed a steaming mug of coffee into his hands instead. "No more drinking tonight. Aki will be back soon, and he'll want you to have a clear head. We have a lot to discuss."

The front door opened again. I glanced up and locked eyes with Shadow as he slipped inside. He inclined his head to me and then took a seat across from Gideon.

"Hello, Shadow," Mina said, placing a hot mug in front of him too. "Have you seen Aki?"

"He's finishing his business with Senan," Shadow said, taking a sip. "He'll be along soon."

"Good." Mina stirred the liquid in the pot on the stove. "Dinner is almost ready."

I watched as the group fell into companionable silence. Gideon pulled a dagger from his belt and polished the blade with the end of his shirt. Shadow stared into his coffee cup as if it had all the answers in the world, and Mina flitted about the kitchen, humming quietly to herself as she pulled bowls out of the cupboards.

It was all so... homey.

A mixture of longing and envy made me want to throw up. My childhood hadn't been easy, and Hammond House was the closest thing I'd had to a home in a long time. The cozy feeling here and the easy silence between Aki's group brought up feelings and memories I thought I'd buried.

I didn't like it, so I turned my thoughts to everything I'd learned today. There was a lot to catalog into my plan for survival. Weapons weren't allowed here, but magic was, and that magic came at a huge cost. The Fae didn't like humans, or Mina, or the queen, or some dude named Asmodeus, and apparently Monster Land was on the brink of war. Aki was trying to stop it with a crew of four—a tall former prince, a man who could change into a dog, a humanophile inventor, and a drunk.

In true Everly fashion, I'd slurped into a primed powder keg, and with my luck, it would explode right in my face.

CHAPTER TEN

Mina had just finished setting the table when the front door opened again. Aki swept inside followed by a man in a brown cloak.

Senan.

Up close, he looked older than I'd first thought—if that was even possible. Wrinkles formed canyons on the dark skin around his eyes and mouth, but his dark eyes were sharp when they landed on me. He examined me like I was a shiny object he'd found on the beach somewhere. "This is the human?" he asked Aki. "Fascinating. I've never seen one up close."

That was saying something, since the dude looked like he was a thousand years old.

Shadow vacated his seat and offered it to Senan, who lowered himself with a grunt of thanks. Aki took his place at the head of the table and Mina set the large pot of soup in the center with a wooden ladle sticking up.

"Thank you for joining us, Senan," Aki began. The rest of the table remained quiet as he spoke. His voice carried a natural authority, and it settled over the group like a blanket. "We're gathered here this evening to discuss our plans for the upcoming weeks. The equinox is fast approaching, and we must secure the gate and capture Bria in order to learn Asmodeus's location."

"It won't be easy," Senan said. He nodded his thanks to Mina as she ladled some soup into his bowl. His long, pointed ears stuck out from his white hair, and I couldn't help but stare at them as he spoke. "With the growing unrest in the city, the queen has tightened security. The royal armory is more well-guarded than ever. I've requested use of those weapons for our city guard multiple times, but I have yet to receive a response."

"I'll send a pixie in the morning," Aki said.

"What makes you think the queen will respond to you?" Shadow sat in the chair next to mine, his eyes on Aki.

"She will." Aki smiled faintly, humorlessly. "I am due for a visit to the castle. And no doubt she's heard about our visitor already."

All eyes swung to me. My blood froze in my veins. From what I'd heard about this queen, it wasn't good for me to be on her radar. Hopefully the plan would go smoothly and she would give us the weapons we needed to take back the portal and get me home before she took an interest in my presence here.

"In the meantime." Aki looked to Gideon. "Spread the word through your contacts, and have the others do the same. In order for us to be successful, we will need more Thiosian support."

Gideon grinned. "I can think of a few groups who would be mighty interested in some weapons of their own."

I raised my eyebrows. Was he talking about the protesters we'd seen today? They hardly seemed like the type to help us out, but what did I know? They'd clearly been itching for a fight; maybe Aki's cause would give them the reason they'd been looking for.

"Shadow, we need to understand the situation at the royal armory. Find out how many guards she posts there, what kinds of weapons are inside, and locate potential entry points should the queen be unwilling to grant our request."

"Yes, sir."

"Mina, we will need equipment beyond our weapons. If what Everly said is true, Bria has somehow gained the ability to use magick. We don't know how many others will be the same. We'll need a solid defense system against her."

Mina nodded. "I'm on it."

"Once we have taken the gate and learned Asmodeus's location, I will alert the others," Senan said, clasping his hands in his lap. "If Queen Elyra refuses to help, we will form our own army to confront Asmodeus."

"What about me?"

All eyes turned to me again.

I ignored them. "Am I supposed to sit here twiddling my thumbs for the next few weeks? Tell me what I can do to help."

Aki looked at me for a long moment. As usual, his expression was unreadable. "The best thing you can do is to stay out of trouble. I'm sure Mina will need assistance in her preparations. Your presence here is largely unknown, even after the events of today, and I'd like to keep it that way. We cannot draw any unnecessary attention to our group."

In other words, he was giving me busy work. I scowled, but remained silent. Inactivity had never been a comfortable thing for me. My skin crawled at the thought of following Mina around for the next three weeks, but it's not like I could do anything to help. I was in an unfamiliar city and I didn't have magical powers like a lot of the Fae did here. Not to mention that, as a human, I stood out like a sore thumb.

It was only a few weeks. Then I would be back home and Mary Beth and I would laugh about this whole experience.

After I punched Peter in the face for leaving me behind at the warehouse and getting me into this mess in the first place.

That thought made me feel a little better.

By the time the conversation turned to less serious topics, I had eaten three bowls of Mina's soup and was working on my fourth. They didn't make food like this at Hammond House. Would Mina consider coming home with me and taking up the position as lead cook? The others would never go hungry if they ate like this every day. It was a far cry from stale bread and canned soup.

Senan left eventually, moving far too quickly for an ancient being, and Gideon busted out the alcohol. This time, Aki and the others joined him. Gideon poured plum-colored liquid into burnished copper cups and Mina passed them around the table. I took a cautious sniff as she slid a cup of the liquid in front of me. It smelled like blackberries. "What is this?"

"Mead," Gideon said. "I brewed it myself for a special occasion."

A ghost of a smile passed over Shadow's face. "What's the special occasion?"

Gideon grinned and raised his cup. "To Bria's defeat."

"It's a little early to celebrate that," Mina admonished.

"It's never too early." Gideon nodded to me. "Thanks to that girlie there, we have all the information we need. It's only a matter of time now. To Bria's defeat!"

"And eventually Asmodeus," Aki added. "Hear, hear."

Everyone clinked their cups together.

When I didn't join them, Gideon looked at me expectantly.

"Yeah, I don't drink." I wasn't a fan of anything that could fog my brain, and this kumbaya moment was making me uncomfortable. I may be stuck here for three weeks, but I had no intention of getting merry with this motley crew. I had to stay focused on my goal of getting home; I wouldn't allow myself to grow attached to any of these Fae. The best thing I could do for myself was to keep them at arm's length. "I think I'll head out for a walk."

Aki nodded to Shadow. "Go with her."

"Thanks, but I don't need a guard dog." Or a handsome wolf/Fae/man who would distract me from my goal.

Shadow raised an eyebrow. "I'm not a—"

"I'm a big girl," I interrupted. "I can take care of myself."

"Shadow will accompany you." Aki's voice held no room for argument. "You don't know Thios or the customs here. He will keep you safe."

I swallowed further protests. Okay, since I was apparently stuck with him, I could use the opportunity to pick his brain. I had pretty much figured out Mina and Gideon and even Senan, but Shadow was as much a mystery as Aki was.

I waited as Shadow took a long gulp of mead and stood to follow me, ignoring my stomach as it fluttered with what had to be nerves.

Nights in Thios were darker than back home.

I stepped out the front door of Aki's house. The cobblestone road was empty in the near pitch black. Far above, moonlight barely filtered through the thick tree canopy. It took a moment for my eyes to adjust as Shadow silently closed the door and stood behind me.

"You don't need to follow me," I said halfheartedly. "Feel free to go away. I won't tell Daddy you didn't obey his orders."

"Hilarious." Shadow brushed past me and stepped into the street. "Are you coming or what?"

"Coming where?"

"You wanted to go on a walk, didn't you?" Even in the near darkness, I could see him raise an eyebrow. "I'll show you something."

He started walking, not bothering to look back.

What was it with males in this place? Did they all wander off and assume females would follow them?

Part of me wanted to go the other way just to spite him, but Aki was right about one thing; I had no idea where to go around here, and I wasn't particularly interested in getting myself lost in the dark.

Reluctantly, I followed Shadow.

He led me around the back of the gigantic tree that was Aki's house, then turned down a path I hadn't noticed before. It was narrow and jaggedly cut stones nestled every few feet in the thick layer of moss covering the ground. I watched Shadow's broad shoulders as we walked. He was eerily silent, his feet making no sound on the soft ground. "How do you do that?"

Shadow glanced over one shoulder. "What are you talking about?"

"Are your feet even touching the ground?" I peered suspiciously at his black boots. "Is this part of your dog thing? Where's your tattoo?"

"Wolf," he corrected. "And that's a personal question. It's not considered polite to ask."

"Why?" I knew why. The tattoo was an Achilles heel, not to be shared with anyone who asked. That's why the Thiosians wore long sleeves all the time. Mostly, I just wanted to see how Shadow would answer. He and Aki were the two puzzles in the group that I hadn't been able to figure out. Gideon was a drunk and Mina was a sweetheart, but Shadow and Aki? They were mysterious, and they appeared to like it that way.

"It's like..." Shadow paused, searching for the right words. "It's like my asking you to share your deepest secret. It's not something you would discuss with a stranger."

I frowned. I'd never shared my deepest secrets with anyone, let alone a stranger. I guess I could give him that. Before I could formulate a reply, we reached the end of the path.

It opened up into the most beautiful garden I'd ever seen. A break in the leaves above sent a shaft of moonlight down, illuminating the area in a silvery glow. An ancient gazebo sat in the middle with mossy stone pillars arranged in a circle and an ancient roof. I rushed past Shadow and down the shallow stone steps, inhaling the sweet smell of flowers and damp grass and all things good in the world.

"This is... wow," I breathed. "I've never seen anything like it."

Brightly colored flowers bloomed everywhere, in large bushes and in the cracks between nearby boulders. Something about the area made my stomach fluttery, like when I rode my bike really fast down a steep hill.

It felt... right.

"Beautiful, isn't it?" Shadow appeared silently beside me, his expression tranquil. "This is Aki's garden, though he rarely uses it."

I glanced at him. "Do you? You don't seem like the garden-loving type."

"Appearances can be deceiving." Shadow shot me a sideways smile as he stepped forward, climbing the stone steps into the gazebo. "It's a great place to hear your own thoughts."

I agreed, though I didn't say so. Instead, I sat on the stone step. "Sorry to take you away from the festivities in there."

Shadow sat beside me. His muscular arm radiated warmth even through the thick fabric of his sleeve. "I'm not one for festivities."

"Now that I can believe." I grinned briefly.

A moment of silence passed as we watched the flowers shimmer in the moonlight. Oddly, it was a comfortable silence. Shadow was still very much a stranger, and I had a feeling he had more secrets than even I did, but something about him felt... comfortable. Familiar.

"To answer your earlier question," Shadow said finally, "I can move so silently because Seraphine gifted me with Spirit magick."

"Spirit magick?" I frowned. Hadn't Mina mentioned that Spirit was one of the five Reyan houses? "Is that why you can change into a dog?"

"Wolf," he corrected automatically. He kept his eyes trained forward, but I saw his jaw tighten. "It's a rare Gift hardly seen anymore. Most of my kind were killed in the past few centuries. I'm one of the few remaining."

A shiver went through me, and my stomach turned at the sadness in his voice. "Was it because of the Schism?" At his surprised glance, I added, "Mina filled me in today."

"Yes. In the past, Spirit Guardians were called to serve and protect the king and queen. Most of them were killed during the war after the Schism. I was young, so I escaped the bloodshed. Others weren't so lucky."

I looked away. I recognized the haunted look in his eyes. It was the same one I saw in the mirror whenever I thought about my parents.

Suddenly, I understood why I was so comfortable around him. It wasn't because he was angsty and unsociable.

It was because he was a kindred spirit. He was alone, just like me.

CHAPTER ELEVEN

I snapped awake, chest heaving. The room was dark, but all my senses were on high alert, ready to fight any unseen danger. I kicked free of the sheet tangled around my legs and stood, scanning the shadows in the corners of my bedroom. It took me a few minutes to convince myself it was just a nightmare; there wasn't anyone—human or Fae—lurking nearby, waiting to kill me as soon as I let my guard down.

I padded over to the window and lifted one of the heavy wooden slats covering it. There was no hint of light outside; it had to be the middle of the night.

With a sigh, I changed into jeans and a thick woven sweater. No way was I going back to sleep now. Maybe a late-night walk would clear my head. The one with Shadow earlier certainly hadn't. It had left me with an unsettled feeling that had translated into nightmares.

The house was silent as I crept downstairs. Shadow was in his wolf form, curled in Aki's chair with his head on the armrest. His tongue lolled out the side of his mouth. He didn't stir when I opened the front door and slipped outside. Some guard dog he was.

The only sound outside was the rustling of leaves far above as I walked down the cobblestone street. I allowed a small smile to curl my lips. Aki wasn't around now to order me not to go out alone. He was right about one thing, though. I didn't know the area, so I wouldn't go far. After my talk with Shadow earlier and my nightmare, I had some restless energy to work off.

Thios wasn't so bad. There was something peaceful about it now, with nothing but faint moonlight shining through the canopy above. No crazy rioters, no annoyingly tall, condescending masked men giving me orders, and no Fae milling around to remind me I was in another world. I could pretend I was back home, wandering Seattle before the rest of the city woke.

Growing up on the streets, lonely had been a constant state for me. I'd never known any other way until I found Mary Beth. What was she doing now? Had she realized I was gone? Did she miss me as terribly as I missed her?

I pushed those thoughts away. Only a few more weeks. I would help Aki get the weapons he needed and secure my way home.

A shadow on the other side of the cobblestone street shifted. I froze, not sure if I'd imagined it, and then continued my leisurely pace, slowing so I could observe the area in my periphery.

There it was again. It was slight; if I hadn't been paying attention, I would have missed it. I stopped walking and turned to face the shadow, ready for an attack. "Hey," I said, my voice echoing in the silence. "I know you're there. Come out and face me."

The shadow jerked and then darted down a nearby alleyway.

"Hey!" I whisper-shouted. Indecision froze me for a second. I looked between the alleyway and the main street, biting my lip. Aki would probably kill me if he ever found out, but curiosity got the better of me.

I took off after the intruder.

Whatever the shadow was, it was small and fast. I barely managed to tail it as it weaved between tree buildings, shimmying through narrow paths and ducking under obstructive tree roots. By the time

I was within grabbing distance, we'd reached the pavilion in front of the Great Tree.

"Stop," I said. I grabbed the small Fae's arm, yanking both of us to a stop. Heaving, I kept a firm grip while I regained my breath.

The small shadow was a Fae child. She barely reached my waist, with thin arms and legs and huge green eyes. Her hair was a halo of tangles around her dirty face. She pried at my hand with an irritated grunt, trying to work her arm free.

"Hold on a second," I wheezed. "I'm not going to hurt you. I just want to talk."

"Let me go," the small girl hissed.

The barely leashed fury and seething hate in the child's eyes made my stomach turn. She reminded me of... me. "I'm not going to hurt you. I'm just a human. See? I'll let you go, but please don't run."

The girl's eyes narrowed. She took a quick step back when I released her arm. She looked like she would run away—I could hardly blame her—but I held my hands up. That made her pause, and she gave me a puzzled look. "Human?"

"Yes, human. I'm just visiting. I don't live here."

"I've...never seen a human before." The curiosity on her face couldn't be mistaken, but neither could the suspicion. A girl after my own heart. "How do I know you speak the truth?"

"You could ask any of the Fae who live in that house I came out of. Aki, or Mina—"

"Mina gives us pastries," the girl said matter-of-factly. That name-drop seemed to have won her over, because she relaxed her stance.

"Us?"

The girl looked over her shoulder and made a come-here gesture with her arms. I looked over her head to see a dozen more children melting out of the darkness and into the pavilion. They were all as tiny as this girl, if not smaller. They wore ragged clothing and their bare feet were stained black with dirt and filth.

The hollowness in their cheeks made something twist in my chest.

The Fae children gathered around me in a loose circle, keeping a cautious distance. I didn't blame them; it's what I would've done at their age.

"A human," the girl exclaimed to her fellows. She grabbed the wrist of another girl, dragging her forward. This girl was about a head taller than the first one. Her shoulders drew back and she notched her chin higher when she met my eyes.

Ah, she was the leader.

"Are you really human?" the girl asked.

"She is," my small benefactor insisted. "She lives with Mina."

The surrounding crowd shifted, whispering to one another. Several of them drew closer, tightening the perimeter.

"I'm human," I assured them. Their leader didn't look convinced, but the rest of the children broke out in murmured exclamations and comments. "Where do you all live?"

The leader crossed her thin arms over her chest. Before she could respond, however, the small girl who had decided she was my friend spoke up. "We live everywhere."

"On the streets?" I saw myself in the smudged, dirty faces looking up at me. My stomach lurched.

"Or in the trees. The forest. We can take care of ourselves." The leader notched her chin higher.

"I'm sure you can." I kept my tone casual. "You know, I'm just like you. I live on the streets where I come from."

"You do?" My small friend's voice was hopeful.

"Kiera," the leader snapped, taking a step forward.

Kiera's shoulders hunched, but her eyes were still bright when they met mine.

"What are you doing up so late?" I asked. "Do you have a place to sleep tonight?"

"No," Kiera said.

"Yes, we do," the leader said, glaring at Kiera.

"Saoirse," Kiera whined. She pointed at the group of children. "It's late, and it's cold."

I looked between them. Saoirse's expression was fierce, but her lower lip trembled as she glanced at the group. Everyone else was silent, watching the exchange with anxious expressions. A cool wind whipped through the clearing, ruffling hair and clothing, and several children moved closer together.

I flashed back to that winter evening when I'd been curled in a ball behind a dumpster. Mary Beth's hand extending out to me. "I know where you could sleep tonight."

All heads swung to look at me.

"I don't have a home here to offer you, or I would. But I know a secret place. It's sheltered from the wind and there's a roof in case it rains. It's close to Mina's house."

Kiera gave an excited hop closer to me. "Yes, yes!"

"We have nothing to offer you in return," Saoirse said.

"I don't have much to offer you either. But I know Mina could use some extra hands with a project she's working on. I'll put in a good word for you. If you stop by the house tomorrow, she'll put you to work and make sure you're fed." Or so I hoped. "We'll consider that payment enough."

All the children looked at Saoirse, waiting for her answer. She searched my face, no doubt looking for the deception she often saw on the faces of the adults around her. I kept my expression uninterested and bland. Finally, she nodded slowly. "Okay."

A quiet cheer erupted from the gaggle of children, and I couldn't help but grin as they crowded close to me, firing a million questions at once. Kiera grabbed Saoirse's hand and jumped up and down, excitement blazing from her tiny, dirty face.

"Come on," I said, gesturing for them to follow me. "I'll show you what I'm talking about."

The gaggle of Fae children followed me down the street. Kiera skipped along next to me as if she didn't have a care in the world.

Maybe I couldn't do much here in Thios, and maybe I didn't have magical powers...but for the next three weeks, I could help these kids. I could help them like Mary Beth had helped me.

That would have to be enough.

I was waiting impatiently at the kitchen table when Mina came downstairs the next morning. Shadow had left shortly after the sun came up without much more than a bleary, "Good morning," and I hadn't seen Aki yet. Part of me was relieved. I needed Mina on my side before I broached the orphan subject with Aki. I had a feeling he wouldn't be pleased with the arrangement.

Mina skipped down the last step, her silver-white braid swinging behind her, and gave me a cheery smile. "Good morning, Everly. You're up early."

"I've been awake for hours."

"Really?" Mina gave me a concerned glance. "You couldn't sleep?"

"No. I need to show you something."

She raised her eyebrows. "Okay...?"

"Come with me." I grabbed her hand and towed her out the front door. My stomach was doing somersaults, but I was doing the right thing. I knew it. Those kids needed me, and Kiera had implied that Mina had helped them before. She was the only one in Aki's crew who might be on board with my plan.

"Where are we going?" Mina asked. "We've got a busy day, you know. I have to make breakfast and get started on the—"

"I know." I turned down the path to the secret garden and gestured for Mina to follow. "I have an idea to help with that."

We entered the garden, and Mina drew up short when she saw the group of children sitting underneath the stone pergola. Kiera and Saoirse sat in the front; Kiera was bouncing in her seat, her eyes alight with excitement.

Mina looked at me. "What—?"

"I told Saoirse that you could use some help." I gestured toward them. "I know you've got a lot to do to get ready for the you-know-what. These kids will help. In return, we can feed them and let them sleep here."

Mina's eyes searched my face. She glanced back at the children, indecision clear in her expression. "Everly, I don't know…"

I lowered my voice. "They need help. And so do we. You and I can't make that many weapons ourselves in just a few weeks. I'll help you get more food; whatever we need to do to get them fed. They'll be a lot safer sleeping here than in the forest."

A tense moment passed. I tried not to look too invested in Mina's answer even as my heart did nervous flips in my chest. If she didn't agree, I'd find some other way to help them. Aki probably wouldn't be on board anyway, so maybe I could—

Finally, Mina squared her shoulders. "Right. Saoirse and Kiera? Come with me. We'll work out assignments for everyone while we make breakfast. The rest of you, stay here and don't cause any trouble. We'll be back soon."

The children cheered. Traitorous burning started somewhere in the vicinity of my eyes as Saoirse and Kiera scurried after us on the path back toward the house. Before I lost my nerve, I leaned close to Mina and murmured, "Thank you."

Mina met my eyes and smiled. "Careful, Everly. I might start to think you have a heart."

"This just made sense. And it means less work for me."

"Right." Mina placed one hand on Kiera's shoulder. "Come on, ladies. Let's get to work."

It was dinnertime when the true obstacle to my plan arrived.

Kiera stood at the counter with Mina, assembling little metal balls for Mina's makeshift weapon. She had explained the concept to me—a handheld device we could throw at our enemies. A special herb powder found in the forest would then explode and knock them unconscious in seconds. It sounded a lot like a grenade, and I was a hundred percent behind the idea. It would be a lot easier to lob one at a group of enemies and knock them out instead of fighting them one by one. Plus, it was something I could use so I wouldn't be completely defenseless in the fight.

"What do you think Aki will say about our... helpers?" I asked Mina.

"He probably won't be happy." Mina glanced up. A pair of copper eyeglasses perched on her nose, magnifying her eyes by several times. I hid my smile as she blinked at me like a bug-eyed alien. Luckily, she moved the glasses to the top of her head before I lost it and started laughing. "Most don't know this, but Aki has a weakness, and I know just how to exploit it."

A weakness? Aki? Color me intrigued. "What?"

"Logic." Mina tapped her temple with a finger. "Ever since Aki left Reya behind, he's had a singular goal, and that's defeating Asmodeus. Everything he says and does is for that purpose. If we can spin this as something that will help him achieve his goal, he'll get on board."

I tucked that tidbit away for future reference. Aki was still a giant mystery wrapped in an enigma; I'd take whatever I could get to figure out what made him tick.

"Aki is scary," Kiera said in a tiny voice. She assembled a metal ball, not looking at either of us. "He always looks so mean."

"He's not mean," Mina said, gently patting Kiera's head. "He's just... focused."

I grabbed a metal ball out of the basket of finished ones and tossed it in the air. "How long have you known him, Mina?"

"Years now. I met him shortly after the Schism. He took me in when nobody else would." She bumped Kiera with her hip. "That's how I know he has a heart. It's just buried deep, like someone else we know."

I wrinkled my nose at her pointed look. "I don't have a heart."

"Sure you don't." Mina shared a smile with Kiera, and Kiera giggled.

Before I could argue, Aki swept into the house as if our conversation had conjured him there. A gust of wind rushed across the room, throwing open the covers of several books sitting on the coffee table, and slammed the door behind him.

"Would someone kindly explain why there are a dozen children playing in my garden?" Aki's voice was calm, but he pinned me with a glare.

Kiera ducked behind me, making herself small. If Aki had a heart like Mina claimed, he sure had it buried deep. I glared back at him, but Mina broke in before I could tell him off.

"They're here to help." Mina placed a steaming coffee cup in Aki's hands. He curled his fingers around it, seemingly without realizing it. "We recruited them."

"That doesn't explain why they're in my garden."

"They needed a place to sleep." Kiera trembled behind me. I shifted so I fully blocked her from Aki's view.

Aki's silver eyes narrowed on me.

"I need assistance with my project," Mina said. "And I'm sure Shadow and Gideon could use some extra hands. These children are adept at traveling the city unseen. Their skills could prove useful as we prepare for the equinox."

Aki looked between the two of us. I held my breath. This was the ultimate test; if he threw Kiera and her friends out, he was just like the monsters I'd seen in Seattle.

"I will not allow them to sleep in my garden." He paused, then huffed. "We will find other arrangements for them tomorrow. Inform Gideon and Shadow of their involvement. They'll find a good use for their skills." With that, he retreated to his armchair by the fire and opened a thick leather-bound book, effectively dismissing us.

"Yes, sir," Mina said loudly, grinning at Kiera and me.

I couldn't help grinning back as I stepped away from Kiera. "Looks like you're all set."

She did an adorable little happy bounce. "I can't wait to tell Saoirse."

I swear my heart grew three sizes. If I could give Kiera and Saoirse and the others a safe place to sleep and a purpose even for just the next three weeks, then maybe this trip wouldn't be a total waste.

For the second time in as many days, a feeling of rightness settled over me.

I should have questioned it, but I didn't. Instead, I leaned into it.

Chapter Twelve

The next few days passed in a flurry of activity. Shadow and Gideon took most of the children and sent them on a variety of errands, everything from scoping out the armory to sending messages to allies and gathering information from the Fae in town. Despite Aki's initial hesitation, he didn't protest when the children continued to sleep in the garden. Kiera and Saoirse helped Mina and me with her improvised weapon. It was tedious work, and I was glad to share the load.

As the girls spent more time with us, they opened up about their backgrounds. Saoirse had been on the streets as long as she could remember, and Kiera had lost her parents two years ago. Saoirse cared for her band of kids, and she was deeply protective of them. Although she never expressed her gratitude, I could tell she was thankful that she didn't have to worry about food or finding a place to sleep for the dozen children she looked after.

A new day dawned bright and sunny, and I lay in bed for a few minutes. Waking up in my own room—without strangers sleeping in a bed less than a foot from mine—was heaven, though part of me would always feel guilty for enjoying it. I watched sunshine filter through the window and inhaled the smells of coffee and wood. If only I could wake up like this every morning for the rest of my life, and if only Mary Beth could be here with me.

A steaming bath was ready for me—another one of Mina's inventions, I'd learned—and I took my time, scrubbing every inch of skin I could reach. Mina had left more clothes folded on the chair next to the bathtub. These were closer to my style, dark green cargo pants and a black T-shirt, complete with black combat boots. She must've finally run out of band T-shirts.

By the time I made it downstairs, Aki and Mina were sitting at the kitchen table eating croissants in amicable silence.

"Good morning," Mina said brightly. "Come help yourself."

I didn't think twice, loading up a plate full of croissants and soft butter. On the back counter, I could see platters of croissants for the children. I would take them over as soon as we finished eating, just as I'd done every morning since they'd started sleeping in the garden. I sat down next to Mina and bit into the first pastry. Seriously, I'd never be able to return to the food at Hammond House. Even Mary Beth might gain some weight if she ate like this every day. I missed her so much.

"Where's Shadow?" I asked Aki, trying to distract myself from the stabbing pain in my heart.

"He had some errands to take care of."

Well, that was mysterious. Shadow reminded me of a ghost more than a person—Fae?—most days. He never seemed truly present with the group, and he disappeared more often than not. "And Gideon?"

"Gideon comes and goes as he pleases," Mina said. "As you've probably realized, he's a bit of a free spirit. I believe he's meeting with some potential allies today. And before you ask, Kiera and Saoirse are in the garden with the rest of the children. We'll bring their breakfast in a few minutes so they can get to work."

A light knock on the door distracted me from saying anything more. Was it Kiera? It was a timid knock like hers.

Mina hurried over and pulled the door open, but there was no one there. Wait, that wasn't right. Something flitted through the air at a dizzying speed and hovered at Aki's eye level in the center of the table. It was a Fae, only six inches tall, with tiny wings moving so fast they were only a yellow blur. He carried a thick envelope twice his size and dropped it on Aki's plate. Aki picked it up and nodded at the small creature, who then flitted away. Mina closed the door behind it and returned to the table as if nothing was amiss.

"Um, what was that?"

"A pixie," Mina said, as if it was the most normal thing in the world. When I gave her a blank look, she laughed. "Sometimes I forget you're human. Pixies deliver messages in Thios. You'll see them flying around in the morning most days."

"Like messenger pigeons?" Come to think of it, I had seen them. Fae came in all shapes and sizes, so I hadn't paid them much attention as I'd seen them flitting around in the air above the main road to and from the Great Tree.

"Sure, if you'd like to consider them like that. They're Fae, just like Aki and I. Delivering messages is simply their occupation."

Aki slid a finger under the white wax seal and opened the envelope.

Mina took it from him and stared at it while he unfolded the parchment paper inside. "Is this seal what I think it is?" she asked faintly.

"Yes."

"What is it?" I asked.

"A message from the palace. The queen has deigned to read my letter." Aki's eyes met mine. "She requests our presence at the palace tonight."

"Our?" I echoed. "Like...me and you?"

"I suspected as much. Elyra has informants in the city, but she's far more concerned about the politics within the palace than what's going on below. A human in Thios was apparently just enough to garner her attention. I doubt it was because of my letter."

"Okay... this is good, right? You wanted an audience with the queen and now you've got one. Maybe she'll give you the weapons you need to take the gate."

Aki nodded, but his expression didn't seem like it was good news. "We'll attend the ball this evening. Shadow will accompany us as a precaution. You'll make an appearance in front of the queen and I'll present my argument and request use of the armory." Aki dropped the letter onto the table and stood, brushing nonexistent crumbs from his cravat.

I must've looked concerned, because Mina placed her hand over mine. "It will be fine. Let's take these croissants to the kids. There's a lot to do before you leave tonight."

I groaned, but grabbed a platter and followed her out the door.

By the time we returned to the house, it was late afternoon and I was cranky and sore. Kiera, Mina and I had spent all day hunched over the tables in her workshop, fitting together small pieces and testing components. The sleep grenades were coming along nicely, but we'd be hard-pressed to finish them by the equinox. We only had two and a half weeks left and at least six weeks' worth of work.

"I've had a few clothing choices prepared for you," Mina said as we entered the house. "I'll help you get dressed."

I wrinkled my nose. "Do I have to wear a dress?"

"Formal attire is a requirement at the palace," Aki said from his armchair in front of the fire.

"I don't wear dresses."

"Tonight you do."

I grumbled about the insanity of fairies and tall, bossy men as I followed Mina up the stairs. She opened my bedroom door and gestured inside with a flourish.

I stepped through the doorway, eyes widening. Two exquisite gowns were lying on my bed. I didn't consider myself a fashionable person, nor did I have any interest in girlie things, but the sight of the satin and lacy confections made something melt inside me. One was emerald green, with a black lace bust and a full bottom. The other was simple, sky blue with long sleeves and no embellishments whatsoever. I pointed to that one without hesitation.

"I thought you might be drawn to that one," Mina said with a knowing smile. Then she giggled. "I actually got the other one for myself."

"Are you coming with us?" Spending the evening with Aki and a bunch of royals sounded stuffy and boring, but it would be bearable if Mina came. I liked her a lot; her bubbly personality and never-ending optimism were endearing. People like her didn't exist in Vagrant Seattle.

"Maybe someday," Mina said. Something flashed across her face, a dark expression I couldn't distinguish. It was gone so fast that I wondered if I'd imagined it. "Here, let me help you get dressed."

She held up the gown while I undressed, then helped me step into it. The fabric slid over my skin in a soft caress, and I shivered. I had literally never touched anything so luxurious in my entire life. Was this what it felt like to be a princess? I'd never given myself permission to wonder about such things. What was Faery doing to me? I was in for a rude awakening when I went back to Seattle. This would all seem like a beautiful dream when I was back to wearing combat boots and only having access to cold showers.

Mina laced up the back of the dress with a delicate white ribbon, and I winced as my breath stuttered out of me. "That's way too tight."

"That's how they wear it at the palace. This way your chest won't fall out if you have to run for your life."

"What?" I said, aghast.

Mina laughed, all bubbly and bright again. "I'm just kidding. You'll be fine. Here, your hair." She grabbed a brush from the vanity next to the bathtub and ran it through the length of my hair, then deftly piled it on top of my head. She jabbed my skull with a series of pins and then stepped back, looking pleased. "Perfect. Fit for royalty."

I turned to look in the mirror; I didn't recognize the girl staring back at me. The dress hugged my curves—what little I had—perfectly, accentuating my hips, and fell straight to my toes. My hair somehow looked elegant, with strands curling down around my neck. "Wow."

"Beautiful," Mina agreed. "Let's get you downstairs. Aki and Shadow are waiting for you."

She helped me slip into a pair of silver heels that looked like they should be at the Grammy's, not in a forest city in fairy land.

As I descended the stairs, heat climbed up my neck as Aki, Shadow, and Gideon all looked up at me. Aki gave a brief nod of approval, and Gideon nearly choked on his whiskey.

"Little lady," Gideon drawled, "you look like a million bucks. Who knew?"

I couldn't stop my gaze from straying to Shadow. He wore his trademark all black, but the fabric was nicer, with silver accents. His book had dropped to his lap, forgotten, and his golden eyes seemed to glow even from here. They traveled from my toes to the top of my head, and warm chills followed in their wake.

I looked away before I did something stupid like smile at him, and stomped to the door—a feat in mile-high heels. "Stop gawking and let's go already."

I prayed none of them could see the small smile that curved my lips when none of them moved for a full five seconds after my declaration.

"Do we get to ride in the air ship?" I asked, following Aki down the deserted cobblestone lane. Shadow trailed beside me, keeping pace with me in my heels. I hadn't been able to meet his eyes since we left Aki's house, but his warm presence was comforting. I wasn't thrilled about the idea of meeting the queen, but I was unreasonably excited about riding on the air ship.

"Yes," Aki replied, and I couldn't help the excited bounce that entered my step. Aki didn't look amused by my excitement, but I caught a smile on Shadow's face before he could hide it.

Evening had fallen over Thios; the shadows stretched anxious hands toward us as we passed. Because the sky wasn't visible from the ground below, the surroundings darkened quickly. A faint mist floated through the air, lending the road an eerie haunted-cemetery-at-night kind of vibe. Chills swept over me as we walked. It was dead quiet; not even a breeze dared to stir the air around us.

Maybe it was nerves that sent dread crawling up my spine despite my excitement.

Before long, we reached the pavilion in front of the Great Tree, where the air ship waited for us. It was just as intriguing as when I'd first seen it during the meeting at the Great Tree, but now that I was closer, I could admire it fully. The bottom looked like an old-school wooden ship from the 1800s, complete with circular windows lining the side. It had an open deck up top, but instead of masts and sails, thick rope along the ship's frame connected it to an enormous balloon above. The balloon was oblong, the length of the ship, and the back end tapered to a point. Large canvas wings extended from either side of the balloon, a bit like sails.

Fae bustled on the deck above, tying ropes and shouting to each other.

Aki started up the long wooden walkway extending from the ground to an open door in the middle of the ship's base. Shadow appeared beside me and extended an elbow. Ignoring the warmth in my cheeks, I tucked my hand into the crook of his arm. I wasn't thrilled about the idea of walking across this narrow plank in these heels or falling to my death before I even met the queen.

A Fae man stood at the ship's door. He was short and thin, but his clothes were tidy. A wide-brimmed hat sat slightly askew on his head, and he gave us a hasty salute as we approached. "Lord Aki, it's nice to see you again."

Aki inclined his head. "Nice to see you, Ollee. It's been too long."

Ollee gave him a brief smile and then looked at us, all business. "I'm the captain of this vessel. Please come aboard. We'll depart shortly."

Aki dropped a coin into the man's outstretched hand and he winked at me as we filed past him.

The interior of the ship was stately, with red rugs lining the floor and elegant wall sconces lighting the dim corridors. As soon as we were inside, I slipped off my heels and ran down the hall. "How do I get up to the deck?" I asked, looking back at Aki. "I want to see us take off."

Aki pointed at the staircase I'd run past with a droll look. I thought about sticking my tongue out at him, but I was far too excited to waste time with his obnoxious attitude. I took the stairs two at a time and emerged onto the deck just as the floor underneath me gave a slight jolt. Shadow grabbed my elbow when I stumbled. I hadn't realized he'd followed me. I shook him off and rushed over to the railing.

The ground fell away, growing smaller as the boat rose straight into the air. A breeze whipped my hair, pulling more strands free, and I gasped as the temperature dropped. The floor swayed beneath my feet and my stomach flipped over itself.

I'd been on an airplane once with my parents, but I'd been too young to remember much. I only knew because my mom had kept a small framed photo of me and my dad at the airport. After my dad left and my mom went downhill, there'd been no time or money to travel. And now that I had Mary Beth to look after, well...

Maybe someday, Mary Beth and I would travel the world. We could buy one-way tickets to exotic places and pick up odd jobs to fund our explorations. All we had to do was get Mary Beth clean first.

Aki stepped up next to me, and Shadow leaned on my other side.

I peered over at Aki, unable to contain my smile. "I can't believe a ship like this exists here."

"This is the queen's air ship," Aki said. "Only those with invitations to the palace and those who work in Reya may board it."

"Mina said the queen doesn't use it herself. Is that true?"

"Not once, in my memory."

"Then why own one? Just to get her workers back and forth?"

Aki shook his head. His black hair whipped around in the wind, but his mask stayed perfectly in place. "I'm not sure why the queen does many things."

We grew quiet, and I watched the ground fade into the distance. The ship rose over the tree line and I gasped at my first glimpse of the Faery sky.

It was magnificent. Although it had been dark on the ground, the sun was barely setting up here. Forest stretched as far as the eye could see, and the sun was half beneath the horizon. Orange and pink streaks filled the sky, painting it with the most beautiful hues I'd ever seen.

"Beautiful, isn't it?" Shadow murmured from beside me. His eyes were on the horizon.

Something in his expression made my heart twist into a knot. "It is," I agreed. "Too bad you can't see it from the ground."

Shadow's eyes darkened. "Most below have never seen the sky. Very few have ever traveled outside of Thios."

The ship tilted slightly, turning away from the Great Tree, and glided over the treetops. Faery's normal trees were tall, but the Great Tree was a behemoth. There was no other word for it.

"What's beyond Thios?" I asked, squinting into the horizon. "It looks like the forest goes on forever."

"Ocean," Aki answered. "A great mountain range to the east. The forest is uninhabited beyond Thiosian borders. It is Seraphine's domain, and largely unexplored."

"Why hasn't anyone explored it? Back home, humans have explored the whole world."

"And destroyed most of it, I hear," Shadow said drolly.

I wrinkled my nose, but didn't argue. He had a point.

It took several hours for the airship to clear the Great Tree's canopy. I wandered the deck, observing the deckhands as they moved about their work. They didn't pay any attention to me, or Shadow who followed two steps behind me. I wasn't keen on having a bodyguard, no matter how good-looking he was, but at least he didn't stop me from exploring.

The ship operated like I imagined the ocean ones did back home. Depending on the direction the ship needed to go, the Fae workers untied ropes and pulled on them, turning the wings attached to the balloon on top of the ship. A team of air magick users stood at the front and back of the ship, using their hands to summon bursts of wind to keep us afloat. Every once in a while, a great gust of wind rocked the ship, causing everyone to stumble. The deck hands never fell over, but I found myself sprawled on the worn wooden floor several times. Luckily, it was clean.

A couple hours into the journey, I wandered up to the second deck, the higher one that looked out over the main deck. Ollee stood by the railing, observing the activity below with a keen eye. I rested my elbows on the smooth wood and leaned over the railing next to him. "How long have you been flying this ship?"

Ollee glanced at me. If it surprised him that I was addressing him, he didn't show it. "Centuries, ma'am."

"Aki said the queen doesn't use it. Have you ever flown her or the king?"

Ollee shook his head. "I mostly transport Reyans who want to visit the market and Thiosians who work in the palace. Aki is the first royal from Thios that I've had the privilege to escort, my lady."

"Oh, I'm not a lady." I raised my hands, palms out. "I'm just here at the queen's invitation. I'm human."

Ollee looked more shocked than if I'd told him I was the queen herself. "You're not supposed to be here," he whisper-yelled, as if I was daft.

"I know." I sighed. "It's a long story. The queen invited me to the palace tonight."

"I'm so sorry, my lady," Ollee said gravely, a fist over his heart. "I will pray for your quick death."

I blinked at him. "What now?"

"A quick death, my lady. Your trial with the queen. May Seraphine watch over you."

My stomach turned over, and I laughed nervously. "She's not asking me there to stand trial. I'm coming as her guest."

Ollee gave me a pitying look and bowed his head. "Well, I'm pleased to escort you."

I turned away, shooting Shadow a quelling look when it looked like he might laugh. I considered asking him if I should be concerned, but then I remembered Aki's expression when he'd read the missive from the queen that morning.

Yeah, I was screwed.

When the air ship finally rose above the Great Tree's canopy, I stood at the railing with Shadow for my first glimpse of the palace. It sat atop a cliff next to the gigantic waterfall that fed the river Thios rested on. The palace towered over everything in the immediate vicinity. It looked to be made of glass; currently it was painted in pinks and oranges, reflecting the last of the sunset behind us. Apparently sunsets lasted for ages here.

The trees were smaller up here—or the homes were larger. Five huge mansions surrounded the palace. As we glided over the top of them, I leaned as far over the railing as I could, examining everything below.

Two of the five mansions had clearly fallen into disrepair. Vines grew over their walls and one of them looked like the ceiling had caved in. The other three gleamed in comparison with marbled white exteriors and shining stained glass windows.

"What are those?" I asked Shadow.

His mouth tightened into a thin line. "What remains of the five great houses. And before you ask," he added, sending me a quelling look, "it's a long story for another time. Those two Reyan houses are gone, killed in the uprising when they allied with Asmodeus."

I searched his face, a thousand questions on the tip of my tongue, but the look in his eyes made me swallow them back. Later. I was sure Mina would answer all my questions later.

The air ship glided past the mansions and settled on the ground in front of the palace gates. Aki stepped up next to us as the crew lowered the wooden walkway. He raised his brows pointedly at my heels, which were still clasped in my left hand, and I reluctantly slipped them on. We went below deck and descended the walkway.

Several Fae greeted us at the palace gates. They were dressed in perfect white tuxedos, their expressions impassive. The gates swung open soundlessly, and the Fae bowed deeply as we passed.

The palace grounds were breathtaking. My initial impression of the palace was partially correct. It was indeed made of glass, some reflective like mirrors, some translucent like normal windows. Shining metal beams supported the heavy glass. I shivered as a breeze ruffled my hair. The air up here was chilly.

Aki tucked my hand in the crook of his arm and we entered the palace itself, Shadow trailing behind us. I gaped like a fish out of water as we followed a servant down long, impossibly tall corridors lined with large painted photographs. The dwindling sun shone through the windows on the right, illuminating the paintings. The subjects of the paintings all looked like the same person, a woman with silvery-blond hair and icy blue eyes. She wore a shimmering silver and white gown that hugged her figure and draped to the floor. As we progressed down the hallway, the paintings changed. They began to show other people, families and couples. They all wore the same silver and white color scheme, although their clothing choices varied.

"Is this the royal family?" I asked Aki.

He followed my gaze and nodded curtly. "Indeed. As far back as our history goes."

"How far is that?"

"Very far. Millenia, perhaps."

Wow. I forced my jaw to snap shut when we reached another silver door. The dim roar of music and conversation drifted even through the closed door. The servant bowed deeply to us again and swung it open to reveal a ballroom.

"Whoa," I breathed as we stepped inside.

CHAPTER THIRTEEN

The ballroom was all crystal and white marble. Enormous crystal chandeliers dangled from the ceiling and white marble tables lined the room. The only color I saw came from the clothing of the party's guests. Fae twirled in an elegant, choreographed line on the dance floor, following the beat of a flowing instrumental piece. Their brightly colored dresses were long-sleeved, covering their bodies from neck to toe, and masks covered their faces. They were nicer than Aki's mask, with sparkling filigree and details and luscious fabric. Unlike Aki's, their masks covered their full faces. I picked out the telltale red, green, and blue that signaled which house each Fae belonged to. Mina hadn't been kidding; there were only three houses left.

A long table lined the wall to the right, laden with gourmet food. In the center of the room, a dais sat above the dance floor and the queen perched on the throne resting there. Her silver dress draped to the floor, and the train was long enough to reach down several steps to the dance floor. Surprisingly, her dress was strapless, revealing the milky white skin of her shoulders and arms. Even from here, I could see her white-blonde hair, identical to the paintings in the hallway.

Aki led me into the ballroom and off to the left, toward an empty marble table. It seemed like the queen hadn't seen us yet. She was engrossed in conversation with a group of Reyans in flowing blue gowns.

"What now?" I asked.

Aki surveyed the party. Even here, in the royal palace, he was several heads taller than everyone around him. "We'll wait until the queen summons us. While I'm here, I have a few inquiries to make. Don't wander and don't tell anyone you're human." He looked over my head at Shadow, a silent warning in his eyes. *Watch her.* Then he gave me a stern look to punctuate his point and stalked away.

"What am I supposed to do then?" I grumbled. "Stand here like a statue?"

"Yes," Shadow said simply. He stepped forward to rest his elbows on the tall marble table beside me. "This isn't the place to wander. The palace is even more dangerous than Thios is."

I somehow quelled the urge to stick my tongue out at him. Everyone treated me like I was a stupid human who would walk into danger around every corner, and it was getting old fast. Yes, the queen might want me dead or imprisoned tonight, but I'd never done well with authority. I wanted to go exploring just because Aki and Shadow had told me not to. Was it rational? No, but I'd stopped fighting that part of me a long time ago.

Shadow shifted beside me. The corners of his mouth were tight, and something glittered in his golden eyes as he watched the Reyans in the ballroom.

"Have you ever been here?" I asked him.

"No." He hesitated. "But I should have grown up here."

That's right; he'd told me that most of his kind had been killed in the Schism. I looked around the ballroom with new eyes. He was technically a Reyan, but he was just as removed from them as Aki was. I lowered my voice. "Does anyone know that you're from the House of Spirit?"

He shook his head. "I don't use my magick in public often, but I'm sure some in Thios suspect as much. Word hasn't reached the queen, though, or she would have indentured me into her service already."

"She can do that?"

"She's the queen." He raised an eyebrow at me. "She can do whatever she wants."

That was a terrifying thought.

We fell into silence, so I occupied myself by watching the dance floor. The dancers moved like it was a professional production, perfectly in sync and flawlessly executing each choreographed movement. A few Fae mingled around the perimeter of the dance floor. Curious eyes glanced my way, but nobody had the guts to come over and talk to me. Shadow's brooding presence was probably deterrent enough.

I sighed, resting my chin on my fists. The palace was beautiful, but it seemed sterile and cold. The mingling Fae's smiles didn't reach their eyes, and they spent more time observing everyone else than paying attention to their conversation partners. I was far more comfortable on the streets of Seattle than in a place like this. My feet ached from the impossibly high heels, and my dress was chafing under my arms.

"Well, hello there," a silky voice said behind us.

I glanced around, ready to tell the Fae woman to back off, but she wasn't looking at me. Her imperious eyes rested on Shadow, and an inviting smile curled her ruby-red lips.

Shadow turned, his dark eyes widening almost imperceptibly. "Evening."

"We don't receive visitors often," the Fae woman said. She didn't spare a glance my way. "Although you look familiar. Have we met?"

Shadow placed one hand on the small of my back, drawing me closer to his side. "I don't believe we have."

"Pity." The woman smiled. "I'd like to rectify that. I'm Riawna, first daughter of the House of Water. And you are?"

The lady had guts; I'd give her that. But there was something venomous about her smile. It didn't reach her eyes, and the way she pointedly ignored me just ticked me off.

It ticked me off even more when Shadow smiled back at her. "Shadow," he said, his voice even deeper than usual. "Pleasure to meet you, Riawna."

Okay, ew. Clearly I was the third party in this conversation. Shadow could play around with the Reyans all he wanted—it's not like he belonged to me—but I didn't need to be around to see it.

I spied a nearby set of double doors and pushed away from the table. Shadow's eyes met mine in a silent warning, but I shot him an unfriendly smile and walked across the ballroom, leaving him alone with the red-lipped woman eyeing him like she was a cat and he was a bowl of milk.

The doors were glass—of course—and I pushed them open to reveal a beautiful balcony beyond. The incessant music dimmed as the doors slid closed with a quiet click.

The sun had set and darkness had fallen. The palace glowed white, shining against the shadows, but a few stars still winked in the sky. I kicked off my heels. The coolness of the white marble floor was heaven on my sore feet. Hiking up my dress, I wandered over to the railing and rested my elbows on it. Out here, it was silent except for the distant roar of the falls.

This was my kind of place.

I jerked when the door behind me opened again and spun around, expecting to see Shadow with a thunderous expression. Instead, a male Fae stepped out and clicked the door closed behind him. He wore the same white tuxedo as many Reyans I'd seen, but he also wore a shining silver cape that reached the floor. It hooked together on the top of his shoulders with crystal pins in the shape of a flower. Aside from his pointed ears and lavender eyes, he looked almost human.

He strode across the balcony and jumped a little when he saw me. "Oh, hello," he said. His voice was deep, but it had a sing-song quality to it. "I didn't see you there."

I looked between him and the door. Aki had said not to talk to anyone, and I'd just escaped an awkward conversation between Shadow and Riawna. This guy seemed harmless, but I didn't really want to incur Aki's wrath tonight. I took a step away from the railing, hesitating.

"No, stay," the man said with a dreamy smile. "This is the best spot. The best."

I bit my lip and forced myself to relax and lean against the railing again.

The man leaned next to me, but he didn't admire the view. His eyes had a glazed quality to them, as if he wasn't really seeing me. I shouldn't have been surprised—I'd seen a lot of strange things since coming to Thios—but something about them made me uneasy. "You're not from here," he said after a moment. "Not from here at all. Who are you?"

"The queen invited me," I said.

"Ah, the queen. Indeed. She's a wily creature, the queen. Never know what she's thinking."

"Uh, yeah." I suddenly wished I'd stayed inside with Shadow and the red-lipped woman.

The Fae man hummed a tune and rocked back and forth, bracing himself with his hands on the stone railing. Something about it made the hair on the back of my neck stand up. "Your eyes," he said suddenly. "Violet, but not really violet. Just like you. You, but not really you."

I blinked at him. My eyes were blue green. "I... guess so?"

"You should beware. This land is dangerous, dangerous indeed. The foundation is cracking, you see. Soon the darkness will come and the light will disappear. Dangerous times indeed." The Fae looked away from me. "I'm very tired."

This guy wasn't right in the head. I looked around, squinted into the ballroom. Shouldn't he have someone watching him if he was like this?

The Fae man swayed on his feet, his eyes closing.

"Whoa," I said, grabbing hold of his shoulder. "Are you okay, sir? I can get you a chair or something."

"The darkness," he mumbled. "The black."

"Okay, hold on to the railing right here. I'll—"

The door to the balcony slammed open. I glanced up to see Aki filling the doorway, Shadow right behind him.

Shadow shot me a death glare, a clear reprimand for running away from him. Well, if he hadn't been busy flirting with the beautiful Reyan, I wouldn't have had the chance to slip away. So really, this whole thing was his fault.

Aki's shoulders were tense as he strode across the balcony, but he froze when he saw the male Fae next to me. Then he dropped to a knee and bowed his head. Shadow followed suit. "Your Majesty."

My jaw dropped for the second time that evening.

The crazy Fae straightened and stepped away from me. His gaze was still distant and unfocused, but he seemed steadier now. He nodded to Aki and Shadow and then smiled vaguely in my direction. "I think I'll sit," he mumbled, and entered the palace without a backward glance.

"W-what...?" I stared after him, dumbfounded, then looked at Aki. "That's the king? I didn't know he was still alive."

Aki slowly stood, his eyes on the door. "Yes. The queen rules with sole authority. The king rarely shows himself these days. I'm surprised to see him here tonight."

"What's wrong with him?"

"He's been that way since the war."

I stared at the door, frowning. "He's kind of... creepy."

Shadow smiled faintly, but it disappeared when Aki gave him a look.

"He wasn't always that way," Aki said. "He was once a wise king, loved by all. The queen has never been interested in political affairs, so the king managed the kingdom. After the war, he wasn't able to run things like he used to. The queen took over, but she hasn't performed to the same standard that the king did."

I eyed him. "You sure know a lot about the Reyans."

"Of course I do. I used to be one."

"Mina mentioned that, but she was light on the details. Want to elaborate on why you're in Thios now?"

Shadow glanced at Aki. Was he wondering the same? Did he not know why Aki had left the palace?

"It's a long, complicated story," Aki said after a long pause. "Perhaps I'll share it someday, but now is not the time."

Now was not the time for a lot of things around here.

Aki extended his elbow for me to take and escorted me back into the ballroom. I waited for him to say more, but he merely pasted a pleasant smile on his face and led me toward the dance floor. Shadow melted into the crowd, probably to watch us from a distance.

"The queen has requested an audience," Aki finally murmured, his lips barely moving. "Remain silent unless she speaks to you directly. I'll handle this."

I wasn't the type to let anyone do the hard work for me, but for once I was grateful. I was so far out of my depth here. With my luck, I'd look at her wrong and she'd yell, "Off with her head!"

Perhaps that was extreme. I hoped it was.

We walked past the dance floor and toward the dais where the queen sat on her throne. I kept my eyes on the floor in front of me, observing the queen out of my periphery. Up close, she was so beautiful it was hard to look at her. Her silvery blonde hair—almost the same color as her dress—fell to her waist in perfect curls. A silver tiara rested on her head, sparkling like a disco ball in the light. Though she didn't wear long sleeves like most other Fae did, I couldn't see her tattoo. I wondered where it was. Did she show her skin because it was underneath her clothing? Or because she was so confident that no one could harm her? Ice-blue eyes regarded us as we approached, and she inclined her head when we stepped onto the dais.

"Aki," she said warmly. Her gown shimmered as she extended one pale, perfect hand.

Aki bowed and kissed her knuckles. "My queen."

"It's been too long." The queen smiled, revealing perfect white teeth. Was there anything about her that wasn't perfect? "Thank you for coming this evening."

Aki straightened, but kept his head bowed. "We're honored that you requested our presence."

"How many years has it been?"

"Fifty or so, my queen."

Fifty? Did Aki not age? I glanced sideways at him, but he didn't meet my eyes.

"Fifty. It feels much longer. The Court has not been the same without you."

Aki smiled politely.

The queen turned her ice blue gaze on me. My muscles froze. Electricity whizzed through every atom in my body. Every hair stood on end, vibrating with static. I felt the urge to shake like a dog, to get the feeling off my skin, but I forced myself to remain still. I kept my gaze respectfully on the ground. I took pride in never bowing to anyone, but I didn't have a death wish.

"A human," the queen said. Her melodic voice turned curious. "They had informed me that a human had entered Thios. I have never seen one up close. Why is she here?"

The human could speak for herself. I gritted my teeth, stifling the comment. Aki's warning echoed in my head.

"Asmodeus," Aki said. "One of his followers abducted her from the human world."

"Really." The queen's gaze swept me from head to toe. "For what purpose?"

"That remains to be seen." Aki clasped his hands behind his back and straightened his shoulders, meeting the queen's gaze. "I have agreed to help her return home. The gate reopens on the equinox. With your consent, I would like to use weapons from the armory to regain control of the gate. As you are aware, Asmodeus has stifled trade between Thios and the human world. Much-needed supplies are dwindling, and the situation may become dire if we do not act quickly."

The queen inclined her head. Her gaze swept from Aki to me. Then she looked to her left and nodded to a tall Fae standing there. He wore the white robes I'd seen all the other servants wearing, but I could see the black tattoo winding out from both of his shirt sleeves and curling onto the skin on the back of his hands. He didn't seem interested in hiding it. As a guard for the queen, maybe he didn't have to.

The Fae made a gesture with his hands, as if he was forming a snowball in front of his chest. The air around us shimmered, and sound from the party behind us was snuffed out. I looked over my shoulder, gaping, but the festivities were still in full swing. It wasn't as if the sound was muffled; it was gone completely. Just like the meeting at the Great Tree. This Fae must have air magick like Aki.

"We may now speak privately," the queen said. She folded her hands in her lap. "I agreed to your audience because I would like to request your assistance, Aki."

Aki bowed his head. "I am at your service."

"I am aware of your dealings with the Thiosians." The queen's voice held barely contained disdain at the mention of Thios. "Tension between the nobility and the Thiosians has escalated of late. While I understand your need to associate with them, I assume this escalation was not your doing. Am I correct in that assumption?"

Aki appeared relaxed, but I saw his fingers tighten behind his back. "Yes, my queen."

I kept my mouth shut, glancing between the two of them as furtively as I dared. Aki was a good liar. I'd need to remember that.

"Asmodeus and the gate are the least of my concerns. No one has heard from him in years, and he wouldn't dare to attack the Court again after his previous loss. But those downworlders are an immediate threat." The queen sat back, folding her perfect hands in her perfect lap. Her expression was pleasant, but her eyes were cold as ice. "Your...involvement with the Thiosians is advantageous in this situation. Though I have assigned Senan as their leader, lately I've had doubts about his loyalty. Perhaps you'll have more success quelling this little rebellion."

This woman was as out of touch as Mina and Aki had said. Senan had been on the Thiosians' side for years, and she was just now questioning his loyalty? Not to mention the fact that Aki was the leader of the so-called "little rebellion" she was asking him to stop. I would laugh if I wasn't about to pee my pants in terror.

Aki bowed his head. "My queen, I don't believe the Thiosians will settle without some concessions from Reya."

"I am aware of their grievances." The queen's ice-blue eyes never strayed from Aki. "The weapons ban is in place to protect them.

And until we settle this matter, I will not open my armory to you or any of the downworlders."

Aki hesitated, but bowed his head again. "I will do as you ask."

"See that you do. Until the equinox, the human will remain in the palace."

My stomach flipped over. Something in the queen's eyes told me it wouldn't be a pleasant experience. I forced my expression to remain neutral even though I wanted to run screaming from this terrifying, perfect castle. The queen's tone was polite, but she had that look about her—one that concealed violence. I'd seen it before. No way was I staying here with this lunatic.

"I'd like to request that the human remain with me." Aki's words were swift. "Asmodeus may not be a threat to you, but we don't know why he wanted her. He may have spies in the castle, and I'd rather not risk your safety. I know Asmodeus better than anyone; I can keep the human out of his reach."

The queen considered us for a long moment. "Very well," she said finally. "She will accompany you when you report back to me. I would ensure that she remains in your care."

"Of course, my queen."

The queen nodded at the Fae to her left and sound flooded back into the space around us. The sudden volume made my head spin. Aki grabbed my elbow and dragged me off the dais and away from the terrifyingly perfect queen. Normally I'd protest the manhandling, but my legs weren't listening to my brain's commands at the moment.

As we walked across the ballroom and toward the palace's front entrance, Shadow fell into step behind us, silent as always. I shook off my stupor and glanced over at Aki. His expression was calm, but a muscle ticked in his jaw. "That... went well?" I ventured.

He didn't acknowledge me.

It wasn't until we'd left the palace and Ollee's ship had lifted off that Aki's shoulders finally relaxed. I stood next to him on the upper deck, Shadow at my other side, and watched the beautifully illuminated palace shrink into the distance. The tension finally left my body as well. I kicked off my heels and sighed in relief as the cold wood decking numbed the bottom of my sore feet.

"What are you going to do about the queen's request?" I asked.

Aki sighed. "I will do what Senan has done for years; I will play both sides. It is too late to stop the rebellion; the Thiosians have been oppressed for too long to make peace now."

My gut feeling since I'd arrived here was right. War was brewing in Faery. It wasn't a matter of if, but when the proverbial crap hit the fan. "Then... what now? We can't fight Bria with no weapons."

Aki stared up at the stars twinkling above us. It was dark, but the lanterns hanging from the railing on either side of us illuminated his expression. His jaw was set, his eyes steely. Shadow shifted beside me, and a quick glance revealed the grin on his face.

I knew what Aki was going to say. I clenched my hands on the railing to stop them from shaking.

Not from fear—oh, no. From excitement.

Aki met Shadow's eyes and smiled grimly. "We're going to take them by force."

CHAPTER FOURTEEN

"I don't like this, Aki." Mina paced in front of the fireplace, wringing her hands, her pale hair flickering orange in the light from the fire.

I sat in an armchair nearby, still in my evening gown, and sipped on my steaming mug of hot cocoa. Part of me craved a cup of Mina's coffee flavor of the day—some Thiosian roast I'd never heard of and cardamom—but it was late and if I wanted to get some sleep for once, hot cocoa was a better option.

Aki sat in the armchair across from me, an ancient text open on the table between us next to an identical mug of hot cocoa. He, of course, hadn't touched it. "I do not see another choice," he said calmly. "The queen will not grant us weapons, and we cannot take the gate without them. The Thiosians in our outfit are not prepared to use their magick against Seraphine's wishes, nor would I ask them to without proper training."

"If she catches you, she'll imprison you or even sentence you to death." Mina's blue face was pale. "You won't be around to fight Asmodeus or help Thios."

I shivered despite the fire warming me. The queen's scary power and her attempt to keep me in the palace were too fresh. But another part of me reveled in the thought of taking the weapons from her.

She was terrifying, but she was also cold and mean and I had never liked authority figures anyway.

"Woo-hoo," Gideon yowled from the kitchen table. "I say, let's give the queen what's coming to her. It's about time we downworlders show her what we're made of."

I met Shadow's eyes across the room, where he leaned against the wall with his arms crossed over his chest. A flicker of a smile passed his lips, and then it was gone again.

"We will not show her anything," Aki said, leveling a look at Gideon before returning his gaze to Mina. "The queen will never know the weapons are missing."

"How?" Mina settled herself cross-legged on the rug in front of the fire, facing us.

"A heist," I said. Excitement thrummed through me. "Please tell me we're going to go all Ocean's Eleven on the armory."

Everyone looked at me like I was crazy. Right; no movies in Faery.

"You know, a heist. We sneak in there, grab the weapons, and sneak out before she realizes we're there."

"Precisely." Aki nodded. "A heist."

"The armory is well-guarded," Shadow said. "There's only one entrance, and four members of the Reyan Guard patrol the front. From what I've gathered, they're the strongest magick users in the queen's retinue. Sneaking past them would be near impossible."

"Then we'll need a distraction." Gideon grinned. "I can take care of that. It's my specialty."

"We'll need you to open the door," Aki said. "Shadow will provide a distraction. We'll need something big enough to draw all four guards away."

"Understood. I have a few ideas."

"While they're gone, I will take the weapons we need and carry them out." Aki closed the book beside him and returned it to the bookshelf next to the fireplace. "For this to succeed, the queen cannot be aware that the weapons have been taken."

"She'll know exactly who took them," I said. "Especially after we just talked to her about it. What can I do?"

"You and Mina will provide the eyes we need to ensure the guards do not return."

"Aw, come on. I have to be a lookout?" I scowled. My first heist and I'd be relegated to the lamest job. Typical.

"Unless you have some magical human powers we're not aware of, girlie," Gideon drawled, "I doubt you'll be much help."

I stuck my tongue out at him, which elicited a snort of laughter from him and Mina and another half-smile from Shadow. Aki remained cool as a cucumber, as per usual.

"We will initiate in a few days," Aki said. "In the meantime, Shadow, I need you to learn the guards' rotations and put a distraction in place. You may work with the others, but I want no one else directly involved. The fewer Fae who know about this, the higher likelihood that we will succeed."

"It will be done."

Aki whipped out a slew of other commands, none of which involved me—the lookout—and everyone scurried to do his bidding despite the late hour. A few minutes later, Aki and I were alone. I watched the glowing embers in the fireplace for a moment, and my skin crawled as an awkward silence ensued. I'd been here for a while now, but Aki and I had never spent a few minutes alone together like this. Not since we'd walked here from the gate. I had so many questions to ask him—about himself, the crew, the queen, and Faery itself. Would he answer them, or would he be cryptic as always?

Instead of asking the important questions—like why he'd left Reya, how we would take the gate, or his history with Asmodeus—I blurted, "Why are you so mean to Mina?"

Aki slowly turned his head, cocking an eyebrow. "Excuse me?"

"It's good to know men are obtuse in Fairy Land too." I rolled my eyes and gestured to the cold cocoa on the table next to him. "Mina obviously likes you. The least you could do is drink the coffee, whether you like it or not."

He looked at me for a long time.

"What's your story with her anyway?" I continued, refusing to be cowed by his silence. "You clearly take her for granted. I'm surprised she hasn't left."

For the first time since I'd met him, something unexpected flickered in Aki's eyes. Something like regret. He leaned back in his chair and turned his head toward the fire, so I couldn't see anything past his ivory mask. "Mina and I have a complicated history. It is—"

"If you tell me it's a long story again, I will kick you in the shins," I warned.

"Actually, it is quite short. I do not pursue romantic... entanglements."

"Entanglements... wow. You're such a poet."

Aki leveled a look at me before turning back to the fire. "If you think me a poet, you might be interested to know that I have loved and lost once before, and it was almost the end of me."

My jaw dropped. If he'd hit me over the head with a shovel, I would have been less surprised.

"My current position does not allow for such things. I care for Mina and I will always appreciate her presence here, but I will encourage nothing further. That time has passed for me, I'm afraid."

This was not where I had expected this conversation to go, and in typical Everly fashion, I had shoved my foot in my mouth.

Aki had loved and lost before. It was difficult to picture this take-charge, emotionally distant, ridiculously tall Fae as a swoony young man in love with a woman. And if he'd lost her... was that why he was so distant now? That part, at least, I could understand. Losing my parents had certainly changed me.

"I'm... sorry, Aki," I finally said. "Did it have anything to do with why you left Reya?"

"It had everything to do with that." Aki stood. "You will not like to hear it, but it truly is a long story, and one that I do not wish to revisit."

I opened my mouth to protest, then snapped it closed. It's not like I had shared any of my past or my inner demons with him, and I certainly wasn't ready to. How could I expect him to do the same? Instead, I said, "I get it. I'm sorry I brought it up."

Aki nodded once. "Goodnight, Everly."

"Goodnight." I watched him disappear upstairs to the bedrooms, then returned to staring at the fireplace.

So Aki had a tragic past. It seemed that everyone in the crew did, except for Gideon. I hadn't figured him out yet. Life was cruel—not just in the human world, but in Faery too. I'd always imagined that the Fae were monsters, and they'd certainly seemed that way from the little I'd seen in Seattle. But since coming here and learning that most of those 'monsters' were courtesy of Asmodeus and his crazy evil plots, I'd realized something important. Aki and his crew, and the other Thiosians I'd met so far, had taught me that humans and Fae really weren't as different as I'd always believed.

And for some reason, that was a comforting thought.

CHAPTER FIFTEEN

Mina had a whole list of tasks for me the following morning. The woman would've made an excellent CEO in the human world.

I started by bringing breakfast to the children we had adopted/hired. They were busy preparing Mina's grenade invention, and progress was moving steadily. Mina had organized them into quite the assembly line, and they happily chatted while they worked. A large crate of metal spheres sat at the end of the line, a second box of keys beside it. From what Mina had explained, the keys would insert into the spheres and turn, activating the components inside. Two seconds later, it would explode and knock out anyone nearby.

"Everly!" Kiera dropped what she was working on and launched herself at me.

Caught off guard, I froze when she squeezed me tight around the waist.

Well, that was new. When was the last time I'd been hugged? I honestly couldn't remember. Mary Beth and I were close, but we weren't touchy-feely. I was sure my parents had hugged me, but I'd buried those memories so deep that they were nearly impossible to find now.

"Hi there," I said, awkwardly patting Kiera on the head as she let me go.

She flapped an arm at the spot she'd been sitting in. "Look at how much we've done! Mina said she's so proud of us. We might even be done before the summer festival next week."

"You guys have done some amazing work," I said. "I knew you would."

Kiera grinned up at me.

My heart stuttered at the innocent trust in her eyes. How did she still have that after living on the streets for so long? Maybe it was different here in Thios, but in my world, innocence like that was beaten out of you at a young age on the streets. I looked past her to the other children who were happily working on their projects. They had full bellies, a roof over their heads, and meaningful work to keep them busy.

I had made that happen.

Well, okay, it was mostly Mina, but my chest swelled with pride anyway.

"You brought breakfast?" Kiera prompted, pulling me from my thoughts.

I held up two baskets overflowing with fruits, vegetables, and soft cheeses. "Mina made you quite the spread."

The other children gathered around as I set the baskets on the smooth stone steps, excitedly filling their laps with food.

I stepped back, smiling, and caught movement out of the corner of my eye. Shadow had entered the garden, silent as always. His dark eyes met mine, and he nodded once. "Mina sent me to fetch you. She needs us to go into town."

I held up the list she had given me. "I can go shopping on my own."

"Can you?" Shadow shoved his hands into his pockets, the picture of confident male-ness. It was equal parts appealing and irritating. "You have a nasty habit of getting yourself into trouble, so she asked me to accompany you."

"I don't need a babysitter."

"Things have been... tense lately." Shadow glanced at the children. "It's best if you have an escort, just in case."

I pursed my lips. Weapons may be banned in Thios, but that didn't lessen the threat of violence. Aki had been right; the Thiosians had been oppressed for a long time now, and they were getting understandably restless. Who knew what would happen now that the queen had ordered Aki to "quell" the rebellion? The last thing I needed was to be accidentally killed in a random protest while shopping for Mina's grocery list.

"Fine," I relented. I waved goodbye to Kiera and the other children and led the way out of the garden. "Let's go."

Shadow followed me without a word.

The cobblestone road to the market was busy today. We passed wooden carts laden with produce and weaved through Fae carrying baskets of goods to sell. Some Fae stood in front of their box gardens within the trees, palms out, and watered their plants using water magick. Others created fire, cooking meat to take to market.

Elemental magick really was amazing. I could only imagine what applications it would have if humans could use it back home.

I ducked as a pixie buzzed over my head, dragging a package twice his size, his tiny face scrunched in concentration.

The postal service would still be a thing, though. Even FedEx was probably more reliable than pint-sized Fae creatures.

Shadow and I reached the market and I led the way from stall to stall, gathering the items on Mina's list. It hadn't taken long for me to get the lay of the land; the market was like Pike Place back home. Each Fae had a designated tent where they set up shop each day to sell their wares. Thanks to Mina's daily visits with me in tow, many of the shopkeepers recognized me now and their suspicious expressions had lessened slightly. Mina seemed to have garnered a grudging respect from many of the Thiosians. Since my arrival, I had accompanied her to gift her homemade gadgets to several of the shops—a portable solar oven to keep one Fae's bread warm throughout the day, a pair of magnifying glasses for a jewelry maker who serviced many of the bored Reyans who visited Thios every day, and even a glove to channel a metal worker's fire. My respect for Mina had grown too; despite the pitying and sometimes downright hostile treatment she received from many in Thios, she kept a cheerful attitude and continued to serve them anyway. I hadn't found the guts to ask her if their treatment was because of her lack of Gift or her love of humans, but I had a feeling it was a combination of both.

If I was in Mina's situation, I wouldn't be so kind. I'd be tempted to give them all the middle finger and keep my incredible inventions to myself.

Raised voices interrupted my musing. I stood on tip-toes to see the shops toward the end of the market, distantly aware of Shadow moving closer behind me. A group of Thiosians faced two red-masked Reyans in front of the jewelry stand. The plump Fae shopkeeper—Warred, if I remembered correctly—wrung his hands nearby, Mina's magnifying glasses swinging from his near nonexistent neck.

I picked up speed, weaving through the Fae crowding closer to watch the escalating conflict. Shadow stuck to my heels, but thankfully he didn't stop me.

"It's a fair price," Warred said as I approached. "The peace stone is rare, and it took my son days to find it in the forest."

One of the Reyans—a male, I thought, judging by the trousers and his deep baritone voice—inclined his head imperiously and said, "You won't make a fool of me, downworlder. I'll not pay more than three coppers for that trinket. It's a fair offer, and you won't find another who will pay more."

"Thievery," one of the watching Thiosians yelled. Several others murmured agreements, and hostility gathered thick in the air.

The Reyans didn't seem to notice, or maybe they just didn't care. I couldn't see their expressions behind their sparkling red masks, but they remained relaxed. The male who had spoken first threw a few coins at Warred. They bounced off his chest and fell to the cobblestone with a barely audible clink. Then the Reyan swiped a delicate necklace from the wooden counter and handed it to his companion, a female Fae in a long gold dress. The pale white stone sparkled even in the dim light from the tree canopy above as the female put it over her head.

"Filthy Reyans," someone yelled as Warred bent to collect the fallen coins. A raucous of agreements filled the air, and the Thiosians pressed closer to the Reyans.

The Reyan man seemed to finally realize the danger, and he raised a hand threateningly at the group, summoning a tight ball of flame in his palm.

I looked back and forth between the Reyans and the angry group of Thiosians. This was going to get ugly, and fast. I didn't see any guards loitering around to break up the fight that was moments away from occurring, but I doubted that the Thiosians—or poor Warred, who just looked defeated—would come out on top. I didn't know the jewelry maker well, but Mina frequented his shop and often stopped to chat even if she didn't purchase anything from him. I suspected he was part of Aki's mysterious rebel group, but Aki took pains to make sure few knew the names of his allies. Warred's wife had passed away a few years before, and he had two children at home to feed. That was all I knew about him, and it was enough.

His livelihood would be ruined if someone didn't stop this.

I stepped forward to do something, magick or not, but Shadow was faster. He pushed through the crowd and placed himself between the Reyans and the Thiosians. His presence and the low growl vibrating from somewhere in his chest were enough to make both sides pause.

A tense silence followed as all three parties sized each other up.

Finally, the group of Thiosians dispersed, muttering angrily to each other. Apparently Shadow's reputation—or maybe Aki's—preceded him.

The Reyans weren't so quick to back down. Instead, the male looked Shadow up and down. His body language was decidedly less aggressive. "I didn't know there were any Spirit users left," he said. "Why are you not in service to the queen?"

"I left Reya when my kin were slaughtered," Shadow said tightly. He nodded to Warred. "Pay the shopkeeper a fair price. If you don't, you won't make it back to the air ship."

The Reyan paused for a moment longer, then grabbed a few more coins from the purse hanging from his belt and tossed them to Warred. He led the female Reyan away, but before they were out of earshot, he turned and said over his shoulder, "You're a disgrace to your house."

Shadow didn't respond, but I saw the way the muscles in his shoulders hardened to stone. The words had struck a nerve. He didn't relax until the Reyans had disappeared down the street toward the Great Tree.

"Thank you," Warred said. "I owe you a debt."

"No, you don't," Shadow said quietly. He returned to my side and led me away. "Continue your work."

We continued our errands, but I couldn't get Warred's expression out of my mind. It had seemed like a minor issue, a disagreement about price, but Shadow's reaction told me it was much more than that. Aki and his crew had mentioned several times now that tensions were high between the Thiosians and the Reyans, and even though I'd seen the protesters at the meeting, I hadn't fully understood what that meant. Constant tension like this had to bubble over sometime, and it would eventually lead to civil war. Especially since the queen was unwilling to do anything about the situation. Some leader she was.

Shadow remained a silent—well, shadow—as we visited two more shops. Finally, I couldn't take my thoughts anymore, so I turned to him. "Is it always like this between the Reyans and the Thiosians?"

He regarded me for a moment. "Yes, though it has been escalating."

"Why don't the Thiosians just overthrow the queen? She's obviously bad news."

"The queen and the houses are immensely powerful. As you know, weapons are prohibited and Thiosians aren't allowed to use their magick for anything beyond their trades. Without weapons or magick, they don't stand a chance against Reya. The queen not only has the houses, but she also has a well-trained army of Reyan guards."

"But you can use your magick," I pointed out. "So can Gideon and Aki. And doesn't Aki have a whole network of rebels? You could form an army of your own."

A ghost of a smile reached Shadow's expression, and my stomach pitched. Man, it was a good thing that little smile was rare. It was capable of making me feel dangerous things. "It sounds easy in theory," he said, clearly oblivious to my internal struggle.

"The situation sounds pretty serious. I don't understand why they wouldn't want to do something about it."

Shadow shrugged, and we began walking back toward Aki's house. "It's difficult to unravel centuries of oppression. Aki's group is working to do just that, but it takes time. With any luck, we'll regain control of the gate and it will turn the tide. An influx of commerce and product from the human world will put Thios in an advantageous position."

I frowned down at my boots. We were still weeks away from the equinox, but what if Aki couldn't convince the Thiosians to join his cause? Even if our plan succeeded and we managed to steal weapons from the queen's armory, we needed Fae to take up those weapons. It would be even better if those Fae could use magick as a weapon too.

If I had a Gift, would that even the odds? Aki and the others used their magick as a weapon, and it made them powerful. Could I do the same?

"What are you thinking about?" Shadow asked, glancing at me. "Your expression worries me."

"Do you think you could teach the Thiosians how to use their magick as a weapon?" I asked, my eyes on the cart ahead of us loaded with potatoes. "If they were willing?"

"Of course. Aki trained with the Reyan Guard when he was a member of the House of Air, and he trained Gideon. But Seraphine originally granted her Gifts for survival. Using a Gift for battle goes against its original purpose, which is why the Mark grows and increases its user's weakness. It's difficult to convince the Thiosians to go against Seraphine's will, even if the Reyans use it that way."

I hesitated. "And what if a... human wanted to get magick? What would one have to do?"

"In order to form a bond with an element, you must perform the Rite," Shadow said slowly. "It is a trial that Seraphine performs, and she determines if you are worthy. But Everly, the Rite is a permanent change. One that can and will most likely end your life early."

"I'm not afraid of death," I said. "I've been flirting with it for years. Could a human perform the Rite or not?"

Shadow looked at me for a long time. "Why do you want to?"

"I don't want to be powerless." I met his eyes, hoping he saw the determination in mine. "I promised myself a long time ago that I wouldn't take a back seat to the events in my own life. If we're going to fight Bria for the gate, I want to help. I want to get myself home."

"We will have many weapons to choose from," Shadow countered. "You could use any of those."

I snorted. "I have no idea how to use a sword. I would accidentally stab myself before someone else."

"Magick isn't something you can use overnight. It takes years of training to master it, let alone use it as a weapon. It won't help you in the fight with Bria."

Okay, I hadn't thought of that. If that was true, then why did I feel such a sudden urge to do it? Was it curiosity? It was like the Stupid Idea that had sent me to the warehouse in the first place to investigate Bria and her men. The Stupid Idea that had gotten me sent to this beautiful, dangerous place. The reason I had met Shadow and Aki and the rest of the Fae. Maybe it didn't make sense, but my instincts had never steered me wrong before. I had to trust my gut.

I released a hard breath through my nose. "That may be true, but how will I know if I don't try? We'll need all the help we can get."

Shadow observed me for a moment more. "A human has never attempted the Rite, let alone succeeded, but it's not forbidden. If Seraphine finds them worthy, any being can receive her Gift."

"Then maybe I'll be the first." I forced a grin. "Who knows? Maybe I'll inspire everyone else around here to do something about the gate and the queen."

"Very well." Shadow flashed that knee-buckling small smile again. "We'll see what Aki has to say."

"Absolutely not," Aki snapped. "It's too dangerous for a human to perform the Rite."

We sat around the dining room table, empty plates and serving dishes scattered on the surface before us. Mina had made another fantastic dinner—homemade rolls, some kind of roasted meat like the one I'd tried in the market, and an array of vegetables I was quickly coming to recognize as native to Thios. I had even helped knead the dough for the rolls, with plenty of instruction from Mina as she prepared everything else. Now that dinner was over and everyone was pleasantly full, Shadow had broached the subject with Aki, and his reaction was as I'd expected.

"Thanks for your concern," I said drolly, "but in case you forgot, you're not the boss of me."

Aki scowled at me from his seat across the table, his arms folded over his chest. "While you're in Thios, you're in my charge. Therefore, I am the boss of you. The Rite isn't a game; it's likely to get you killed."

Gideon snorted a laugh into his coffee cup, spraying the whiskey-laced brew all over Shadow, who was seated next to him. Shadow's expression didn't change as he dabbed at his sleeve with a napkin, gaze moving back and forth between me and Aki.

"I don't see why you care," I said. Nobody bossed me around; I had been alone for too long to let that stand. "It's my choice to make. If I die doing it, that's my problem."

"And I'll have to answer to the queen for your dead body." Aki pushed his coffee cup away. "Even if you were to successfully complete the Rite, it takes time to strengthen your elemental bond. You won't be able to learn to fight before we retake the gate, and magick has no place in the human world."

He had a point. If someone saw me using magick in Seattle, I'd be locked up in a secret lab somewhere as the government's science experiment faster than I could say whoops. But I could hardly back down now, nor could I explain that my gut was telling me to do this, and I had to listen.

I met Shadow's eyes, and he inclined his head. He didn't understand why I needed to do this either, but he hadn't protested after his initial questions. He seemed to trust that I knew what I was doing, even if it was dangerous. That made me feel all warm and fuzzy inside, though I would never tell him that.

Aki didn't care about my wellbeing; he was more worried about how my death would affect his vendetta against Asmodeus and the queen—and I could respect that. It's the way I would have thought about it too. If I wanted to gain his support, I had to appeal to his logical side like Mina had suggested when we'd tried to convince him to let Kiera and Saoirse help us.

I took a sip of my coffee—dang, Mina was a coffee genius—and forced my heart to calm. It wasn't easy. "The queen never needs to know. I'll do the Rite somewhere private. If I die, you can tell the queen I went back through the gate. Or that Asmodeus killed me. Whatever you want. If I succeed and I can't learn to use the magick before we take the gate, I'll go back home and it will be my problem. You have nothing to lose by—" I swallowed hard and spit out the rest— "allowing me to do this. You only risk to gain a potential magick user in the fight against Bria. Shadow says none of the other Thiosians are willing to learn to use magick to fight, but I am."

Aki regarded me for a long moment. The rest of the table was silent, and all eyes were on their leader. Finally, he said, "You make a good argument. Very well. You can perform the Rite after we take our weapons from the armory. I won't allow it to interfere with that. Understood?"

I nodded, fighting the urge to raise a triumphant fist in the air, and shared a smile with Shadow.

Mina shoved her chair back from the table. It screeched against the floor, and we all swung around to look at her. "Sorry," she said too brightly. "Now that it's all settled, I need to clean up. Anyone want some pie?"

"Pie." Gideon tucked his napkin into the collar of his tunic. "You have no idea how much I want some pie, Mina darlin'."

I snorted to myself. Yeah, pie was clearly what Gideon wanted.

"Shadow, have you worked out the details for tomorrow evening?" Aki asked, ignoring Gideon as usual.

"Yes." Shadow leaned forward. "Ollee has agreed to assist us."

"Ollee? The air ship captain?" I asked. Somehow I hadn't pictured the jolly Fae as a revolutionary type, but it seemed that all the Thiosians had reached the point where fighting back seemed to be the only option.

"Yes. He has agreed to crash his ship."

"Crash his—what?" I demanded. "He loves that ship!"

"He does, but we need an event big enough to draw all four guards away from the armory door."

"An air ship full of Reyans crashing to the ground ought to do it," Gideon drawled, shoving a crusty piece of fruit pie into his mouth.

Aki stood, declining a piece of pie from Mina with a shake of his head. "Excellent plan, Shadow. And you have steps in place to ensure that the guards stay there long enough for us to complete our task?"

"Of course." Shadow shot him a wolfish smile.

I settled into my chair, digging into the pie Mina had placed in front of me. This was going to be a heist for the history books—if Faery had such things.

CHAPTER SIXTEEN

It was early the following evening when we left for the queen's armory. It was situated beyond the pavilion, between the Great Tree and the air ship landing area, and rarely frequented by Thiosians. The building's aging stone walls were covered with moss, effectively disguising it from the occasional passersby.

I stuck close to his tall form as we reached the base of the Great Tree. The evening's silence was only broken by the wind rustling through the leaves in the canopy far above us. Mina and Gideon were close behind me; Shadow was the only one missing, off getting into position for the air ship's crash. It was growing dark, but still early enough for the ship to be carrying Reyan and Thiosian passengers, but there were plenty of growing shadows to limit visibility while Aki robbed the armory.

Aki stopped walking abruptly, and I bounced off his back. He grabbed me by the arm before I could fall to the ground.

"Sorry," I muttered, righting myself. "Where is—?"

"Shh." Aki's gloved hand found my mouth, silencing me.

I peered around him, squinting. The squat armory building was less than a hundred yards away. Two lanterns illuminated a weathered wood door and the two guards standing on either side of it. They might as well have been statues for how little they moved.

They were garbed like most of the Reyan Guard I'd seen, with shining armor covering their bodies from neck to toes, disguising the location of their tattoos. I still didn't understand the reason for their armor; it's not like the Thiosians had any weapons to attack them with. They clasped their hands in front of them, prepared to wield their magick to protect the armory.

I shifted from foot to foot, keeping my eyes on the armory's entrance. I itched to get this thing moving, even if Mina and I were only lookouts. Just being part of such a daring heist was equal parts exciting and terrifying, and that combination was my jam. Fear of the queen catching us still niggled at the back of my mind, especially because I didn't have any magick to defend myself, but that would soon change. The thought made me giddy.

A wolf's howl echoed in the distance, haunting and beautiful. Shadow's signal that he was in position.

It was go time.

Aki nodded to me. "You and Mina, head to your designated places. Sound the alarm if you see anything suspicious."

Mina touched my arm, her fingers cold, and smiled as if to reassure me. She looked more nervous than I felt.

We snuck away from Aki and Gideon, taking position on either side of the cobblestone road so we could see both the armory and the air ship landing area.

A hoarse shout filled the air, and I glanced up in time to see Ollee's air ship descending much faster than it typically did. Ollee was a speck at the helm; it was too far and too dark to see his face, but several screams echoed his shout.

The armory guards shifted, muttering to each other and craning their heads to see what the fuss was about.

That's when the ship crashed.

The ground shook beneath me—from the ship's collision or aided by Gideon's magick, I didn't know. Boards creaked, wood splintered, and the screams intensified as the air ship crashed into the landing area and skidded along the ground. It dragged across the dirt several hundred yards and then slowly tipped, landing on its side in the landing area furthest from the armory.

"The air ship," one guard yelled. Sure enough, all four of them ran toward the crash, leaving the armory door wide open for the taking.

I pumped a fist in triumph as they ran past me. Shadow's plan had worked perfectly. Hopefully the ship wasn't too damaged; it was Ollee's livelihood, and I knew how much he cared for it. Next time I saw him, I would thank him for this sacrifice.

Across the way, Aki and Gideon emerged from their hiding place and approached the armory on silent feet. Gideon rolled his shoulders, then lifted one foot and brought it down hard on the mossy earth. A fissure formed in the dirt, streaking toward the door like a bolt of lightning. A muted crack sounded, like a tree falling in the distance, and the door swung open on silent hinges. Luckily, the chaos from the crash seemed to have masked the sound; no one glanced back this way.

Aki and Gideon disappeared inside the armory, and I kept my eyes on the air ship. Shadow had promised them five minutes to get what they needed and get out. It should be plenty of time, especially if they used Aki's magick to collect and carry the weapons. In the distance, I saw the guards using their magick to create a hole in the ship's bottom so the passengers could escape. A crowd had gathered, making it hard to distinguish who was who, especially now that it was getting dark.

A minute passed. Then two.

I bounced on the balls of my feet, every muscle coiled and ready to spring. Across the way, I saw Mina looking the opposite direction, ready to signal if needed. Where were Aki and Gideon? They had to hurry, or...

Wait.

Something shifted in the darkness in front of me. A slit of moonlight flashed on metal. Armor.

The Reyan Guard—two of them were coming back.

I jerked around to look at the air ship. There was still a crowd gathered around it, and I could see at least some guards still helping the evacuation efforts. Where had these guys come from? They were moments away from discovering that the armory had been breached. It was too late for me to use the signal; Aki and Gideon would never escape without being seen. And if they were seen, the queen would know something had happened and that Aki had something to do with it. The whole operation would be ruined, Aki and the crew would be imprisoned or killed, and I'd never get home.

I had to do something.

I sprinted out of my hiding place and planted myself on the street in front of the two guards. "Help," I said, injecting as much panic into my voice as I could muster. It wasn't hard, considering the situation. "The air ship crashed. There are Fae stuck inside!"

"We know," one of the Reyans said irritably. "The others have it under control."

"But can't you help? I'm sure some are injured."

"It was a minor incident," the other Reyan said. They tried to step around me.

I matched them, blocking their path. "But—"

Something thumped onto the cobblestone road, rolling to a stop in front of the guards' feet. A hissing sounded, followed by a plume of blue smoke. In the space of a breath, the two guards collapsed to the ground in a heap.

I looked up and past them, gaping at Mina. She held a second metal ball in her hand, her eyes wide and frightened. "What are you doing?"

"I couldn't let them get past you," she whispered.

"I had it under control."

The armory door opened behind us, and Aki and Gideon emerged. A gust of wind followed behind them, carrying an array of swords, spears, shields, bows, and arrows. Aki took one look at the guards and jerked his head for us to follow him while Gideon restored the door and repaired the fissure he'd made in the ground.

By the time the guards awoke, we were long gone, but the plan had gone terribly wrong.

We somehow made it back to Aki's house without incident. Between the late hour and the air ship's crash, we saw no other Fae on the road. We made a pit stop somewhere in the forest to stash all the weapons. Gideon used his magick to create a huge hole in the ground, closing it up after we carefully placed the weapons inside. I was convinced that only Gideon could find it again, because I had no idea where we were.

By the time we returned to Aki's house, the sky was tinged with the light gray of dawn. Mina made fresh coffee for everyone—whiskey for Gideon—and the group sat in somber silence. We had gotten the weapons we needed, but the plan had not been a success.

"Do you think the guards will realize we attacked them?" I finally asked.

"I doubt it," Mina replied. "They didn't see me throw the grenade. They likely won't remember the few moments before they fell unconscious."

The front door opened, and Shadow slipped inside. He plopped into a seat next to me, bright-eyed and bushy-tailed despite the long night we'd all had.

"What the hell happened to you?" Gideon boomed. "You were supposed to keep the guards occupied."

Shadow didn't spare Gideon a second glance. He met Aki's eyes. "I apologize. The crash wasn't as severe as we'd hoped. I detained the guards as best I could, and I was pulled away before I could catch the other two."

Gideon snorted. "You're a lousy guard dog if you can't keep a few guards busy."

"And you're a lousy thief if you can't grab a bunch of weapons and get out before you're caught," Shadow shot back.

"It is done." Aki sipped his coffee—black, to Mina's dismay—and set his cup on the table. "We will accept whatever consequences follow. For now, we will consider this a success. We retrieved the weapons we need, and with any luck, the guards won't remember what made them fall unconscious."

I hoped that was true. But in my experience, the best-case scenario never happened.

Gideon shot Shadow another dirty look, then engaged Mina in conversation about breakfast options. He wanted pancakes—loads of pancakes—and Mina vehemently disagreed, opting for fruit and bread instead. Their argument escalated, and I tuned them out as Shadow leaned over to me.

"It's almost dawn. Are you ready for the Rite?"

"After pulling an all-nighter robbing the most powerful Fae in the kingdom?" I forced a smile. "Of course I am."

"The Rite is not to be taken lightly," Shadow warned. Something like concern crossed his expression. "It is a feat of mental strength like you cannot imagine."

I didn't doubt it. But my whole life had been a feat of mental strength. I had done everything necessary to survive, and I was damn proud of how far I'd come. The Rite was the next step I needed to take to protect myself, especially if the queen was gunning for us, and I wouldn't let it stop me.

"I'll be ready," I said to Shadow.

And I would be. Because there was no other option.

CHAPTER SEVENTEEN

The sky had barely lightened with the first gray of dawn when it was time to perform the Rite.

I followed Aki and Shadow down the path to Aki's garden. Mina had found other accommodations for the children last night; we had agreed they should make themselves scarce for a few days in case the queen tried to take action against us for our weapons heist. She and Gideon had volunteered to remain at the house and keep an eye out for movement from the Reyan Guard while I performed the Rite. According to Aki, the garden was the perfect place for it; secluded and quiet. Apparently, if I was interrupted during the process, it could kill me.

Nothing to worry about. I wasn't nervous at all.

Aki led me to the ancient stone gazebo. A single mat lay on the flagstone floor, surrounded by brightly colored flowers blooming in the early morning light. "Have a seat," he said, indicating the red woven mat in the center of the floor.

I did, sitting cross-legged. Normally I didn't respond to orders well, but nerves made me more compliant than usual. Okay, fine. I was a little nervous.

"Sit straight," Aki instructed. "Rest your hands on your lap."

I followed his directions, ignoring the butterflies fluttering in my belly. I felt as if I was standing on the edge of a great precipice. My next step would send me falling into the abyss, and though I'd told Shadow I was ready, my body longed to scramble up and out of here before I made a horrible mistake.

The Rite couldn't be that bad. Seraphine seemed like a nice lady; she was all about nature and peace and all that.

"We perform the Rite during a deep meditation," Aki explained. "I'll guide you into it. Once you are ready, Shadow will cut your hand and we will let your blood flow into the earth. This will connect you with Seraphine, and she will test your worthiness."

"Sounds like my idea of a good time," I said, voice shaky.

Shadow kneeled in front of me. His dark eyes caught mine, and the steadiness there was reassuring. "You'll be fine, Everly. If there's any human tough enough to pass Seraphine's test, it's you."

"Damn straight." I let him see a small smile. "Let's do this."

"Stare straight ahead. Let your eyes go unfocused," Aki instructed. His voice drifted to a soft, musical tone. "Take a few deep breaths. In through your nose and out through your mouth. Focus your mind on the feeling of the breath moving through your lungs. Now, let your eyes fall closed."

I closed my eyes. Meditation was a little woo-woo, but I had decided to follow my gut and I couldn't back down now. My chest rose and fell with the power of my breath, and I focused on that feeling. I imagined it as a swift wind blowing over the countryside. Tall grass bent one way, then the other, with the power of the oxygen entering and exiting my lungs.

"Take notice of your body," Aki's voice said, drifting over the scene in my mind. "Perform a sweep from head to toe. Notice where you're comfortable, where you're uncomfortable. The feeling of the mat underneath you and the breeze on your face."

I did, but I started at my toes because I'm rebellious that way. My inner gaze swept up my legs, taking stock of the stick poking me in the thigh. I didn't shift, merely observed the discomfort and moved on. Before I reached the top of my head, my body disappeared.

I was standing atop a hill—the one I'd seen in my mind. The land around me stretched for miles in rolling, grass-covered hills. My breath still rustled the grass back and forth, but I heard no sound. The land around me was eerily silent. I looked down at myself, held my hands up to examine them. I had a body after all, and I was wearing clean jeans and a nice T-shirt; the nicest I'd ever owned. The skin on my arms and hands was clean and unblemished. The scars from various scrapes and cuts over the past few years had disappeared. Were those even my arms? I wished I had a mirror to check, but the hair falling down my chest was the same color as mine.

The surrounding grass danced with the power of my lungs. It bothered me that it was so quiet, but something about the scene was strangely peaceful. The sky was clear blue. Off in the distance, though, clouds formed disturbingly fast. They began as white fluffy things, then morphed together and turned dark gray, then black. I stood on my hilltop, watching them curiously.

They grew and grew until a black wall stretched across the horizon. Lightning flickered in their depths, but I could hear no thunder.

The grass around me began to move erratically as the clouds shifted and moved in my direction. Darkness stretched, reaching toward me with cloudy black claws. The grass moved faster and faster, accelerating with the beat of my heart.

Then it all stopped.

The grass was still, the sky was pitch black.

I felt more than heard a disturbance above me, and I tipped my head back. A single shaft of blackness descended from the cloud-covered sky. Lightning flashed again, but it was as if the shaft absorbed it. As if it was the essence of darkness itself and nothing could penetrate it. I froze, watching it move toward me. Part of me wanted to move, to run. Adrenaline rushed through my veins, but my limbs wouldn't obey my brain's command. My brain wasn't even working. All I could do was stare as inky black darkness enveloped me.

When I opened my eyes again, I was floating.

Or rather, I didn't have a body at all. I was just a spirit drifting through a sea of black.

I blinked, and it was as if a golden screen clicked on in front of my eyes.

A little girl skipped down the street, dark pigtails bouncing, her small face radiant as she beamed up at the two adults holding her hands. Her parents lifted her, swinging her between them as they walked, and the toddler whooped with joy.

The little family looked...

They looked happy.

The parents smiled at each other, and the man leaned over their daughter's head to give his wife a long kiss. She giggled and blushed beautifully, love shining in her eyes as she looked up at him.

My heart jackknifed in my chest—if I had a chest in this form. My family. Had we really been like that once? It was such a contrast from the childhood I remembered. I stared at the little girl, jabbering in nonsensical half-English as she pointed at a Fae walking in the opposite direction across a nearby street. The way her parents —my parents—crooned and patted her on the head, exchanging a conspiratorial smile. My father with his dark hair and eyes, his tan skin, his quick smile. My mother, freckled and fair, her blue-green eyes—the ones I'd inherited—sparkling with life and love and laughter.

It made me want to throw up. It was a life I couldn't remember, a life I'd spent years wishing for.

Before I could speak, think, or wish I wasn't seeing this, the mental screen clicked off and blackness swallowed me once again.

When I awoke, I was in a bed. Not the bed at Aki's house, and not the one in Hammond House either.

But it was familiar. Achingly familiar.

Unmoving, I looked around the room. The small desk in the corner, the closet exploding with half-folded, wrinkled clothes. The walls adorned with scribbled pictures created by small hands. The pink comforter wrapped around me like a cocoon, a dozen small printed roses smiling up at me from the fabric.

My bedroom. My childhood bedroom.

I moved to get out of bed, but my body didn't obey my command. Soft snores brought my attention back to the room. Were those my snores? But I was awake.

No, I wasn't. It's like I was trapped in my body, an unwilling passenger along for the ride.

My bedroom door opened, and if I could control my eyes, they would have widened. A woman slipped into the room, her dark hair mussed from sleep. She had blue-green eyes like mine, and freckles dusted her nose and cheeks. She was like an older version of me, but she was beautiful. And healthy. And nothing like how I remembered her.

My mother sank to her knees next to my bed. Her beautiful face was sad, her cheeks wet and her eyes red. "Evie," she whispered, touching my hair. "Evie, wake up."

The body I inhabited stirred, but the actions weren't my own. I watched it all as if it was a movie, and I was in the main character's body.

"Mama?" said a sleepy child's voice.

"Hi, honey." Mom smiled for my benefit, but it didn't reach her eyes. She touched my cheek. "Did you have a good sleep?"

"Good sleep," my sleepy voice echoed with a barely contained yawn. "Where's Daddy?"

"Honey... I need to tell you something. Come here." Mom gathered me into her arms and cuddled me close. "You know I love you, right?"

"Yeah."

"And your daddy loves you. We both do." Mom took a shuddering breath.

I remembered this day. I'd only been five years old, but the memory of it had stuck with me for my entire life. It was the start of the only life I could remember. I wanted to scream, to run, to shout at my mother not to speak her next words. The words that would shatter my childhood in an instant. But no matter how I fought, I was only an unwilling witness to this moment.

"Daddy... Daddy's gone, honey. And he's not coming back."

My childish sobs echoed in my head, bouncing around until I thought I would lose my mind.

The world went black, as if I'd closed my eyes for an instant.

When I opened them again, I wasn't in my mom's arms anymore. I was standing in the living room of the apartment I'd shared with my mother when I was thirteen. It was dilapidated, abandoned. Cobwebs dusted the corners of the ceiling, and empty pizza boxes littered the coffee table and floor. The TV was on, set to the news, but it was muted. The apartment was silent. Empty. Cold.

No... not empty.

I didn't want to see this. I didn't want to be here.

Despite my mental protests, my feet crossed the aged wood floor, kicking plastic cups out of the way as I approached a closed door at the end of the hall. Surprisingly steady fingers reached out and grasped the knob, turning it. The metal creak of the door's hinges was loud in the silent apartment.

My mother's bedroom was dark. A sliver of light peeked through the mostly closed curtains, illuminating the end of the mattress on the floor. A bare foot sticking out of the blanket, the skin leeched of color. There was no sound. No movement from the bed as I approached. No signs of life.

No, no, no. I didn't want to see her. I didn't want to relive this memory.

In slow motion, my hand reached out and grabbed the blanket, pulling it back to reveal a shadow of the woman who had been my mother. Her dark hair was ratted around her face, and her T-shirt and sweatpants were stained and torn. But it was her eyes I couldn't look away from. They were blue green, like mine, but they stared sightlessly at the ceiling.

My scream tore from my lungs, echoing in the deathly silent air.

A sudden whoosh sounded behind me. I flipped around, somehow in control of my body again, and I stared as the closet door flew open. Yawning blackness greeted me, roiling clouds churning within the darkness. It spilled out, rushing toward me, and I welcomed it. Anything to get me out of here, away from the memory of my mother's dead eyes.

When I blinked, I was standing on the grassy hilltop again. As quickly as they came, the dark clouds shot up into the sky and exploded in a bright flash of light, leaving the sky clear blue again. I stared at it, blinking rapidly in the sunlight.

A sound behind me had me flipping around again. A few feet away stood the most magnificent creature I'd ever seen. It was the size of a moose and it looked like a stag, but it was covered in silvery-white fur. Huge antlers protruded from its head, but they didn't end in sharp, jutting points like normal antlers I'd seen. Each one split into four branches, each branch curved into a C-shape ending in a small glowing orb. The creature's legs were long and thin, with corded muscle, and ended in glowing hooves.

It was the same creature I'd seen at the Great Tree, the one that had disappeared before I could point it out to Shadow.

The creature stood silently. It was facing my direction, and its eyes were pitch black, like the clouds that had enveloped me earlier. It made a huffing noise and pawed at the ground with one hoof, its eyes never leaving mine.

I raised my hands. "I won't hurt you," I said softly.

The creature snorted and shook its head, massive antlers swaying through the air. Then it took a step closer.

I forced myself to remain still. Would it attack me if I tried to run?

The creature approached until it was a foot away. Then, with its soft nose, it bumped my hand.

I will not hurt you, little one. The voice was in my head, feather-light.

I stared at the creature. "What are you?"

It didn't respond. Instead, it bumped my hand again. I lowered it, palm up, and the creature bumped it a third time.

Do my will, the voice said. Then it lowered its head and touched its nose to the top of my left foot.

Warmth started in my chest and worked its way outward, spreading through my limbs from head to toe. It was warm at first, gentle, and then it grew in intensity until I thought I would burn from the inside out. I think I screamed, clutching my chest, but I made no sound.

The creature watched as I collapsed to the ground, writhing in agony.

A hand grasped my arm and I flew backward—or it felt like I did.

My head snapped back and my eyes flew open. I expected to see the creature above me, but instead I saw Shadow. Aki stood behind him, his face expressionless behind his ivory mask.

"Everly," Shadow said. "You're okay."

Breathing hard, I glanced around. I was back in Aki's garden, and I wasn't burning alive.

But I *was* burning.

I fumbled with my shoe, untying the laces and yanking it off, followed by my sock. There, on the top of my left foot, was a black tattoo the size of a quarter. It glowed with an orange hue, and the surrounding skin was red and irritated.

"Everly," Shadow said softly.

I jerked my gaze up to him.

"You did it." He placed a gentle hand on my shoulder, that heart-squeezing smile curling his lips. "You passed Seraphine's test. You got your Mark."

CHAPTER EIGHTEEN

It was only a matter of time before the other shoe dropped.

That's what I kept telling myself as I helped Mina make croissants and a sausage casserole for breakfast. I didn't feel any different now that I had an elemental bond, except for the slight burning in the tattoo on my foot every once in a while and the bone-deep exhaustion that made me want to sleep for at least a week. Shadow had suggested that I rest, but I was too keyed-up to sleep, and if I was awake, I might as well do something useful with my time. After the Rite, Aki had disappeared to meet with Senan and report on our successful break-in at the armory. Shadow had slipped away soon after, citing orders to keep watch on the Reyan Guard and prepare Aki's network for retaliation.

Now I found myself back at Aki's house, mere hours after I completed the most sacred ceremony in Faery, chopping vegetables for a breakfast casserole.

Mina was uncharacteristically silent, rolling and folding croissant dough without a glance in my direction. She hadn't said a word to me outside of her directive to cut vegetables and put them in a nearby casserole dish. Was she worried that we'd be arrested for the break-in at the armory last night? It was a distinct possibility, especially after the way we'd had to deviate from our original plan.

Hopefully with Shadow and Gideon's ears to the ground, we'd have some warning before the Reyan Guard showed up at our door. There hadn't been any movement during the night, and I hoped that was a good sign.

By the time breakfast was ready, the rest of our group had returned. We gathered around the table and dished our plates while Shadow and Gideon gave Aki their reports.

"I have alerted our network of last night's events," Gideon said, nursing a glass of whiskey with his breakfast. "So far, there has been no chatter on the streets about the break-in last night. Everyone is too busy discussing the air ship's crash."

"No movement from the Reyan Guard either," Shadow added. "No extra patrols or increased presence at the armory. It's as if nothing happened."

"Maybe the missing weapons haven't been noticed." Mina poured coffee into Aki's mug and returned to her seat across from me.

"Perhaps, but I doubt it." Aki took a sip of the coffee, frowned, and returned it to the table. I didn't miss the crestfallen expression that crossed Mina's face as he did. "We must assume that she's aware of the missing weapons and that she suspects we are behind it. She may not act on that to avoid drawing attention to the incident, but I have no doubt that she'll retaliate somehow."

I swallowed hard. What retaliation could he be referring to? If I was lucky, the equinox would arrive and I'd be back home before I ever had to find out. I had no desire to see the inside of a Reyan dungeon.

Aki turned his attention to me. "Congratulations on your successful Rite, Everly."

Gideon whistled, raising a glass in a toast. "I didn't think you could do it, darlin'. I'm impressed."

I know; I'm a bad-ass. That's what I wanted to say, but instead I grinned at Shadow, who inclined his head in silent acknowledgment. Somehow that made my heart warm more than anyone else's praise.

"We will begin your training today. You must learn to deepen your bond and control your element. Without it, you risk hurting yourself or someone else, and—"

A knock sounded at the front door.

We all fell silent, and five pairs of eyes went to the filigreed wood separating us from our visitor.

The silence stretched for what felt like an eternity, and then the knock sounded again.

Aki nodded at Mina, who pushed her chair back and crossed the living room area to swing the door open. Reyan guards didn't come crashing in, demanding that we get on the floor with our hands above our heads. For a brief moment my stomach hollowed out in relief, and then I heard the telltale buzz of a pixie's wings.

The purple-winged pixie flew right past Mina and toward the kitchen table, dropping an envelope with a distinctive white wax seal on the space next to Aki's plate before exiting the way she came in. I held my breath as he slid his finger underneath the wax and popped it open, unfolding the thick paper.

"The queen requests an audience," he said after scanning the letter's contents.

A rushing sound in my ears drowned out the sudden outburst of questions from the rest of Aki's crew. This was it. The queen knew. She was summoning us to the palace so she could hang us for our crimes. Or would she kill us with her magick? Maybe her guard from the House of Air would steal the breath from our bodies like that protester had done to me.

I would never see Mary Beth again—oh, Mary Beth. I had been so busy that I hadn't thought about her lately. Guilt threatened to make my throat close. What would happen to her if I never returned? Would she ever make it off the streets? Would she ever get clean, or would she end up like my mother had?

"Everly."

I yanked myself out of my mental death spiral. Gideon, Aki, and Mina were arguing about what the summons meant, but Shadow's gaze was only on me. The calm in his expression centered me. It would be okay. Just because she had chosen this moment to summon us didn't mean that she knew about the armory.

Oh, no... what if she knew I'd performed the Rite? Panic threatened to drown me again.

Shadow leaned forward and placed his hand over mine. The warmth of his skin was like a defibrillator to my system, dissipating my shock and returning clarity to the situation.

Wait—Shadow was holding my hand. That crossed so many lines that I had drawn in the sand between me and anyone else. Even worse, I liked it. The weight of his hand on mine felt natural, like there was nowhere else it should be. If I just turned mine over, I could curl my fingers around his, and then I could never let go.

Now was not the time for this line of thought. I pulled my hand away and settled it in my lap, but I shot him a thankful look before I did. If he was disappointed, he didn't show it, and I swallowed hard, tuning back in to Aki as he addressed Mina and Gideon.

"We will answer the summons," Aki said decisively. "Elyra expects us to fight or flee, but we will do nothing to draw suspicion. Even she wouldn't dare to punish us unprovoked. It would cause outrage in Thios, which could lead to rebellion and a headache she would rather not address."

"Then why does she want you to come to Reya?" Mina asked. Her face had paled to a sickly shade of light blue, and she grasped the still-open door so tightly that her knuckles turned white.

"To instill fear," Aki replied, standing. "She wants us to know that she's in control. We will answer the summons, give her what she wants, and she will not retaliate further."

If only I shared his confidence. I felt more like I was climbing the stairs to the gallows, the noose already tightening around my neck.

It was mid-morning when we boarded the air ship back to Reya. Apparently, Ollee and the stranded Reyans had spent the night repairing the ship's damage. Ollee was a talented captain; he had crashed convincingly without causing permanent damage to his prized vessel.

It was just me and Aki this time; Shadow had remained at home per Aki's request. I wished he was here; his steady presence would go a long way to soothe my nerves. I flashed a weak smile at Ollee as we boarded and tried not to read into the pitying smile he sent back. Mina had offered a dark purple gown for me to wear, all satin and sleek lines, but I didn't feel nearly as confident as I had the first time I'd visited the palace—not that I had felt much confidence then either.

The palace sparkled in the afternoon light as the air ship touched down on the wide lawn. I followed Aki down the ramp, and two Reyan guards led the way through the immense double doors. We walked through a labyrinth of stairs and rooms, down the hall full of portraits, and past the crystal-chandeliered ballroom where we'd met the queen last time. I half expected the guards to lead us straight to a dank dungeon somewhere, but a few minutes later, they opened a door to an elegant throne room.

It was a long room with a white marble floor and an enormous ceiling. Stone pillars lined the walls on both sides, leading the way to a dais at the end that supported two thrones. Guards stood at attention, one between each pillar, each holding a long spear. They didn't point the spears at us, though. They didn't even acknowledge us as we passed, marching down a long white rug leading to the queen—and maybe our deaths.

Elyra sat upon the bigger throne. The king was nowhere to be seen. She wore a shimmery white dress today, nearly the same color as her skin, and its long train pooled on the floor at her feet. Her ice-blue eyes regarded us as we approached, and she sat unnaturally still, a predator waiting for her chance to pounce. She looked more human than most of the Fae I'd seen, but something about her made my skin crawl. "Aki," she said, her tinkling voice like glass shattering against the marble floor. "Thank you for your prompt response to my summons."

"Anything for you, my queen." Aki bowed low, and I followed his lead. He seemed relaxed, but he had to be as anxious as I was. He'd spent years gathering support to go after Asmodeus, and one wrong move could bring it all crashing down. It wasn't just my trip home at stake—it was Aki's entire mission.

"I see the human has survived so far," Queen Elyra said, her pale eyes moving to me. I quickly dropped my gaze to the floor, ignoring the sweat dripping down my back. "Nothing to report about her behavior, I assume?"

I tensed. Was this a trap? Did she know about the Rite? Was I about to die a quick death?

"No, my queen," Aki said smoothly. "All is proceeding according to plan."

I dared a peek, and my stomach flipped when a feline smile crossed Queen Elyra's face. That was an "I'm-going-to-eat-you-for-dinner" kind of smile. The smile a lion might give a gazelle before snapping its neck. "Very well. I summoned you here to report on your progress after our last discussion."

"Yes, my queen."

"I have been informed that several members of my houses have been accosted while visiting Thios, and tensions remain high with the downworlders. It appears you have made no progress acting upon my request."

Aki clasped his hands behind his back, his gaze on the wall above the queen's throne, expression complacent. "I will investigate the matter, my queen. I'm sure you're aware that it's not a problem to be resolved overnight."

"You disappoint me, Aki." The queen's voice turned frosty, and her power crackled through my bones. The temperature seemed to drop twenty degrees in an instant. "I expected more from you. You were a loyal servant to me in the past, so I'm willing to give you another chance. Quell the rebellion, or you will join your little human in the dungeon for whatever remains of her miserable life. I'm in no mood for a war, but I will not hesitate to handle the matter myself if you cannot."

My blood turned to ice, and I had to force myself to remain still.

Aki, to his credit, merely bowed his head and said, "Yes, my queen."

Queen Elyra looked down her nose at us for a long moment, as if daring us to disobey her. I had a rebellious streak, but I didn't have a death wish; I kept my eyes on the toes of my sparkly heels. Well, that was impractical. How was I supposed to run for my life in heels?

If only I had at least figured out how to summon a spark. A spark was all it would take to get out of here. I could light the queen's dress on fire, or maybe some curtains. Aki and I could make a break for it while the guards tried to put it out.

Yeah, right. My panic—and the queen's magick zipping through me—had to be melting my brain.

The silence stretched long enough that I imagined a dozen different escape attempts in graphic detail, and then a few of the

Reyan Guard escorted us out. The queen must have given them some signal that I'd missed in my crazed imaginings.

As I followed Aki's tall form out the way we came in, I couldn't help feeling like a guillotine was going to drop on us at any moment. But nothing happened. We left the palace, boarded Ollee's air ship, and floated away from the Falls before I finally let my shoulders relax. I glanced up at Aki, who stood silently at the railing next to me. "That was too easy, wasn't it?"

He looked down, meeting my eyes. The ivory of his mask reflected the moonlight before we descended below the Great Tree's canopy. "Yes. Far too easy."

"I thought so." I swallowed a gulp. "Even if you succeed in taking the gate, the Thiosians' rebellion won't go away. It will only get worse. And the queen..."

"Will most likely imprison me." The finality of Aki's words made chills skate up my spine. Or maybe that was the dropping temperature as we descended into the shadows. "She likely suspects that I play a role in the rebellion. She brought me there today to provide my one and only warning."

"If she thinks you're involved, why not just arrest you now?"

Aki's white-gloved hands grasped the railing in front of him. "Believe it or not, the queen and I used to be... friends. I think she granted me this warning because of our history. She won't do it again."

I gaped at him. Every time I learned something new about Aki's past, it prompted a hundred more questions. I wished he would tell me the whole story, but he was about as open as a hardshell clam. From what I'd gathered, it sounded like an awful story, so it was understandable that he didn't like to share, but I liked to at least know something about the Fae I had associated myself with. It made me nervous to have so many questions about my companion.

Okay, that wasn't completely true. I wanted to know more about Aki's past because I wanted to understand him. Because I was beginning to...care about him. About Aki, Mina, Shadow, Kiera, and even Gideon.

And that made me very...antsy.

CHAPTER NINETEEN

Magick sucked. Or I sucked—the jury was out on which.

I sat with my eyes closed, hands resting lightly in my lap, and tried to calm my mind.

"Deep breaths," Aki's firm voice said from behind me.

I was two seconds from throwing this meditation mat at his head. Instead of giving in to the urge, I snapped my eyes open to glare over my shoulder at him. "It's not working."

"You're not trying."

"Yes I am. I haven't been sitting here staring at my eyelids for the past hour because it sounded like a fun time."

Aki leveled a look at me. I was coming to recognize it as his exasperated, 'I don't have time for your shenanigans' expression. I was the best at getting it out of him. He unfolded from his position on the floor and paced away from me, gloved hands clasped behind his back. "Seraphine's Gift is temperamental," he said, staring out at the garden. "She may have granted you a bond with fire, but it is your responsibility to develop that connection and learn to harness it."

I scowled at my foot, where my Mark was hidden beneath my left boot. "I still don't understand how meditation is supposed to help me do that."

Aki turned to face me, releasing a long breath as if grasping at the fraying ends of his patience. "Did you emerge from the womb knowing how to talk?"

I huffed. "Obviously not."

"Then you must understand why you did not emerge from the Rite knowing how to harness your magick." Aki lifted a hand and held it in front of him, palm up. A breeze swept past me, carrying dust and leaves and small twigs toward the tall Fae as if drawn to him like a magnet. It ruffled his hair before coalescing into the palm of his hand, swirling in a tight sphere with a whistling sound. Aki didn't bat an eye as it swirled faster and faster, pulling debris into its orbit until it grew to the size of a watermelon. Then it imploded, shooting air and dust in all directions. Aki's coat tails whipped out behind him and my hair blew back from my face, and then stillness fell in the garden again.

Okay, holding a fireball in my hand sounded cool, but air magick clearly had its perks. I'd seen Aki in action a handful of times, but it was amazing to see it up close. If magick drew on the elements within a user's body, Aki should be breathless all the time. But he was unaffected by the exertion.

"Magick is a skill to be trained," Aki continued, ignoring the fact that my jaw was hanging open. "Fire is bonded to you now, part of your body and soul. If you cannot trust the bond, you cannot harness its magick. Something is holding you back, and self-reflection is vital for you to determine what is causing your roadblock and how you can overcome it."

I stared at the floor. That was all well and good, but after what I'd seen during the Rite yesterday, I had no desire to dive back into the nightmares in my mind.

My mom's sightless eyes flashed across my memory, and I shivered. If using my magick required me to relive those moments again, I'd lose what sanity I had left. There's a reason I had locked those years up tight and thrown away the key.

Not that I would ever tell Aki that. There was only so much weakness I could show him before he decided I wasn't worth his time. I'd seen it before, with my so-called foster parents and various government officials at the homeless shelters I'd frequented before I landed in Hammond House. They could handle Rough-and-Tough Everly, but Vulnerable Everly? That was a deal-breaker.

I loosed a sigh and sat back. "I think Mina... needs my help with something. Probably. Can we pick this up again later?"

Aki raised an eyebrow. He looked like he wanted to challenge my weak excuse, but Shadow chose that moment to trot into the garden in wolf form.

I jumped to my feet and bounded down the pavilion steps, grateful to escape Aki's too-keen eyes. Shadow met me there, his eyes no less sharp but far more forgiving. I waited while he shifted into his Fae form and unfolded from a crouch, looking far too appealing in his all-black clothing. "Hey," I said brightly. "Need something?"

Shadow's eyes swept over me, eliciting tingles despite my annoyance over my failed magick use, and then flicked to Aki. "If you're not too busy."

"Nope, we were just finishing up. Thanks for the lesson, Aki. We'll pick it up again tomorrow." I linked my arm through Shadow's elbow and dragged him away before Aki could call us back. A thrill went through me; he was warm even through his sleeve's thick fabric. Besides the little hand-holding moment we had yesterday, I had never touched him like this. Was that why I felt the urge to do it now? Or maybe it was because my mom's lifeless face still hovered in the back of my mind, or maybe because I had the feeling that Shadow understood me better than anyone here. We were kindred spirits somehow; I knew it even though I knew as little about his past as he did about mine.

And I needed a kindred spirit right now. Or a distraction. Or both.

Shadow let me tow him all the way out of the garden and down the cobblestone street before he spoke. "Running from the situation will hardly make it better."

I stopped walking and glared halfheartedly up at him. Of course he'd read me so easily, and of course he wouldn't let it go. "Can't a girl ignore her problems without everyone nagging her?"

A smile tugged at Shadow's lips. "Not when we're days from a battle where the solution to those problems will become necessary."

"Ugh, I know." I released his arm and shoved my hands into my pockets. He kept pace with me as I continued walking. "I don't love the idea of hiding while you all attack the bad guys, but I doubt my street punches will do much to hurt Bria's Fae. And I doubt this magick thing is going to work out before then."

"I told you it wouldn't be easy," Shadow said, moving around a mountain of a Fae lumbering down the middle of the street before returning to my side.

"And I didn't believe you."

"Not surprising."

I side-eyed him, allowing a smile. "I don't make a habit of trusting Fae, after all."

"Of course not." Shadow's dark eyes twinkled. "We would eat you as soon as look at you."

I almost laughed. To think I'd grown up believing that the Fae were man-eating monsters. I hadn't had much evidence to suggest otherwise, but after living in Thios for the past couple weeks and seeing the way the Fae lived, it was ridiculous to even think about. Some nights, as I lay awake fighting the remnants of another nightmare, I wondered if the Fae were more human than most humans were. Sure, Asmodeus was a bad egg and he had lots of minions—like Bria—who followed in his footsteps, but I'd witnessed more human qualities from the Thiosians than I'd seen in years living on Seattle's streets. Thios had its problems with the queen and her crazy laws, but I'd experienced more kindness from Mina and Aki and everyone else than I could remember ever feeling in the human world.

And I was days from going back there.

I waved a hello to Warred and stopped at his market stand, staring at a shelf of bracelets without really seeing them. Between accompanying Mina on her visits and saving him from those Reyans, we had become friendly. I still suspected he was part of Aki's mysterious rebel group. I'd never gotten confirmation, but he was far too familiar with Mina to not be involved somehow. We would probably see more of him when we attacked the gate in a few days.

Just days left.

I was days away from sleeping in a room with a hundred other people. Days away from fighting Peter for every dollar I could earn and waiting for the inevitable moment when Mary Beth went too far with Zayne and his wares. Days away from returning to my existence as a nobody, only caring about myself and Mary Beth and struggling to survive with no greater purpose and little hope of a future.

But Mary Beth needed me. I was all she had in the world, her only hope of surviving to see age thirty. I couldn't abandon her like I had abandoned my mom. Like my dad had abandoned us.

I didn't belong in Thios. But had I ever belonged in Seattle?

The air beside me moved, and a musky smell reached my nose as Shadow leaned forward. His strong fingers gently closed around something on the table in front of me, and I blinked as he handed it to Warred.

"Excellent choice." Warred grinned, showing fangs, and took the coin Shadow fished out of his pocket. He bowed and winked at me, dropped something back into Shadow's hand, and turned to help another customer.

Shadow's dark eyes met mine. He opened his hand to reveal a bracelet, a polished red stone resting in the middle of a simple band woven from hemp-like string. "To celebrate your new bond with the element of fire," he explained, tying it around my right wrist and knotting it securely.

I turned my hand this way and that, admiring the way the stone glinted in the sun.

When was the last time someone had given me a gift? I honestly couldn't remember. To my utter horror, the back of my eyes burned. I blinked hard before I did something idiotic like start crying and cleared my throat. "It's... really something. Thank you."

"You can wear it to the summer festival," Shadow said gruffly. "I'm sure Mina'll find something suitable to wear with it."

With that, he walked away. If I wasn't so busy gawking at the bracelet and two seconds from bawling like a baby, I might've wondered at the faint pink that had tinged Shadow's cheeks, or the way his lips had tugged into a smile as he turned away.

That night, images of my father haunted my dreams.

He left when I was five years old, so I didn't remember much about him, but I knew his face from the framed picture my mom had kept on her nightstand. In that photo, he was a head taller than my mom and his eyes were crinkled with laughter. My mom was laughing too, her freckled face lit up in a way I couldn't remember ever seeing before. They were cuddled close, my father's arm around my mom's shoulder, and he held a baby—me—cradled in his other arm.

During my mom's downward spiral, while she was out with another guy or in a drugged haze, I'd spent hours staring at that photo with a mixture of longing and disgust. I'd longed for that happy time to be my reality, and I'd hated my father for leaving.

Now, in my nightmare, my father was a faceless shadow haunting our tiny apartment. He watched as my mother overdosed, as I was taken away by social services and placed in a foster home with foster parents who cared more about their monthly paycheck than taking care of me. As I ran away and struggled to survive on the streets. He was there in the shadows as I slowly froze to death behind a dumpster in an alley, when Mary Beth found me and offered me her hand. As I pulled my life together and finally started earning money and found us safe haven at Hammond House.

All along he watched, my faceless shadow, silently judging everything I did and said, hovering over me like a thundercloud promising a torrent of misfortune. No matter what I did, I couldn't get away from him. I couldn't forgive him for leaving, for making a single decision that altered the course of my life forever. That killed my mother. That had almost killed me.

He was here in Thios, too. Watching as I meditated in the garden, judging as I wrestled with my magick.

He was in my bedroom at Aki's house, a looming shadow standing at the end of my bed—

I jerked awake and scrambled back, slamming the bed's headboard into the wall. My gaze flew upward, but the space at the end of my bed was empty. Cold sweat dripped between my shoulder blades, and my cotton T-shirt stuck to my skin.

It was just a nightmare.

I put a hand on my chest, willing my heart to settle even as I searched every corner of the room, alert for anything that might be out of place. The stone on my bracelet caught the light, and my gaze snagged on it. Releasing a heavy breath, I slid to the edge of the bed and jammed my feet into my boots. No way was I sleeping in that bed again tonight. I didn't even want to stay in this room.

I considered retreating downstairs to cuddle in front of the fire, but Aki had been spending late nights there recently, researching or whatever he did with his old books. I wasn't in the mood for a lecture or an explanation, so I wrapped my blanket around my shoulders and moved to the window overlooking the rope bridge that stretched between Aki's house and his neighbor. The window opened silently, thankfully, and I slipped outside. It was still dark and the street below was silent as I dropped to sit, my feet dangling over the side.

What kind of messed-up nightmare was that? I hadn't dreamed about my father in years. I would never stop hating him for what he'd done, but I'd stopped wasting thoughts on him a long time ago. So why had this dream happened now? Was it because of the Rite?

I shivered. I'd mentally prepared myself for nightmares about my mom's death. After all, that had seemed to be the biggest challenge within the Rite. This one had caught me completely off guard.

"Everly?"

I jumped and looked over my shoulder. Mina stood at the open window to my bedroom, her silvery-white hair hanging loose and wavy over her shoulders. She wore an old Simple Plan T-shirt and polka dotted pajama pants, and she looked wide awake.

"You couldn't sleep either?" She climbed out the window and sat beside me, shivering in the night breeze.

Wordlessly, I unwrapped my blanket burrito and spread half around her shoulders. "Just a nightmare."

She shot me a sympathetic smile. "I had nightmares for weeks after my Rite."

"You did?"

"Mm-hmm. They say it's pretty common." Mina shrugged her narrow shoulders. "It'll pass. Want to talk about it?"

I shook my head. "What are you doing awake?"

"Oh, I can't sleep with everything going on. I just keep making to-do lists and wondering what I'm missing."

I glanced at her. She had dark purple circles under her eyes, noticeable even against her blue skin. How long had she been having trouble sleeping? I could only imagine the burden on her shoulders. Aki was the leader of the rebellion, but Mina was the true mastermind behind it. Not only did her inventions help the Thiosians survive without supplies from the human world thanks to Asmodeus's monopoly on the gate, but her weapons would be vital in Aki's plan to regain control and capture Bria. No wonder she wasn't sleeping.

Aki had told me he was grateful for Mina's presence, but did he realize how important she was to his cause? How much she cared about him and what he stood for, and the sacrifices she made to help him succeed? If I had someone who cared like that for me, I would certainly treat them better than Aki treated Mina, lost love or not.

"Anyway." Mina smiled brightly. "Any luck using your magick yet?"

"No. It's going nowhere fast." I swung my legs gently, eyes on the cobblestone street below. "I have a feeling it won't help much during the fight."

"It might not, but you don't need magick to be useful. I'm proof of that." Mina bumped her shoulder against mine, jostling the blanket around us. "You've got my grenades, and Aki will be with you. He'll make sure you get home safely."

I smiled at her. "Thanks, Mina. I don't know what any of us would do without you."

"Oh, you'd get along just fine." Mina's smile was strained. "I just do what I can."

"You may not have magick, but you're the lifeblood of this operation. Without you, everything would be a mess. All of us would be exhausted and starving, and most of Thios would cease functioning entirely without your inventions."

Mina laughed, a delicate tinkle that echoed in the darkness. That seemed to break her out of whatever doubt had crept into her mind, because we fell into comfortable silence as the sky lightened.

It was funny, but I wasn't as concerned about making it home safely anymore. I was more worried about helping Mina and Aki and the others retake the gate. That was an odd feeling for me. I'd spent the last four years living by the motto that everyone had to look out for themselves. I included Mary Beth in my circle of protection because I owed her, but I had never believed I could help anyone else, let alone tried.

Aki's fight for the gate was above my head. Aside from opening the path for me to go home, it shouldn't concern me.

So why did I feel a sudden determination to master my magick and help Aki capture Bria and accomplish his goal?

CHAPTER TWENTY

The next few days passed in a blur of activity as the summer equinox approached. I spent mornings helping Mina with her grenades and organizing the children's daily tasks. In the afternoons, I met with Aki and Shadow in the garden and they attempted to teach me how to use my magick.

Shadow had been right; I couldn't wave a magic wand and use the Gift Seraphine had given me. No matter how much I meditated and how hard I tried to harness the magick, flames wouldn't spring from my hands. The tattoo didn't grow, but my frustration did. With each day that passed, I grew more anxious about our attack on the gate and less sure about my decision to perform the Rite. What good were magical powers if I couldn't even use them?

After an annoying morning staring at the inside of my eyelids and attempting to find my zen—with no luck—I stalked out of Aki's garden with a hefty burst of rage and nowhere to put it. Instead of veering toward Aki's house, I paced into the forest, looking for something, anything, to direct my excess energy at.

I found Gideon.

He stood in a clearing not too far from Aki's house. A quiet "thwump, thwump" led me there when I finally slowed down enough to let my blood settle.

Gideon stood with a bow at the ready, an arrow nocked on the string. He looked surprisingly steady, his gaze concentrated on an upturned log at the other end of the clearing. As I watched, he released the string and the arrow whizzed through the air, embedding itself into the middle of the stump with a "thwump."

Wow. So Gideon had skills beyond using his bare feet and his Gift.

I ignored the stab of jealousy.

"Are you spying on me, darlin'?" Gideon drawled without turning around. He lowered the bow and grabbed another arrow from the quiver at his back, placed it, and drew the string tight again.

"How did you know I was here?" I stepped through the brush and into the clearing, approaching him.

"You stomped through the forest like a herd of elephants. I'd wager all of Thios heard you." Gideon loosed the string again.

Thwump. The arrow struck home.

"Impressive," I murmured. "Should you be using that in the open? What if the queen's guard sees you?"

Gideon finally glanced at me, a hint of a smile on his lips. "They rarely patrol this area. And if they did, I'd love to get some practice in before the equinox. How's the magick training going?"

"It's not." I scowled, my eyes on the tree stump with six arrows in a perfect group. "I'm going to be pretty useless in this fight."

"You're only human." Gideon lowered the bow. "It takes most Fae years to master their Gift. I'd be mighty impressed if you could do more than a spark right now."

"I can't even do that," I admitted.

"I wouldn't worry. You can sit and look pretty; leave all the fighting to us monsters."

I winced. "Who told you about that?"

"Does it matter?" Gideon grinned. "The important thing is that you've changed your tune."

"I have. I know the Fae aren't monsters." I glanced sidelong at him. "Most of them, anyway."

Gideon snorted a laugh.

I couldn't help but smile. "How did you get dragged into this fight? You don't seem like the revolutionary type."

"Why? Because I like whiskey?" As if to emphasize his point, Gideon grabbed a foggy bottle from a nearby rock and took a long swig. "We're not always what we appear, little lady."

"I've gathered that much. How did you meet Aki?"

Gideon set the bottle back on the rock and hefted his bow again, shooting another bullseye as if he could do it in his sleep. "I met him during the war. He saved my life."

That hit home. Mary Beth's face immediately came to mind, and I suddenly understood Gideon's loyalty to Aki. "How?"

"Asmodeus—or rather, one of his followers—killed my sister. I went after him, of course, a dead man's mission. Aki stopped me from getting myself killed and told me to use my life for a different purpose. And here I am." Gideon lowered the bow and turned to face me. "And the whiskey? It was my sister's favorite drink. She was an alcoholic if I've ever met one."

I searched his face. For the first time since I'd met him, I saw the sorrow behind his grin. The meaning behind his drinking. No wonder the others never mentioned his addiction to the bottle. Mina was the only one who tried to circumvent it by constantly shoving food in his hands instead. Gideon was a trickster, the comic relief of the group, but he had a tragic past like everyone else.

"I get it," I said quietly. "I lost my mom a few years ago. I still want to kill the one responsible."

If only I could kill drugs and addiction. It was a revenge I would never see.

"Here." Gideon shoved his bow into my hands. "You ever shot one of these?"

"Uh, no. They aren't very common in the human world." I accepted the change of subject—I wasn't eager for this conversation to go into touchy-feely territory either—and glanced down at the bow, hefting it in one hand. It was lightweight and the wood was smooth against my fingers.

"They should be," Gideon said. He cleared his throat. "They're mighty fine weapons. It's a shame the queen banned them, or I would use them more. Want me to give you a lesson?"

My first instinct was to refuse, but clearly my magick training was going nowhere. At least if I had a bow, I could attempt to help when we took back the gate. Or at the very least, avoid getting myself killed. If all else failed, I could poke my attackers in the eye with an arrow. "Yeah," I said to Gideon. "I guess that'd be nice."

Gideon stepped up behind me. "Hold the bow in your left hand. Raise it up—yes, just like that. Keep your left arm straight."

I copied the stance I'd seen Gideon use. The bow was surprisingly comfortable.

Gideon handed me an arrow and showed me how to nock it. He placed my fingers on the end of the arrow, one above and two below. "Now pull the string back nice and tight." He guided my hand back until it reached my cheek. "Shoulders relaxed. Deep breath. And—release."

I let the string slip between my fingers. The arrow whizzed through the air.

Thwump.

The arrow struck home on the upper right side of the target, vibrating with the impact.

My chest warmed with pride, and I looked up to see Gideon grinning at me. All traces of seriousness were gone, as if our conversation had never happened. "Well done, darlin'," he said. "You're a natural."

I fought my answering grin and failed. "Thanks."

Gideon took the bow from me and quickly nocked an arrow. Before I could blink, he let it fly. Even from this distance, I could tell his aim was off and he would miss his group. But with a light stomp of his left foot, the ground rumbled and the log rolled to the left.

Thwump.

His arrow hit the middle of the target, right in the center of his group.

"That's cheating," I said. "Is that why you're such a good shot?"

Gideon winked. "It's not cheating, love. It's using all the tools at my disposal. First rule of battle; there is no such thing as cheating."

He tried to pat me on the head, but I dodged his hand.

His smile didn't falter. "If you practice for a few days, you should be able to hit a target at close range. It won't be much, but at least you'll have a weapon you can use."

I eyed him. "Are you offering to coach me?"

"I wouldn't go that far." Gideon strode toward the log to retrieve his arrows. "But if I happen to be here every morning between now and the equinox, I suppose I could teach you some tricks."

I grabbed the bow from him and extended my other hand for an arrow. "Show me again."

The day before the summer equinox, I sat with Shadow in the garden and tried to meditate for the millionth time. Aki was off somewhere preparing for tomorrow, so Shadow had volunteered to teach my "lesson."

I shifted uncomfortably on the mat, eyes closed, and finally growled, "It's not working."

"This isn't a skill to be developed overnight," Shadow answered dryly.

I opened my eyes and glared at him. "Or at all, apparently."

Shadow's lips twitched. "It takes time and practice."

"You've told me that a million times. How am I supposed to practice if I can't even draw on anything to do it?" I pushed to my feet. "This is stupid. Clearly I'm not meant to do this."

"Seraphine doesn't make mistakes. You're simply impatient."

"Yeah, well, we're literally marching into battle tomorrow morning and my biggest weapon doesn't work. Excuse me if I'm a little frustrated about it."

"For many, it takes years of practice to strengthen their bond and harness their magick. Even if you could access it now, it wouldn't help you tomorrow." Shadow stood and extended a hand. "Come on; let me show you something."

I shouldn't cross that line, but what could it hurt? I was leaving tomorrow; I'd never see Shadow or Thios again, and I was sick and tired of denying myself the things I wanted. If I wanted to hold a dude's hand, I was going to do it.

I placed my hand in his, and a thrill went through me as our fingers intertwined. It was warm and strong and dang if it didn't set off a million butterflies in my stomach.

Sheesh, I was acting like a lovesick puppy.

Wait—who said anything about love?

Shadow led me out of the garden, oblivious to the meltdown happening in my head. We emerged onto the main road and converged in the traffic of heavy carts laden with food and Fae heading toward the Great Tree. Instead of following the flow of traffic, though, Shadow turned off the main road and led the way down an alleyway.

"Where are we going?" I asked, shoving all my unproductive thoughts into a box and sealing it tight. I hadn't been this way before. Most of Mina's tasks involved staying on the main road, in the market, or near the Great Tree. I'd been so busy getting ready for the equinox that I hadn't taken much time to explore the surrounding area beyond that, aside from my morning archery lessons with Gideon.

"Just wait," Shadow said lightly.

It grew quiet as we moved further from the main road. The only sounds were our quiet footfalls and the rustling of leaves in the giant tree canopy above us. I tried to ignore the way Shadow's warm, strong hand clasped mine and the way my body wanted to respond. His dark shirt moved across the muscles in his back as he walked, and pockets of sunlight illuminated the blue tones in his black hair.

Okay, so the Fae was gorgeous. Whatever. I had to stop these thoughts before they went any further.

We walked for what felt like ages before Shadow finally slowed his steps and pulled me off the path and behind a tree root the size of a school bus. I opened my mouth to ask more questions, but he held a finger to his lips. I narrowed my eyes—he may be cute, but even cute couldn't give me orders—but I obeyed.

The sound of voices drifted to us as we circled around the tree root. Shadow stopped and leaned back, gesturing for me to look.

In the clearing beyond, a large crowd of Fae gathered. I recognized Warred's thick frame—I knew he was part of the rebellion!—and a few others I had seen around the market and during outings with Mina and the others. I'd known Aki had more followers than just Mina, Shadow, and Gideon, but it was another thing to see them gathered in one place.

Aki stood in the center of the group, addressing the Fae in a voice barely loud enough to reach us. I strained to hear his words.

"My friends, you are here because you understand the threat Thios is facing. The queen has taken away your rights for far too long, and she must be stopped. It is time to make a stand against her and fight for equality—for yourselves and for your friends and families."

The group rustled, their quiet murmurs of agreement filling the air.

"Tomorrow is the summer equinox, and the gates to the human realm will be opened. Asmodeus has controlled the gate in the forest for years now, cutting off trade with the human world. Without that trade, Thios has been reliant upon the Reyans to provide commerce and keep our market running. We have secured weapons from the queen's private armory, and we must use them to take control of the gate. This is a dangerous task, but it is the spark we need to ignite a flame and claim independence from Reya once and for all."

A quiet cheer erupted from the crowd.

Shadow tapped my shoulder and nodded for me to follow him. We snuck away from the group and back into the forest.

"These are the Fae who will help us tomorrow," Shadow said. "You don't need to worry about harnessing your Gift right now. We have all the strength we need to take the gate."

It was a straight-up army. A small one, but an army nevertheless.

But something bothered me. "I thought Aki's primary goal in taking the gate was to find Asmodeus. Why didn't he mention anything about that just now?"

"Aki is a strategist above all else," Shadow said, pulling aside a branch so I could pass. "Right now, Thios's major concern is Reya. Asmodeus is a distant threat in their minds, so they wouldn't be motivated to help if he focused on that."

"It feels a little shady to lead them astray like that."

Shadow shrugged. "Aki wants to help them with the queen too. It's just not his primary goal."

I let that slide as we emerged back into the crowded heart of Thios. Despite my misgivings about Aki's speech, hope sparked in my chest. With this many Fae helping, maybe we could do it—take the gate. Maybe I would see Mary Beth again. It had been my goal since I arrived here, but part of me hadn't dared to believe it could actually happen.

Now we were here, mere hours away from my ticket home, and we had a small army behind us. It was against my nature to believe that good things could happen to me, but I wanted so badly for it to be true. If there was ever a time to push my inhibitions aside, it was now.

So I let that spark of hope simmer in my chest, and I chose to believe it.

CHAPTER TWENTY-ONE

The night before our attack on the gate, we went to a party.

It wasn't the way I would've preferred to spend the evening, but Mina had insisted. It was the summer festival, a huge celebration that happened once a year at the Great Tree. According to her, there was food, music, dancing, and live entertainment. The Thiosians drank and danced and partied the night away. It sounded like a good time, except that we were supposed to go to war the following morning.

"Oh, stop brooding," Mina said when I expressed my doubt about the wisdom of attending the party. "We have made the preparations. There's nothing more we can do tonight, so we should celebrate."

How could I argue with that? So I put on the pretty sage green dress that Mina provided and met the group downstairs.

The entire crew was there. Aki looked serious as ever, sporting his signature old-fashioned suit and white gloves. Mina was gorgeous in a bright yellow dress, her silver hair falling in silky waves down her back. Gideon leaned against the wall by the door, an amber bottle already in his hand. And Shadow sat in a chair by the fireplace, dressed in all black.

"You look beautiful," Mina said with a grin, grabbing both of my hands. "This will be so much fun."

Gideon saluted me with his bottle and took a long swig. "Let's do this."

Mina wrinkled her nose. "Are you drunk already, Gideon?"

"Always."

With a frown, Mina grabbed a hunk of bread off the counter and tossed it to him. "Eat that and sober up." Then she linked her elbow with mine and tugged me toward the door. "Come on. Let's go!"

The pavilion in front of the Great Tree was the most crowded I'd ever seen it. Small balls of flame flickered in the air above like a hundred tiny string lights, no doubt summoned by one of the Fae in attendance, and Fae of all shapes and sizes were packed into every open space. Loud music filled the air, barely audible over the buzz of conversation and drunken laughter. There were no protesters this time, luckily, and everyone seemed to enjoy themselves. Delicious smells came from food stands to the right, and the area in front of the Great Tree had been cleared for dancing. Fae shouted and laughed, moving their bodies to the beat of the music.

It was magic.

I glanced at Mina and returned her grin. "This is cool."

"Told you." Mina extricated her arm from mine and pranced toward where Aki was already disappearing into the crowd. "Aki, don't be a stick in the mud. Come dance with me!"

Gideon watched her go, rubbing one hand over his beard. There was something in his expression that was far more serious than the Gideon I'd come to know in the past few weeks.

"What's the matter?" I asked, leaning over to peer into his face. "Don't be shy; ask the girl to dance."

Gideon grumbled something that sounded like, "Where's the booze?" and staggered toward the food stands.

Before I could ponder on his strange behavior, someone tugged on the back of my dress. I looked around and down to see Kiera grinning up at me, Saoirse right behind her. She wore a dark blue dress, her usually tangled hair nicely combed. She looked adorable.

Kiera did a little spin, giggling as her dress flared around her. "Look, Everly! Mina got us some dresses for the festival. What do you think?"

"You look like a princess," I said, grinning. "You look beautiful too, Saoirse."

Saoirse didn't smile, but her cheeks turned a pretty shade of pink. She grabbed Kiera's hand and towed her away. "Come on; let's get some food for the others."

Kiera waved over her shoulder as they went, practically skipping after her friend.

I was left standing alone with Shadow. For some reason, I didn't want to meet his eyes. So I clasped my hands in front of me and watched the Fae merriment. It was weird to see the Thiosians acting so carefree. They were usually so serious and hardworking; it was strange to see them so relaxed. The happiness in the air was contagious, and I glanced at Shadow.

He was watching me with that smile. Then he extended a hand. "Care to dance?"

"I don't dance," I said.

But this was more than an offer to dance. His golden eyes held the promise of something more, something deeper than the conversations and brief touches we'd shared so far, and I wanted so badly to accept it. Even though I was leaving tomorrow. Even though I was beyond broken, and nightmares kept me up at night. Even though he was Fae and I was human.

To hell with it. To hell with it all.

I put my hand in his, embracing the electricity that zinged through me when we touched. "But I guess I'll make an exception."

Shadow led me to the dance floor. Before I could attempt to move in something resembling a dance, he swept me into his arms. One hand held mine and the other went around my back, pulling me flush to his body. The thought crossed my mind to knee him in the groin for being handsy, but I was too busy swooning like a halfwit. He spun me in a dizzying circle and we joined the dancing throng.

So this was dancing. I'd never done it before, aside from occasionally shaking my behind at Peter when I beat him to a gig.

Dancing was...nice. Shadow's arms were warm and strong, and he swept me around the dance floor as if he was born to do it. We were one being, a tangle of arms and legs moving in perfect sync. My breath—my very heartbeat—matched his. Everything else fell away. I didn't hear the surrounding chatter, or the music, or even my own thoughts. There was just me and Shadow and our eyes locked together in a silent conversation that neither of us understood. Our faces were inches apart, and it seemed only natural for me to close the gap. For our lips to meet, to meld together so we could truly become one.

My lips curved into a grin. We were a breath away from the most magical kiss in either realm, and if there was ever a time in my life that I felt happy, this was it.

Then the world went to hell.

CHAPTER TWENTY-TWO

Laughter turned to screams.

I didn't hear it at first—I was too busy making googly eyes at Shadow—and didn't notice anything was wrong until a large Fae man shoved between us.

Sound flooded back into my awareness. The music had stopped. Screams flooded the air, and somewhere I heard shouting and the clang of weapons.

"Reyan Guard!" someone screamed.

Shadow grabbed my hand, but I was yanked away from him in the crowd. On the other side of the pavilion, a red-orange explosion sent everyone scurrying to safety. The beautiful flickering lights above us went out. Fae shoved at me in their haste to escape. I couldn't see Shadow or Mina or anyone else in our crew. I could barely stay on my feet, but if I fell, I knew I would be trampled to death.

I started shoving Fae back, using my elbows to create a bubble of safety.

Another explosion sounded behind me. This one was close enough that the shock wave sent me and everyone around me to the ground. Ears ringing, I tried to stagger to my feet, but a heavy Fae man—the one who had shoved between Shadow and me earlier—

had fallen on me. Was he unconscious? Dead? I yanked hard, but I couldn't bend my knees to get any leverage. He had me pinned.

"No, no, no," I muttered, scrabbling against the stone ground with my fingers. If another explosion went off, I wouldn't be able to escape.

Fae ran around me, jumped over me, and nobody gave me a second glance. On the other side of the pavilion, the Reyan Guard had converged on the area. They were using a combination of weapons and magick to attack the unsuspecting Thiosians. Fae fell to the guards' swords, bows, and magick blasts. Terrified screams rent the air. Smoke filled my lungs, choking me, and the smell of burning flesh filled my nose.

As I watched, a gust of wind knocked a few guards off their feet. I followed the direction it had come from and saw Aki approaching the intruders. His long coat flapped behind him and his expression was thunderous as he lifted a hand, creating a tornado that threw the guards back a few more paces. Beside him, Gideon staggered forward. The earth shook under the guards' feet, and then with a loud crash, a section of stone separated from the ground and launched a guard into the air like a catapult.

The guards responded in kind. One held up a hand and an orb of water appeared in his palm. The water split into a bunch of droplets and the guard launched them at Aki and Gideon like bullets from a machine gun. Aki blocked them with a wall of wind and Gideon launched a large rock at the guard's head. He dove to the side and it missed.

I yanked hard again, trying to break free from the heavy Fae's body. Nothing. I screwed my eyes shut.

If there was ever a time for me to figure out my magick, this was it. Some fire power would be helpful right about now.

... Nothing.

What use was this power if I couldn't even use it to help my friends?

In the midst of the Fae scrambling to escape, a black shape caught my eye. It was going the opposite direction of everyone else; coming toward me instead of running away. I focused on it, trying to distinguish what it was through the mass of fleeing bodies.

A large black wolf dodged through the crowd, its golden eyes focused on me.

Shadow.

I would've sobbed in relief if I wasn't so annoyed that I had to be rescued.

He reached me and without a word—not that wolves could talk anyway—he moved to the Fae man on top of me and shoved his nose underneath him. With our combined effort, we shoved the Fae off so I could scramble out from underneath him. Another explosion rocked the ground, but it was on the other side of the pavilion, opposite from me. I stood behind Shadow, using him as a buffer against the crowd so I wouldn't be knocked flat again, and looked for Aki and Gideon.

They stood side by side, twin expressions of fury on their faces as they faced what had to be the entire Reyan Guard. They moved together, one defending while the other attacked, protecting each other and the fleeing crowd from the guards' magick. Where was Mina? Kiera? Saoirse? Were they alive? Had they been injured in any of the explosions?

I took a step forward. Why weren't any of the fleeing Fae turning around to fight? Aki and Gideon couldn't defeat the entire Reyan Guard by themselves. Someone had to help them.

Something yanked at the fabric of my dress, and I looked down. Shadow had the gauzy green fabric in his teeth, and his canine eyes burned into mine. I got the message, even though he hadn't spoken a word: You can't help them.

But I wanted to. Oh, how I wanted to.

If only I had brought some of Mina's grenades, or a bow. If only my stupid magick would work.

If only...

"Everly!"

I snapped my head around at the pleading voice. It was impossible to see anything through the smoke and dust and the chaos of fleeing Fae, but I would recognize that voice anywhere. "Kiera," I screamed. "Kiera, where are you?"

"Help me!"

I dodged around a tall, thin female Fae who staggered past covered in dark purple blood. Then I saw her, huddled next to an overturned barrel. It must have been filled with mead at some point, because the muddy ground around it smelled like fruit and alcohol. Her dress was torn and she was covered in mud, her hands over her ears. I sprinted across the distance, ignoring everything around me. "Kiera!"

Just as I reached her, a dark figure rose behind the barrel. His armor was dented and dirty, and his twin curved horns intensified the snarl on his face. He raised a single hand, and a sword glinted dangerously in the evening light.

"No," I yelled.

A canine form whizzed past me and leaped at the guard. They both rolled out of sight behind the barrel.

I dropped to my knees next to Kiera and hauled her into my arms. Her tiny body shook, rattling my bones, but she was warm and she was alive.

She was also really heavy for such a small creature.

I dragged her away from the barrel and toward safety. The explosions had settled now, but I could hear the battle raging between Aki and Gideon and the Reyan Guard. I had to get Kiera out of here before another straggler decided we'd be an easy target.

Kiera buried her head in my neck, sobbing. Before I could ask her what had happened or where Saoirse was, a yip announced Shadow's arrival. He didn't look any worse for wear after tussling with the guard who'd tried to attack Kiera. He trotted to my side, ears twitching, and nipped at my hand.

I don't know why I understood what he wanted, but I did. I pried Kiera from my neck and placed her on his back.

Questions would have to wait. As much as I wanted to help Aki and Gideon, I had to acknowledge that I wouldn't be useful in this fight. The best thing I could do was keep Kiera safe, and that meant doing something that chafed my pride almost more than I could handle.

I had to run. Away from the danger and away from my friends who were fighting for their lives.

Gritting my teeth, I grasped Shadow's scruff and allowed him to lead me into the fleeing Fae crowd.

The other shoe had finally dropped, just as I'd known it would.

Hours later, after the Reyan Guard finally retreated to whatever hole—or skyward palace—they'd crawled out of, I stood in what remained of the pavilion. It was nothing more than a battle-scarred field now. Deep crevices and craters marred the once-cobblestone ground, evidence of Gideon and other earth users' magick, and much of the greenery had been burned in fire resulting from the explosions. The tables, chairs, and decorations from the summer festival had been burned or blown away during the fight, leaving behind nothing but a reminder of the queen's iron fist.

Mina and Saoirse had escaped the attack unscathed, but dozens of others hadn't been so lucky.

Dozens.

I followed Mina as she flitted around the pavilion, organizing volunteers and creating a system to help the dead and wounded. The Thiosians seemed grateful for her help, but I felt every gash, broken bone, and miserable expression as if it were my own. Guilt made my feet leaden, and I could barely lift them as I trudged around the scarred ground, fetching water and supplies so Mina could attend to the wounded.

This was our fault.

We had stolen from the queen's armory, and this was her response. She had attacked her own people and killed dozens during what was supposed to be a celebratory evening. She'd known most of Thios would be gathered here tonight. Aki had inspired the Thiosians to dream of a better life than the one they'd been handed, and this had been the result.

"Everly."

I shook off my miserable thoughts and blinked at Mina. "Sorry. What?"

She gave me a sympathetic look. She looked as tired and defeated as I felt, her dress dirty and torn, but she put on a good show for the others. "Will you fetch Gideon? We need his help to repair the ground. I think he's at Senan's house with Aki."

"Yeah... sure." I trudged away from her.

Fae bustled about, but the area was eerily quiet besides indistinct murmurs and the wails of Thiosians who had lost loved ones in the attack. Chills swept across my skin as I passed a female Fae clutching a single small shoe, silent tears running down her violet cheeks. A little while later, a male Fae stared blankly at what remained of a shop on the edge of the pavilion.

It was Warred, the jewelry maker that Mina often stopped to talk to. He glanced up as I passed, but he didn't appear to recognize me.

I stopped. "Warred?"

He blinked at me. "Oh, Everly. I didn't see you."

"Was this... your shop?"

"It was." He looked back at the smoldering pile of wood, his mouth twisting into a grimace. "My main one, anyway. Took me a lifetime to save up for it."

I swallowed hard. "I'm so sorry. Is your son safe?"

"He is." Warred clenched his fists. "But who knows if he will remain that way. Without my shop, I'm ruined."

"I'm so sorry." I wanted to say more, to ask if he still planned on helping us tomorrow, but the words wouldn't come. After everything that had happened tonight, it seemed insensitive for me to worry about something as simple as going home. Taking back the gate had a greater purpose than my return, but was that purpose truly more important than the Thiosians' lives? More important than Warred's livelihood? Than a female Fae's child?

Judging by the defeated expressions in the eyes of every Thiosian I passed, the queen had already won. Her attack had destroyed more than the pavilion. More than the Thiosians' will to fight.

It might have destroyed Aki's entire rebellion—and maybe my return home, too.

I placed a hand on Warred's shoulder and pushed on toward Senan's house, which lay just outside the pavilion. Unlike many others, it had been spared during the attack. Was that because the queen still thought Senan was loyal to her?

The door swung open at my brief knock and a dark-skinned Fae ushered me inside. I found Aki, Gideon, Shadow, and Senan in a dim study lit by a small fireplace. Senan sat in a high-backed chair in front of the fire, his wrinkled face grave, and Aki sat in a chair across from him. Gideon bent over a desk by the small window. He'd been worst off after the fight, with a wicked gash across his forehead and a slight limp from a lucky shot to his knee—or so he told me.

Shadow stood in a corner, arms folded over his muscular chest. I met his eyes when I walked in, and he inclined his head to me.

Somehow he didn't have a scratch on him after the fight. I hadn't thanked him for saving my life, and I wasn't sure I could find the words if I tried. Our almost-kiss felt like a lifetime ago. I wished I could go back to that moment, to that optimistic, lighthearted version of myself.

"Everly," Aki said. "Did you need something?"

"Yeah. Sorry to interrupt." I glanced at Gideon. "Mina said she needs you to help fix the ground in the pavilion."

Gideon straightened with a wince. "Her wish is my command."

"Are the wounded receiving treatment?" Aki asked.

I nodded. "Mina has everything set up. She's helping with the... dead, too."

"Seraphine help us," Senan muttered.

"Dozens dead," Shadow said from the corner. "The queen is as ruthless as Asmodeus."

Aki steepled his white-gloved hands in his lap. The fireplace sent shadows dancing across his ivory mask. "We cannot allow her to remain unpunished for this attack."

"What are you going to do?" I was afraid to ask. I knew what his answer might be.

"We continue as planned. Tomorrow, we take the gate. We will capture Bria and then move on to Asmodeus. And after we neutralize Asmodeus..." Aki's eyes turned steely. "I will remove Elyra from her seat of power."

I swallowed hard, watching as everyone reeled from Aki's pronouncement. From the things I'd heard and seen since arriving in Thios, I knew Aki's rebels had been moving in that direction, but such an open pronouncement was dangerous. I was sickened and angry that the queen had treated her people this way, that the Thiosians lived in constant fear of another attack, but... Aki was talking about a revolution. Overturning a seat of power that had ruled for generations. If human history was any indication, the outcome would be bloody. Apparently Asmodeus had tried that already during the Schism, and look what had happened to him. Most of Aki's crew—and many Thiosians—probably wouldn't make it out alive.

Part of me was glad I was going home tomorrow and wouldn't be around to witness it.

But another part of me... another part of me wanted to give in to the burning rage in the pit of my stomach. To fight the injustice that the Thiosians had suffered and do my part to make it right.

Faery wasn't my world. The Thiosians weren't my people. But...

I wanted to fight with my new friends.

CHAPTER TWENTY-THREE

I didn't sleep that night.

Instead, I lay in bed and stared at the ceiling. It was my final night in Aki's home. Tomorrow, I would return to Seattle and Mary Beth. I would go back to riding my bike and taunting Peter and trying to keep Mary Beth away from the drug trade. I would sleep in my crappy bed with a hundred other crappy beds nearby and dodge the Hammond House employees until they kicked me out.

I inhaled the woodsy scent in the air, savored the soft sheets underneath me and the clean clothes I wore.

If only I could bring Mary Beth here. She would love Thios and the simple life the Fae made here. She and Mina would hit it off immediately and Mina would teach her to love coffee more than she loved drugs. I would help Aki with his revolution and maybe let down my walls enough to let Shadow sneak in. I would adopt the homeless Fae children and spend all my time with them and Mina and Mary Beth.

It sounded like a dream, and it was.

I could never bring Mary Beth here. Humans weren't allowed, and even if they were, Thios was about to become one giant bloodbath. It already had, after the queen's attack tonight, and it would only get worse.

Besides, trouble followed me everywhere I went—always had—and at least in Seattle, I knew what the trouble looked like and how to fight it. Here, I was completely out of my element. I couldn't use my Gift to defend myself and weapons weren't allowed. The queen had started a war tonight, Asmodeus was a threat looming in the distance, and Aki was bound and determined to somehow defeat both of them, no matter who died in the process. This place was a death trap.

I sighed and rolled over, watching as the sky slowly lightened through the window.

I just had to get through today. We would storm the gate with our small army, Aki would capture Bria, and I would go home. Back to what I knew. Back to where it was relatively safe. Back to Mary Beth.

Mary Beth needed me. She was the closest thing to family I had left. I couldn't get myself involved in a war in some other world and risk my chance of getting back to her. Aki could take care of Thios. It was my responsibility to take care of Mary Beth. I was the only one who could.

When Mina poked her head in the door to wake me up, I was sitting on the bed, fully clothed and ready to go.

She smiled kindly. "You couldn't sleep either?"

I shook my head. "I'm ready to get this over with."

"Me too. Everyone is downstairs."

I followed her out the door and down the spiral staircase. It was still mostly dark outside, but the main floor of Aki's home was bustling. Kiera and Saoirse stood at the counter, sorting grenades and packing them into crates that we would take with us. Aki and Shadow bent over a map on the table, discussing something in low tones. Gideon stuffed the pockets of his duster full of bread and cheese, preparing for the magick he would use in the battle ahead. A white bandage had been wrapped around the gash on his forehead —Mina's work, no doubt—and it was bright against his ruddy skin.

I snagged a croissant from the plate on the counter and ruffled Kiera's hair as I passed, heart tugging. This would be the last time I saw her. She looked up at me, her tiny face still dirty and haunted from the attack last night, and I almost choked. Would she and the others be okay after I left?

This situation royally sucked. Thios and Seattle waged a battle in my heart, pulling me in two directions until I was sure I would tear in half. I should have never allowed myself to grow close to anyone here. Then maybe I wouldn't feel like I was screwed whether I stayed or went.

Shadow's golden eyes met mine, slamming the dagger in further and giving it a twist for good measure. "You doing okay?"

"Fabulous." I gave him a wan smile. "Ready to get this over with."

Aki rolled up the map on the table and handed it to Mina, who placed it on the bookshelf. "The group will gather in the forest in twenty minutes, and then we will travel to the gate. Everly, you'll stay with Shadow while Gideon and I head the main attack. Once their defense is broken, you will slip inside so you can go through the gate. We'll capture Bria."

"Am I really supposed to stay back while all the fighting is happening?"

Aki gave me a level look. "You can't access your magick yet, and your archery skills are too new to be relied on. It will be safer for everyone if you stay back with Shadow until it's safe to go through the gate. You can provide support with your bow if necessary."

"Fine." As much as I hated the idea, I could hardly fault his logic.

Aki nodded once, satisfied with my disgruntled answer. "Let's go."

Mina opened the front door, and the male Fae filed through.

I paused, meeting her dark blue eyes. A million thoughts flitted through my head, a million things I wanted to say, but all I could get out was, "Thanks for everything."

Mina smiled, eyes bright. She pulled me into a tight hug. "Good luck," she whispered. "You'll always have a home here if you need it."

I squeezed her, swallowing hard past the sudden lump in my throat. I wasn't a crier and I wouldn't start now, so I bit the inside of my lip until it bled. When I pulled away from Mina, my eyes were dry. Then I hugged Kiera and even Saoirse. "I'll see you guys later."

My heart twisted as I left Aki's house for the last time and followed Aki, Gideon, and Shadow into the early dawn light.

It was a silent walk to the clearing where we were supposed to meet Aki's small Thiosian army. I followed closely behind Shadow, watching his strong back as he strode down the path. He, Aki, and Gideon wore all black. Aki even wore black gloves today instead of his usual white ones.

When we arrived, the clearing was empty.

I stopped short, meeting Shadow's eyes as he looked over his shoulder at me. He didn't look concerned at the lack of army waiting for us, but when I glanced past him, I caught the way Gideon's fingers tightened on the bow he carried in his left hand. The way he glanced up at Aki, quickly smoothing his expression into amusement when he said, "Do you suppose they overslept?"

Aki didn't answer; just strode into the middle of the clearing, his eyes slowly searching the trees and underbrush surrounding us.

I moved closer to Shadow, silently cursing the ball of lead sitting heavy in my gut. I knew this feeling; it was the one I always got before the proverbial other shoe dropped. I had felt it the morning I found my mom dead in her bedsheets, when I'd seen the aftermath of last night's attack, and when I had gone after Peter into that warehouse.

"They're not coming, are they?" I whispered to Shadow.

"No," Aki answered for him. His back was to us. "They are not."

"Well, hell," Gideon said. He limped to Aki's side. "The Reyan Guard scared everyone off."

"It appears so." Aki turned, clasping his gloved hands behind his back.

"So what now?" I looked between the two of them. "We should talk to Senan. Maybe he could—"

"I doubt Senan has the power to help us," Shadow said quietly. "Last night's attack was a warning. Many Thiosians lost their shops. Their homes. Their loved ones. It will take years for them to recover, even if we take the gate and open trade with the human world again."

"And there's no guarantee the queen won't send the Guard to finish the job a day, a week, or even a month from now." Aki looked to Gideon. "Our attack will have to wait until the next equinox. We will use the time to build alliances and properly train an attack force. In six months' time, we will easily take the gate."

"Six months?" I echoed. "You're kidding. Tell me you're kidding."

Aki met my eyes. "I am not."

The ground rolled beneath my feet, and a quick glance at Gideon proved he wasn't responsible.

Six months. Six months. Six months. The words echoed with the beat of my heart.

What would happen to Mary Beth in six months? A few weeks was one thing; six months was impossible. She would fall back into her old habits without me there to keep her out of the gutter or the hands of her old "friends." By the time I got back, she'd be in too deep for me to save her. She'd end up like my mom, dead, without a soul to mourn her, and I'd have to add her name to the list of people I couldn't save.

"Everly." Shadow rested a warm, heavy hand on my shoulder. "I know you're upset…"

"Upset?" I shrugged him off. "No. I'm not upset. I am furious." I glared at Aki. "You promised to get me home—not six months from now—but now."

"We can hardly attack the gate with just the three of us, darlin'," Gideon said. "We don't have much of a choice."

"That's bull and you know it. You three are the most powerful Fae in Thios. If anyone can do it, you can."

Aki's dark eyes bored into mine. "Our goal is to defeat Asmodeus and remove Elyra from her seat of power. I will not compromise it by attacking the gate without proper preparation."

"Right. Your goal." I clenched my jaw so hard that my teeth ached. Of course his goal mattered more than his promise to me. Why was I even surprised? I'd always lived by the rule to look out for myself first. Why should I expect anyone else to live differently? "Well, thanks for nothing."

"Where are you going?" Gideon asked as I stalked away from them.

"Home." I picked up my pace. "And don't even think about following me. I'm so pissed right now, I'm liable to deck you, magick or not."

Aki said nothing as I disappeared into the forest. Typical.

I stomped through the underbrush. Why was I so angry? Nothing had ever come easy to me; I'd known from the beginning that getting home wouldn't be as easy as it sounded. Aki and his crew may be able to put off their goals for six months, but I couldn't. Mary Beth probably didn't have that long. I'd wasted enough time here already.

I didn't notice I had a tail until Shadow stepped in front of me, blocking my path with his slim form. I drew up short, and my traitorous eyes stung as my gaze collided with his. He looked... sympathetic, and that ticked me off.

"I said not to follow me." My voice held far less venom than it should have.

The corner of his lips tugged up. "Since when do I take orders from you?"

"I'm not in the mood for your jokes right now, wolf boy." I tried to push past him.

He held firm. "Everly, wait. Where do you think you're going?"

"I told you. I'm going home."

"You realize how ridiculous that sounds. You can't fight your way through the portal by yourself."

"Watch me."

Shadow did. His golden eyes peered into mine, and damn if my heart didn't tug a little. Or a lot. My dumb brain went back to that almost-kiss, to that heartbeat in time where my life hadn't been royally screwed up, where the future had been full of possibilities. For the millionth time, I wished I had slammed our lips together before the queen had ruined everything.

But now... now, it didn't matter. Aki had proven that I wasn't one of his precious crew members; maybe I never had been. He didn't care about the promise he made or the fact that I had Mary Beth waiting for me back at home. And Shadow... Shadow was one of Aki's most loyal crew mates. He would never go against Aki's wishes and jeopardize everything they had spent the last however many years working for. Maybe if we'd had more time... Maybe if I wasn't human and he wasn't Fae...

If I had a penny for how many times I'd wished for my life to be different, I'd be a billionaire by now. But I was also a pragmatist, and wishing my life away wasn't my style.

So I squared my shoulders and said, "I have to get home, Shadow. Today. Please don't stop me."

Whatever he saw in my face must've convinced him, because he just nodded. "Be careful. Bria is dangerous. Do whatever you can to avoid a fight."

"I can honestly say that, for the first time in my life, I'm not itching for a fight," I said dryly. Then I cleared my throat. "But... I'll be careful. Thanks."

Shadow looked like he might say more, but then he just nodded again and lifted a hand in farewell before disappearing into the forest.

I watched him go for far longer than I should have.

CHAPTER TWENTY-FOUR

Bravado aside, I had no idea how to get home without Aki's help.

I wandered the forest, shuffling past farmland and over the bridge leading to the outskirts of Thios. Bria and her lackeys would guard the cave with their magick, no doubt expecting some kind of attack, but maybe... maybe I could get past them. Maybe I could sneak in like I had in the warehouse.

Okay, last time I'd gotten caught and dragged through a portal to another world. That probably wasn't the best plan.

Shadow had told me to be careful, but what did that mean exactly? How was I supposed to get past them without fighting? Bria and her goons had magick. My magick was still nonexistent, and I'd be more successful hitting them in the head with my bow than shooting them with an arrow.

I blew out a breath and tipped my head back as I walked, staring at the tree canopy far above. Fluffy white clouds drifted by, briefly obscuring the giant leaves and branches rustling in the breeze. I focused on the sound, allowing my mind to go blank as my feet moved of their own accord.

I'd never been the praying type, but I found myself thinking about Seraphine. She was an all-powerful goddess who could bestow anyone with the Gift of magick—not that it had done me any good —and she believed in balance and peace and all that. Well, Faery certainly wasn't peaceful right now. Queen Elyra was playing the evil dictator and Asmodeus was being all creepy in the distance, slowly starving the economy and inciting conflict between Thios and Reya.

I stopped walking, and my shoulders slumped. What was I doing? No way was I getting past Bria without getting myself killed or captured. I was a human, for Pete's sake. I couldn't fight my way past a bunch of evil Fae with no plan and no backup. I was prone to trouble, but I wasn't stupid. Unless...

I glanced back up at the sky and swallowed hard. "Hey, uh, Seraphine? If you're up there, or... wherever you live... could you help me out here? I shouldn't be here, and I think we both know it. But I can't get back without some help, and Aki... well, he's not feeling very helpful at the moment."

Nothing but forest sounds greeted me.

"I've never asked for heavenly help," I ventured further. "But you gave me this tattoo, so I think maybe you'll at least listen to me. If you're there... just give me a sign or something. Please. I need your help."

Nothing happened.

I waited for what felt like an eternity, and then I scoffed and started walking again. What a waste of time. Heavenly beings had never helped me before. If God—or Seraphine or whatever—were real, where had they been? Why had they let my dad run off and my mom drown her sorrow in drugs and alcohol? Why had they made me an orphan at thirteen years old?

No, I was on my own. Just like I always had been.

A soft snort sounded to my left, jerking me out of my thoughts. I stopped, the toes of my boots wet from the damp moss underfoot, and swung my head around to look for the source of the sound.

It was the white stag.

I stumbled back a step and slipped on the damp moss, falling hard on my butt. It looked just like I had seen it in my dream, and even earlier at the Great Tree. Tingles swept across my skin like I was standing next to an electric fence as it glowed faintly, illuminating the area in an ethereal white light.

Hello again, young one. The voice was feather-soft in my head, like a whispering breeze across my mind.

"You... you're real." I got to my feet slowly, half afraid that any sudden movements would make the creature disappear.

The stag lowered its head, its huge antlers swaying through the air. *As real as you are.*

"Did... Seraphine send you?"

The stag chuffed, its nostrils flaring. *The Great Mother hears all. I am here to help.*

I glanced over my shoulder. Could anyone else see this? Was I going crazy? I was talking to a magical stag. But then again, I was in a magical land that no one on earth knew about; nothing should surprise me anymore. "I won't say no to some assistance," I said finally.

Won't you? Accepting assistance seems difficult for you.

I blinked. The magical stag was psychoanalyzing me now? "I just want to get home."

You cannot do it alone.

"Yeah, I got that. That's why I... asked Seraphine. I don't suppose you have some magical powers that could clear out Bria's men for me?"

That is not my purpose here. The stag stepped forward, its hooves quiet on the mossy ground. *The one called Aki will assist you. It is his purpose.*

"He won't—"

You cannot do it alone.

"Yes, you said that already." I tried to keep my voice level. "If you... work for Seraphine, surely you know what's been going on here lately. I can't wait another six months for Aki to decide he's ready."

You need not. The stag reached me and lowered its head. I stared into one coal-black eye. *You shall take the gate. Today. Aki will assist you.*

"How?"

The creature touched its velvety soft nose to my forehead. My feet fell out from beneath me and then I was falling, falling, falling into darkness. I blinked once and found myself standing outside the cave where the gate was. Two male Fae guarded the cave's entrance, eyes alert as they scanned the area. One was big and burly, with curling black horns protruding from the side of its head, and the other was tall and thin and looked more like a snake than a Fae. Darkness yawned behind them, and I knew the gate was just inside. I was less than a hundred yards from it, but I couldn't move my body.

Wait—I didn't have a body. I was a floating ball of nothingness, observing the scene but not really there. It was just like the Rite.

You will take the gate today, the creature's voice said in my head. *Bria uses an unnatural Gift. It must be destroyed.*

I wanted to reply, but I didn't have a voice. So I thought my response instead. *What do you mean, unnatural?*

You must act. If you do not, it will mean the end of all in Thios.

That was heavy—heavier than me getting home. The creature was talking about end-of-the-world level stuff. The end of this world, anyway. *Aki won't attack today. He wants to wait until he can gather an army.*

There is no time to wait.

Before I could reply, the world went black again. I felt a whooshing sensation, and then I was back in my own body. I hadn't moved; my feet were still slightly damp, sunken in the mossy ground, and I still stood in front of the stag.

The stag eyed me, then turned and kneeled, baring its back to me. *We must make haste. Come.*

I cautiously grasped the creature's neck and swung onto its back. I wobbled when it stood but kept my seat.

Then the creature took off.

I bit back a screech and threw my arms around the stag's neck in a wild effort to stay on its back. It didn't slow at my obvious distress, and I scrabbled around until I found a semi-stable seat. My hair blew back from my face as the gigantic trees whizzed past us faster than humanly possible.

We reached Aki's house ridiculously fast. It was still early, and the streets of Thios were thankfully deserted. Surely the Forest Spirit would draw a crowd. The stag stopped and I slid off its back, breathing hard like I was the one who'd just run a dozen miles in a few minutes.

"Something tells me he won't miraculously change his mind, even if he sees you," I said.

He shall not see me. The burden is upon your shoulders now.

I blinked. "How am I supposed to—"

The stag touched its nose to my right hand, and my palm burst into flames.

I screamed and jumped back, shaking my hand as if I could dislodge them. They didn't go out. If anything, they burned brighter. I jerked my head up to scream at the stag for help—

The stag was gone. Of course it was. A quick look up and down the street proved it had vanished into thin air.

I bit out a curse and stumbled to the front door of Aki's house.

Aki and his crew sat at the table and all eyes swung to me as I burst inside, holding my hand as far away from my body as humanly possible.

"Everly?" Mina asked, eyes wide.

"Help, help, help!" I screamed.

Aki surged to his feet and crossed the room in two long strides. "What happened?"

"Is that—magick?" Gideon asked from the table. "Did I have too much whiskey?"

I brandished my hand at Aki. "Turn it off!"

Shadow was by my side in an instant. He placed a hand on the small of my back, and the warmth grounded me.

"It's your Gift," Aki said. He bent forward until he was eye-level with me. "You're the only one who can turn it off."

I looked frantically between him and my hand. "I don't know how."

"Deep breaths," Shadow said from beside me. "Just like we practiced."

I was closer to hyperventilating, but I tried to slow my breathing. Now that I wasn't in a fog of panic, I realized the fire didn't hurt. It was kind of... tingly. As my breathing calmed, the fire settled until it was a tiny flame in the palm of my hand, and then it went out completely.

"Good," Aki said. "That was... very good."

I glanced up. Was that surprise on his face?

He straightened, resuming his mask of indifference, and I looked past him to Gideon and Mina. Gideon looked like he'd seen a ghost, and Mina looked like I'd stolen her favorite cookie, though she quickly hid it behind a bright smile like she always did.

"Everly, what happened?" Shadow asked, drawing my attention back to his face. "Where have you been?"

"I was on my way to the gate, but I was... distracted."

Aki raised an eyebrow—the only one I could see. "Distracted by what?"

"The Forest Spirit."

The following silence was thick with awe, wonder, and disbelief.

"I'm serious," I added. "He found me in the forest, and he says we need to take the gate. Today. Bria is into some bad stuff and we need to stop her."

"Everly," Aki said flatly. "I will not be tricked into—"

"I told him you wouldn't believe me." I flounced past him and dropped into a chair at the table, ignoring Gideon's wide-eyed stare as I grabbed a roll from the basket in the center. It was pleasantly warm. A shudder went through me, and I realized I was cold. As if I'd spent the day outside in one of Seattle's December sleet storms. So this was magick's aftereffect. Air users grew winded, earth users grew hungry, water users were thirsty… and fire users grew cold.

Mina wordlessly handed me a steaming mug of coffee, and I smiled in gratitude as I took a sip. It warmed me from the inside.

"You… can speak to the Forest Spirit." Gideon's voice was full of skepticism.

I glared at Aki as he took the seat across from me. "Yes, I can. Or at least I did."

"None that I know have ever seen the Forest Spirit, let alone spoken to it," Aki said in a low voice. "Are you certain?"

"How many glowing white stags with pitch black eyes are wandering this forest? You know what, no. Don't answer that." I took another sip of coffee—it was heaven—and set it on the table as warmth slowly returned to my body. "I told him you wouldn't believe me, and then he touched my hand and that happened." I waved my now flame-less hand haphazardly around the table. "The stag said that if we don't stop Bria now, it will be the end of Thios."

Everyone stared at me in shock. I waited, expecting an outburst of questions, arguments, and exclamations.

Finally, Aki lowered his head and said, "The Forest Spirit only visits those that Seraphine deems worthy. If she sent it to you, then we must do her will."

Now it was my turn to stare in shock. My jaw could have hit the table.

Aki looked around, meeting the eyes of each of his crew members. "We take the gate. Today."

CHAPTER TWENTY-FIVE

It was surreal to walk out of Thios, across the bridge, through the farmland, and into the dense part of the forest. It had only been a few weeks since I'd traversed this distance following Aki on my first night here, but it felt like a lifetime ago. This time, Aki, Gideon, and Shadow accompanied me. Aki and Gideon walked a bit ahead. A smooth wooden bow and arrows bounced in the holster on Gideon's shoulder, even more pronounced with his limp. Aki stood ramrod straight, as usual, and walked casually with his hands clasped behind his back. He didn't bear a weapon—I doubted he needed one—and there was a new tension in his shoulders. After the attack last night and the Thiosians' refusal to help, and not to mention the Forest Spirit's dire warning, I had a feeling this battle meant more to him than ever before. He seemed determined to capture Bria, take the gate, defeat Asmodeus, and unseat the queen, makeshift army or not.

The forest was quiet as we made our way to the cave. I dimly registered the familiar surroundings as we walked; last time, I'd been so out-of-my-mind scared that I hadn't paid much attention as I'd followed Aki.

"Are you looking forward to going home?" Shadow murmured from beside me.

I glanced at him. Was he as conflicted as I was? Did he feel the same mixture of relief and sorrow at the idea of me returning home? "Yes and no," I admitted. "I have...things at home that I need to take care of. I won't miss the daily threats of death I get here, but I will miss these trees." I glanced up at the tree canopy far above. "And I'll miss Mina's cooking."

A ghost of a smile appeared on Shadow's face. "Just Mina's cooking?"

"If you're looking for a sappy goodbye, you won't get one from me." I bumped his shoulder with my own, ignoring the pang in my chest. "That's not how I roll."

"Big surprise." But he smiled down at me, and his eyes communicated far more than his words did. I flashed back to the summer festival, that moment before the queen ruined everything, and wished again that we could have had that kiss. I could have taken the memory home with me, and then maybe I wouldn't feel so empty right now.

I returned my attention to the path in front of us. Staying wasn't an option, and the moment for kissing had long since passed, so what was the point of dwelling on it?

We hadn't even reached the cave when the first pair of Fae thugs stepped out of the trees. I pulled out my bow, the smooth wood a familiar weight in my hands by now, and nocked an arrow, but it wasn't necessary. Gideon took one staggering step forward, and his bare feet sent a shock wave through the mossy earth that shot the enemy Fae into the air. Shadow was on them in a flash, his wolf form snarling and dragging them into the bushes. A moment later, Shadow trotted back out, ears perked for further signs of danger. He remained in wolf form as we continued our trek to the cave.

We met two more groups of Fae on the path. Shadow and Gideon dispatched them quickly while Aki and I stayed back. Aki was saving his strength for the real battle—Bria—and I sat with my bow at the ready, but I never had the chance to draw it.

I felt for the small satchel at my belt as we drew close to the cave. It held a pouch of Mina's sleep grenades. I was saving them for the main fight, as Aki had instructed. I had strapped a long dagger to my other hip in the event that I tangled hand-to-hand with a Fae thug, and my quiver was full on my back. On the long walk here, I'd tried to summon my fire magick again, but that familiar block was back. Whatever the stag had done to unlock it had faded, and I was back to my non-magical self.

"Almost there, darlin'," Gideon said, looking over his shoulder at me as he stuffed a block of cheese in his mouth. Mina had prepped him well. In his long duster, I couldn't tell if his tattoo had grown from all the fighting, but I suspected it had. He had barely touched his bow; he seemed content to use his feet to smash his way through our enemies. That was fine by me.

"Stay close to the trees," Aki instructed me. "Use your bow to provide cover. Gideon, Shadow and I will engage Bria."

"Yeah, yeah." I snickered at his unspoken command: Stay out of the way. We don't have time to protect you.

I would do as he asked, even though conforming to his rules went against every fiber of my being. I didn't have a death wish, especially now that I was so close to going home. At least I had the bow and the grenades to help from a distance.

We reached the clearing in front of the cave, and an army waited for us.

At least, an army compared to the three Fae and one human we had. At least ten Fae guarded the dark cave entrance, their vicious expressions matching their battle-ready stances. Our two sides stared at each other for a moment in silence. Was Aki waiting for some signal to attack these fools?

"I wondered when you would show," a sultry voice said from the darkness.

I squinted into the cave entrance, but I couldn't see Bria. I would recognize her voice anywhere, though; it was beautiful and creepy and it had haunted my nightmares since she'd sent me through the gate and into Faery.

A bright orange glow interrupted the blackness a split second before a ball of fire—literal fire—shot out of the cave. The sudden light blinded me, and I saw Aki disappear in a blur before Shadow tackled me around the waist in human form. We fell to the mossy ground and rolled away, his arms tight around me.

Heat blasted past us, and I could swear I smelled burning hair. The tree behind where we'd been standing burst into flames.

Shadow released me and rolled into a crouch. "Find shelter," he barked, then shifted back into wolf form and sprinted toward where Gideon was engaging the enemy Fae. With a powerful leap, he landed on the back of one that had been about to grab Gideon from behind and knocked him to the ground with a vicious snarl.

I scrambled to my feet as another Fae spotted me and approached. He was a hulking, fur-covered creature with horns spiraling from his head.

I recognized him. He was the one who had dragged Arthur into that alley.

It seemed like ages ago, but I'd never forget this monster.

What were Bria and Asmodeus doing with all the homeless people they had taken? I'd always thought they devoured them somehow, but now I knew better. Had they kidnapped them and brought them through the gate like Bria had tried to do to me?

I couldn't think about that right now.

I pulled an arrow from my quiver and readied my bow, backing up a step.

The Fae raised a staff. A gust of wind blew through the clearing, smacking me in the face and knocking me backward. I landed on my butt and rolled, coming up to my feet in a smooth motion. Somehow I managed to keep my bow in my hand.

Something in the air felt... wrong. I'd seen air magick used several times now, and it hadn't felt like this. The electricity—the magick—that crackled through the air felt evil and vile and dirty.

Now I understood what the Forest Spirit had said. This magick wasn't natural. Seraphine wouldn't have let these fools complete the Rite.

I hesitated, eyeing the Fae warily as Gideon shouted, "What is this? This isn't magick."

Over the Fae thug's shoulder, I saw Gideon dodge a huge rock thrown by the snake Fae I'd seen in the Forest Spirit's vision, but the Fae wasn't touching the ground with his hands. He didn't appear to be doing anything at all to wield the magick—or whatever it was. I had no idea who Gideon was talking to, but Shadow growled in response, leaping over a fallen Fae to tackle another one.

Bria and Aki had disappeared; they were probably fighting inside the cave.

I brought my attention back to the Fae in front of me. He smiled cruelly and waved the staff again. I dove to the side, avoiding another gust of wind, and shot an arrow at him. It swerved around him as if hitting a force field of air. As far as I knew, it wasn't possible to wield magick like this. Gideon was right; whatever this was, it wasn't magick.

We needed to finish these thugs quickly and get in there to help Aki. I had complete confidence in Aki's ability to fight, but we weren't fighting fire with fire. We were clearly fighting a new magick none of us had seen before, one that could be the "end of Thios."

I grabbed a sleep grenade from my pouch and turned the key, then tossed it at the Fae thug and backed up a few steps. Mina's gadget worked like a charm; the makeshift grenade exploded with a bright blue flash and a loud boom. The thug staggered back, blinking and shaking his head. He was so surprised that he didn't use his wind to push the grenade away from him. The excess gas knocked him out in three seconds flat.

I grinned. Oh, this was going to be fun.

Gideon and Shadow were still fighting with the rest of the Fae thugs. Nobody seemed to care about little ol' me, and I took full advantage. Slipping into the underbrush, I skirted the battle, loosing arrows at the enemy Fae whenever I had a good shot at their backs. They were strong, and a single arrow could hardly stop them, but it did cause a momentary hesitation—the opening my friends needed to get the job done. Whenever I saw an opportunity, I lobbed more sleep grenades into the fray. In just a few minutes, Bria's small army was taken care of.

It was official; Mina was a genius, and I was a badass. This puny human could hold her own in a fight.

Gideon wiped his brow with one hand and stuffed a hunk of bread into his mouth with the other. He managed a grin even though he looked exhausted. "Remind me to kiss Mina later. The woman is a miracle worker."

"I don't think she'd appreciate that," I said, following him toward the cave. "And what about me?"

Gideon winked. "Not bad, for a human."

I ignored the warmth in my chest at his praise and shot him a sideways grin. "I had a decent teacher."

Shadow made a huffing sound, his canine version of a chuckle, as the three of us plunged into the darkness.

CHAPTER TWENTY-SIX

As soon as we crossed the cave's threshold, the temperature dropped sixty degrees. I'm not kidding; it was like walking from the hottest summer afternoon to the coldest winter morning in the space of a breath. It felt like when I'd used my magick earlier, but a glance at Gideon and Shadow told me they felt it too.

Orange light illuminated the dark cave. Aki's slender shadow towered over us, his phantom head nearly touching the ceiling. He stood face to face with Bria. Her hood had fallen back, revealing purple-gray skin and creepy white eyes. The pair slowly paced in a circle, their gazes never straying from each other. Both had their hands splayed defensively. A ball of orange light glowed in Bria's right palm, and a gust of wind sent the ends of Aki's suit coat flapping.

Gideon eased away from me, his eyes on the pair. "Stay out of the way, darlin'," he said. "This could get ugly."

Without looking to see if I complied, he ran along the wall toward the battle. His bare feet didn't make a sound on the stone floor—they had to be cold—but the ground rumbled as he drew on his magick. Shadow disappeared farther into the cave, presumably to flank Bria's other side, his dark fur blending in with the darkness.

I watched in awe as Bria shot a ball of flame at Aki. He dodged to the left and shot a gust of wind at her in return, which she deftly avoided.

My breath shuddered out of me in a puff of misty smoke. Why was it so cold in here? I had expected it to be cooler than outside, but this was crazy. My arms and legs had gone stiff even under my long sleeves and pants.

Gideon approached Bria from behind. He touched his palm to the cave wall and a large slab of stone broke away. It spun slowly in the air, large enough that Gideon had to duck out of the way as a sharp piece swung past his head. With a small gesture, he sent the stone soaring toward Bria's back.

Bria rolled out of the way just in time to avoid the missile. The stone smashed into the ground where she'd been standing a moment before. She backed away, keeping both of them in her sights. "It's been a long time, Aki," she said. There was no indication in her voice that she was worried about their battle.

"How do you wield magick?" Aki's deep voice boomed in the cave, reverberating off the stone walls.

"Wouldn't you like to know?" White teeth flashed in Bria's dark face. "Let's just say it was a Gift."

"Seraphine would never allow it," Gideon said.

Bria simply smiled, fingering a gold pendant around her neck.

Then the cave exploded.

A wall of heat blasted me backward, slamming me into the wall. My head cracked against the stone, my vision blurring in a sea of stars, and I crumpled to the floor. Dimly, I heard Aki shouting something. I shook my head, trying to clear it, but the bright light had blinded me.

Somehow, the air grew even colder.

"Everly. Everly, get up!"

I blinked my eyes and shook my head again. Finally, my vision cleared to see Shadow kneeling next to me in human form. He looked uninjured, thankfully. He hauled me to my feet. Beyond him, Gideon lay in a crumpled heap against the far wall. Horror snapped me back to awareness. Was he still alive?

Aki rushed forward, his coat tails billowing behind him, and used both gloved hands to shove a wall of air at Bria. It knocked her off balance, and she rolled even as she shot another ball of flame at Aki's head. It swerved around him at the last moment, deflected by an invisible wall of wind.

"Stay here," Shadow said, and shifted back to wolf form. He ran at Bria from the side and leaped, barely avoiding a ball of flame she summoned at the last second.

I glanced toward Gideon. No way was I staying here when he might need my help.

Teeth chattering, I stumbled along the cave wall, skirting the battle as I made my way to Gideon's side. Luckily, Bria was too busy fighting both Aki and Shadow to pay me any attention. I fell to my knees next to Gideon's prone form and used shaking hands to roll him onto his back. His face was black with soot, but his chest moved. He was breathing. I sent a silent thank you to the heavens.

A loud yelp had me spinning around to look at the battle again.

Shadow landed on the ground, smoke curling up from his black fur. He shifted back to human form, his face a snarl of pain, and grabbed for his left arm. Even from here, I could see that his skin was red and blistered and burned. Luckily, that wasn't where his tattoo was. I had yet to see its location, but that burn was severe enough that it would have broken his Mark, which would have meant instant death.

My stomach lurched at the thought, and I glanced back down at Gideon. He didn't appear to have any severe wounds anywhere; I hoped his Mark was safe too.

Aki and Bria stood a few feet apart in the middle of the cave, locked in a silent battle. A wall of air shimmered between them. Aki's wall of wind was barely holding back Bria's wall of flame. For the first time since I'd met him, Aki looked strained. His two gloved hands shook in front of him. Bria stood in an identical pose on the other side of the wall of magick, grimacing with concentration.

I looked between the two of them, then to Gideon and Shadow.

We were losing.

Aki was breathing hard, mere moments from losing his grip on his magick, and Shadow and Gideon were down for the count.

I had to do something. She would burn my arrows to a crisp before they reached her, so my bow wasn't an option.

I had to fight fire with fire.

I got to my feet and took a deep breath, closing my eyes. I tried to focus on the feeling I'd gotten when I completed the Rite; that zen feeling I'd felt when I slipped into the grassy field where I'd met the stag for the first time. That tingly feeling when I'd held my flame in the palm of my hand. "Come on," I breathed. "Come on, magick..."

Nothing happened.

I opened my eyes again with a curse, just in time to see Bria's face change from concentration to triumph.

Her flames broke through Aki's wall of air and slammed into him. He flew backward, flipping through the air in a rush of heat. I screamed as he hit the wall hard and fell to his knees. He was still conscious, but he was breathing hard. His body couldn't keep up with the air he'd expelled with his magick, while Bria looked completely unaffected.

Gideon was still unconscious. Shadow was struggling to his feet, but he was badly burned.

No, no, no.

We were going to lose.

Bria took a step forward, an evil smile spreading across her face. "It pains me to see you this way, Aki," she said gleefully. "Asmodeus will be pleased to—argh!"

Her hand flew to her chest, to the amulet hanging there. The golden stone glowed a bright orange, brighter than the balls of flame Bria had been throwing at us. Her face contorted with pain and she yanked the necklace off. She reared back as if to throw it, but her hand burst into flames. Unlike me, the flames seemed to hurt her. She screamed as the fire licked up her arm and reached her shoulder. Her dark purple skin bubbled and blistered, and she threw herself to the ground, rolling to put the flames out.

What the...?

Aki staggered to his feet, breathing hard. Shadow took a step toward her, clearly unsure of what to do.

But I didn't hesitate.

I grabbed my last sleep grenade and turned the key, tossing it at Bria's feet. It exploded instantly, illuminating the cave in harsh light and deep shadow. The bright purple gas plumed upward, but Bria's reflexes were good. She rolled away and to her feet, tossing the pendant to the ground. The instant the stone left her hand, the flames were extinguished. Her movement had put her close to the entrance of the cave; the smoking sleep grenade created a barrier between us.

Bria stood in the entrance for a moment, her eyes darting between us and the gate. Something like fear crossed her face before it contorted into a snarl.

"This isn't over," she seethed, backing up. Before any of us could move to stop her, she disappeared into the light and ran away like the coward she was.

Aki waved his hand weakly, and a light brush of wind pushed the rest of the gas out through the opening of the cave. It would disperse before it reached Bria's retreating form, but at least it wouldn't knock all of us out.

Silence fell.

"What...just happened?" I said finally, my voice a small echo in the vast space.

Shadow crossed the cave, cradling his injured arm, and dropped to one knee next to Gideon. "We lost."

I looked to Aki. "But you have control of the gate now."

Aki shook his head. "The gate may be in our control for now, but we have no army to defend it without the Thiosians' support. And without Bria, we have no way of finding Asmodeus. We have failed."

I released a breath, blinking at the puff of white mist, and glanced back toward the cave entrance. A glint of metal caught my eye, and I walked toward it. Bria's pendant lay next to the cave wall. Cautiously, I picked it up. The smooth stone was no longer glowing; it wasn't even gold anymore. It had faded to a dull gray.

"What is this?" I asked Aki, crossing back to hand it to him. "Is this how Bria controlled that fire?"

"I don't know. I've never seen anything like it." Aki turned it over, examining it from all sides, then slid it into the pocket of his jacket.

Shadow pulled something from his pocket and waved it under Gideon's nose. He stirred, and his eyes blinked open. It didn't take him long to gain awareness enough to look around at our dirty, disheveled faces. "Why do y'all look so glum? Are we dead?"

"Bria escaped," Shadow said, glancing at Aki.

"Seraphine curse us." Gideon blinked. "I need a drink."

CHAPTER TWENTY-SEVEN

I sat in the cave with a still-disoriented Gideon while Shadow and Aki took care of the unconscious Fae thugs outside. I had no idea what they planned to do with them. I doubted the queen would get behind the idea of locking them in her dungeon, but maybe Aki could use them to get information on Asmodeus's location. Shadow had seemed doubtful when I voiced the idea; he didn't think they were high enough on the totem pole to impart anything useful.

Gideon worked his way through a foggy amber bottle of liquor. He had pulled it from an interior pocket of his leather duster, and it had somehow remained intact through all the fighting.

The gate loomed in front of us, its etched pillars and scrolling design glowing with a slight blue hue. The stone shimmered like the surface of a still lake. It had opened a few minutes ago, shortly after Aki and Shadow had left the cave. It would be open for the rest of the evening, and then it would close again until the next equinox. Aki wasn't confident that he could keep control of it without the Thiosians' help, but at least there wouldn't be any Fae thugs coming through here for a while. I had no idea how many other portals there were in Seattle—I hadn't thought to ask until now—but at least there would be a few less monsters roaming Seattle's streets at night.

Gideon wordlessly offered me his bottle.

I looked at it, then met his eyes. With a shrug, I took it from him and took a long swig. The alcohol burned a path down my throat and into my belly, and I coughed. It had been a while since I'd had alcohol. It still tasted terrible.

Aki returned a few minutes later with Shadow trailing behind him, back in human form now. Even dirty and exhausted, Aki still carried himself with a sense of decorum as he approached where Gideon and I sat with our backs against the hard cave wall. He extended a hand and helped Gideon to his feet, and Shadow did the same for me.

"What now?" I asked.

"You go home," Aki said simply.

I glanced at the gate. "Just like that?"

"You fulfilled your end of the bargain. I have control of the gate, even if Bria escaped. It won't open again for months." Aki nodded. "You're free to go."

I hesitated, glancing at Shadow and Gideon and then back to Aki. "What will you do?"

"I don't know about you all, but I'm going to ask Mina to make me a feast," Gideon drawled. "I'm going to eat until I burst, and then I'm going to sleep for at least two days."

Something panged in my chest at the thought of Mina, but I ignored it. I was going home. I had to.

"We will continue what we have been doing," Aki said. "We will find Asmodeus."

"What about the queen?"

Aki's expression turned grim. "We will deal with her as well."

I swallowed hard. "The Forest Spirit said that Bria's magick was unnatural, and it seemed like using the fire didn't even affect her until it went crazy at the end. What do you think it means?"

"I do not know." Aki straightened his shoulders. "But it's not your concern."

He was right. I knew he was right. I didn't belong here, and Mary Beth needed me. She was the only family I had. I couldn't—wouldn't—abandon her like my parents had abandoned me.

But something still caused me to hesitate.

Shadow placed a hand on my shoulder, and I turned to search his face. I wanted nothing more than to launch myself at him, to wrap my arms around his waist and never leave. To stay here and find out if this thing between us could grow into something more.

Before I could talk myself into turning away, Shadow leaned forward. My eyes fell closed as his lips brushed mine. They were warm and gentle. They held promises of tenderness and a relationship without walls, of support and comfort and everything I'd never dared ask for.

A throat cleared.

Shadow pulled back and my eyes fluttered open again.

Gideon was grinning from ear to ear, and Aki studied the other side of the cave, looking extremely uncomfortable.

I put a hand to my tingling lips and stared up at Shadow.

He gave me that devastating half smile, his eyes endlessly gentle, and said, "It's time to go home."

I didn't want to go. I wanted to stay here with Shadow and Aki and Mina and Kiera and even Gideon. I wanted to learn how to use my magick and shoot a bow and help Mina make dinner every night.

Mary Beth's face flashed in my mind's eye, and I forced myself to turn away from the three of them and approach the gate, reaching out a hand.

"Everly."

I looked at Aki over my shoulder.

For the first time since I'd arrived in Thios, his expression softened into something like a smile. "Take care of yourself."

I swallowed hard, holding his gaze and studiously ignoring Shadow. If I looked at him one more time, I would never leave. "Thanks. For keeping your promise."

I wanted to thank him for so much more than that, but I didn't have the words. And if I was honest, he wasn't one for sappy tributes and neither was I. Hopefully he understood I was thanking him for sheltering me and teaching me. For putting up with me despite my prejudices and bullheadedness. For introducing me to Mina and Shadow and the rest of his crew, who felt more like family to me now than my own family ever had.

I never thought I would say this, but I would miss Faery.

Before Aki could reply, I turned away and pushed through the gate, slipping through the hard stone surface with a slurp.

CHAPTER TWENTY-EIGHT

When the world stopped shifting under my feet, it was light outside. I blinked against the afternoon rays streaming in through the high warehouse windows. The brick wall behind me still shimmered slightly, beckoning me to call this whole thing off and go back to Thios.

But I couldn't. I wouldn't.

The warehouse was empty, as I had suspected it would be. I walked out through the front doors. Only weeks ago, I'd watched Peter go inside and had made the foolish decision to save him. That decision had changed my life—changed me—forever. I wasn't the same Everly who had been dragged into Faery. I'd flirted with death more times than I could count in the past few weeks, but I'd also learned more than I'd thought possible. I'd met some incredible monsters and found out that they weren't monsters at all. I'd learned what it felt like to be a part of something, to have a goal bigger than myself. I had come as close as I ever would to falling in... I couldn't even think the word... with someone.

Yeah, I was different now, but Seattle was still the same and Mary Beth was waiting for me. It was time to go home.

My bike wasn't where I left it—big surprise—so I began the long walk back to Hammond House.

Now that I was back in Seattle, going back to my old life had lost its appeal. Aki may have control of the gate now, but he had no army to defend it. Surely Bria would take it back. Would she realize that I had gone back home? Would she come after me for foiling her plans?

Maybe I could leave town. I had some money saved, which I had miraculously kept safe during my time in Faery. I could take Mary Beth and settle in a new city somewhere. Go-Cart had branches in most major cities, so I'd be able to make money again. We'd lose our lodging at Hammond House, but honestly, it wasn't that great anyway. We had a roof over our heads, but the food was terrible and the social workers were too pushy. We could live on the streets for a while. I'd learned how to take care of myself over the years; I could protect Mary Beth until we found a place to live. Maybe I'd even rent an apartment and get Mary Beth a therapist to help her through her drug problem.

Hell, maybe I needed a therapist too. The past three weeks had been nothing short of traumatic.

I spotted a run-down gas station and jogged across the street. Screw this walk; maybe they had a phone I could use to call a taxi. I had been careful to keep my spare money inside my boot during the past three weeks, preparing for my return home.

The bell over the door tinkled merrily as I stepped inside.

"Hey there," a voice called from somewhere. A door behind the register opened and a portly man appeared. If my bedraggled appearance surprised him—tangled hair, dirty face, soot-stained clothing—he didn't show it. "What can I do for you, sweetheart?"

"Do you have a phone I could use?"

He reached under the register and pulled out an old corded phone. He slapped it on the counter and turned away, giving me a bit of privacy. I picked up the handset and quickly dialed information. While I waited on hold with a local taxi service, I let my gaze wander the counter. My stomach growled at the clear display of cookies and doughnuts next to the register. I should save my money for bus tickets out of the city, but hell, I'd been kidnapped and taken to another realm. If I wanted a cookie, I was damn well going to buy myself a cookie. I opened the door and pulled out a cellophane-wrapped double chocolate chip cookie, and my eyes landed on the newspaper rack next to the counter. I froze.

This had to be a joke.

"Um, what's the date today?" I asked the man behind the counter. I couldn't stop my voice from shaking.

He turned around. His smile slipped for the first time, and he raised his bushy brows at me. He pointed a chubby finger at the newspaper. "September tenth," he said, as if I was blind.

The phone fell from my numb fingers, clattering to the counter. "But it... but it should be April twentieth."

The guy looked at me like I was crazy. "Pretty sure it's been September all month long." His eyes wandered down, taking in my appearance. "Are you all right? Have you taken something you shouldn't have?"

I shook my head vehemently and turned, sprinting out the door before he could question me further.

No, no, no. This couldn't be happening. Seraphine, or God, or whatever jerk controlled the events in my miserable life, had to be laughing their heads off. That was the only explanation for the way fate had screwed up my life over and over again.

I didn't stop running until my lungs were so constricted that I couldn't breathe anymore. Miraculously, I ended up on the outskirts of downtown and only a few miles from Hammond House. I braced a hand on the cement wall of a high-rise apartment building and bent over, breathing shallowly.

Five months. It had been five months—not three weeks—since Bria had kidnapped me. Had nobody thought to mention that time moved differently in Faery? If I could go back through that portal and strangle Aki, I would.

I pushed away from the wall and began walking again. There was no use panicking about it now. I had to form a plan.

I would go to Hammond House. My bed was probably gone by now, but Mary Beth would still be there. I could explain to Helen that I'd been indisposed. She probably wouldn't believe me. Most likely she'd think I was off on a drug-induced bender. Hammond House had strict policies in place, and they never deviated from them. That was fine, since Mary Beth and I would leave town soon enough. I just hoped they'd kept my stuff. I'd been smart enough to keep most of my money with me, but there was a small amount stashed in an old suitcase I'd gotten out of a dumpster and kept under my bed. I could only keep so many bills in my shoes and pockets, and I'd need every penny I could get.

By the time I reached Hammond House, it was just after seven o'clock. The doors had been opened and the line had disappeared. Everyone was inside eating dinner. The lobby was quiet when I stepped inside. Helen looked up at the sound of the door, and her eyes widened in surprise.

"Everly?" She looked me up and down, and her mouth formed an O. "What happened to you? Where have you been?"

I didn't bother answering her questions. "Where's Mary Beth?"

The woman blinked. "Mary Beth...?"

"Yes," I said irritably. "Is she here for the night yet? I need to talk to her. You know what, never mind. I'll go look myself."

"Hey, wait—" Helen scrambled to her feet as I stormed past the front desk. Her heels click-clacked on the tile behind me.

Nobody noticed me when I entered the dining area. I didn't see any faces I recognized, but that wasn't surprising. Turnover was high at Hammond House. Most people stayed for a month or two at most, then either found a job and transferred out or resorted back to homelessness. I doubted Mary Beth could hold a job with her level of addiction, so she had to be here somewhere. She never missed a free meal.

I scanned the dining room, but I didn't see her.

Helen caught up to me, breathing hard. "Everly—"

"Where is she?" I rounded on her. "Don't tell me you guys kicked her out. You know how helpless she is!"

The woman hesitated, and her expression made my stomach drop to my toes. Something like terror sparked in my chest.

Pity. She was looking at me with pity.

But that didn't make sense. If she knew where I'd been for the past three weeks—uh, five months—then she would definitely look at me with pity, but everything was fine. I was back, and I had a plan to get Mary Beth out of here. I was done scraping by every day, waiting for the other shoe to drop on my life. I was ready to get Mary Beth clean and live a real life, maybe get a proper job someday and live somewhere that had my name on the deed.

"Everly..." Helen's voice was soft. "I haven't seen Mary Beth in months."

I stared at her. That spark in my chest exploded into a ball of flame, threatening to burn me alive. Mary Beth... the only reason I'd left Mina and Shadow and Kiera... was gone.

Fate had screwed me over yet again.

Continue the Series

Continue the Rising Elements series with Oath of Flame, releasing on 8/5/2022. Pre-order now on all major retailers!

If you enjoyed this book and want to see more, please show your support by leaving a review. Reviews are so important to me as an author, and they help other readers find my books.

To hear about my newest releases and behind-the-scenes info about my work, you can join my mailing list by heading to my website at www.cearanobles.com. Or if you have any comments, you can shoot me a note at cearanoblesbooks@gmail.com. I love hearing from people who have read my books, and I answer every email I receive!

You can also follow me on these pages:

Instagram - www.instagram.com/cearanoblesbooks

Facebook - www.facebook.com/cearanoblesauthor

My website - www.cearanobles.com

Thanks for supporting me and my work!

Acknowledgments

Some say that writing is a solitary affair... and some are very wrong. The truth is, this book wouldn't be in your hands today without the help of some extraordinary people, and I'd like to take a page or two and thank them personally.

To my husband Grady, thank you for acting as my creative sounding board and for giving up your weeknights so I could get some work done. You are my creative director and co-business owner and overall life partner, and I would be lost without you!

Everly's story blossomed thanks to Alexandra Dawning's flawless editing. She took my little book and guided me to bring out its best. This story wouldn't be the same without her!

To my beta and ARC readers (there are too many of you to name), THANK YOU for falling in love with Thios like I did and hyping up release day so others could do the same.

I learned so much from the Bookstagram community, especially Victoria McCombs and Annabelle McCormack. Thank you for sharing your knowledge with me! And a special thank you to the 20Books group on Facebook; its members inspire me every day to take my writing and my business to the next level.

And lastly, thank YOU, dear reader. Without your support, I wouldn't be able to make a living doing what I love. Thanks for taking a chance on this story. You're the best!

ABOUT THE AUTHOR

Ceara Nobles is a Utah-based author of romantic suspense and fantasy novels. She graduated from the University of Utah in 2016 with a B.A. in Computer Animation, then realized she hated it. Now she spends her days juggling her side hustle as a line editor and her true  love of authorship. When she's not busy writing, you can find her chasing her toddler, road tripping with her hubby, or hiding in bed with a chai and a good book.

www.ingramcontent.com/pod-product-compliance
Lightning Source LLC
Chambersburg PA
CBHW010635100726

47900CB00011B/2832